CONTENTS

STARBOURN

THE PALE HORSE

DAVID HART

Star Bourn: The Pale Horse by David Hart

Copyright © 2026 by David Hart

Book Cover by Tom Edwards

First edition 2026

To my Lord and Savior, who gave me this passion and drive to get as far as I have. Thank you.

PART I

01

[Newton System, Einstein Cluster.]

[Local system time: 1500.]

"An easy search and recovery mission, Captain Severre."

That's what Captain Dannaver told me when we boarded the *Triumphant*. "Just head out beyond Newton, find the freighter, search it, and ping its location back to the *Triumphant* for pickup."

Of course, the rest of my team and I knew it was a load of bull. Nothing was ever that easy. Otherwise they wouldn't be sending out Star Bourn.

As the elite operators within the Marine Corps., we were tasked with pirate raids, special reconnaissance, counterterrorism, so on and so forth. Even though the nature of our missions became less critical throughout the decades since the

Star Bourn's formation in the First Contact War, a task like this seemed like a stretch.

Still, it wasn't worth arguing with the captain and getting written up over it, especially since the Cross-Branch Authority Act passed last year allowed the Navy to give us missions. As a result, we decided it best that we play along. The op was set to commence in twenty minutes, so only two of us were able to take showers, those two being Kenneth "Loudmouth" Morales and Jack "Fixer" Crews.

I was tempted to use my rank to be one of the two to take a shower, but those bastards needed it more. They fell right into a mud pit on our way to a rebel base. The mud did wonders to keep them hidden from our enemies, but apparently some got under their armor, and everybody who's done an op on Hera Falls knows how bad the mud can stink after a while.

They walked out of the showers in their black skinsuits, grins plastered on both their faces. I was about to give them crap for how that looked, but Marissa A. Daniels, or as we called her, M.A.D., beat me to it.

"You two enjoy yourselves?" she asked.

"As a matter of fact, I did," Fixer said, "Unlike the rest of you in your sweat boxes, we actually smell halfway decent now."

"Sweat box" was a nickname we came up with for our body armor. Even though our helmets had minimal air conditioning, the rest of our bodies always ended up drenched in sweat by the end of an op. After a while you get used to the feeling. The smell, though? Almost enough to make the average grunt gag.

"Only halfway?" Nathan "Flyby" Wu asked. While M.A.D. and I laughed, he kept his signature straight-faced expression.

"Alright, alright. Let's pick up your body armor and get to Hangar Bay Three. I don't want to be late for another op," I said, already heading to the nearby armory.

Those of us who were still in our armor held our helmets between our arms and waists. Even with our helmets' air conditioning, there was nothing quite like a breath of fresh air. Well, as fresh as recycled starship air can be.

On our way, a particularly pretty sailor took notice of our skinsuit-clad partners. Those undersuits didn't leave anything to the imagination, hence the name. Loudmouth gave her a smile and a wink, which made the poor girl turn red and walk faster. I elbowed his ribs, which earned me a feigned innocent response.

"What? I only smiled," Loudmouth protested.

"Yeah, we all know what a smile from you means," I said with a chuckle.

We entered the armory, and Fixer and Loudmouth left us to retrieve their armor from the back. The *Triumphant* had been on patrol duty in the Newton System for six months at this point, so the marines aboard didn't feel the need to armor up daily. Sergeant Beucock, the NCO in command of this marine detachment, would've certainly been reprimanded if the higher-ups found out about this, but who am I to rat him out?

About halfway into the armory, we realized we weren't alone. A tall man stood at the back of the compartment where the Star Bourn armor was stored. He turned around, and my eyes widened in surprise for the briefest of moments.

It was Colonel John Miller.

After my dad died during the First Contact War, Miller filled the hole left behind. He was the only person close to me who took my decision to become a Star Bourn seriously from the get-go. We worked together once or twice, but we hadn't seen each other for some time.

All of us snapped to attention, which he promptly waved off.

"As you were. We're leaving early. If we get done in ten minutes, we'll be able to make it back in time for dinner," Miller said.

"You're coming with us?" I asked abruptly.

"Yeah. Is that a problem?"

"No, sir," I said without missing a beat. While I haven't worked with Miller much, I've heard enough about *Legion*—as he's known—to know that he doesn't take crap from anybody, no matter how close they are to him.

"Good," he replied.

Loudmouth and Fixer suited up faster than I've ever seen before. Whether this was because of Legion's presence, the prospect of dinner, or both, I couldn't say. Still, they armored up in record time, and the six of us were off to hangar bay three.

The walk was mostly quiet. Nobody wanted to crack jokes or wink at cute sailors in the presence of the legendary Legion. We also had our helmets on, so any attempts at flirting would go unnoticed anyway.

Abruptly cutting through the silence, Miller asked, "Where's your sixth member?"

"KIA, sir. Command has been giving us back-to-back missions, so I haven't had the time to find a new Star Bourn," I answered.

Miller nodded, "I'm sorry to hear that, captain."

The rest of the walk was silent, which I was grateful for. The loss of Oracle, our sixth member, was still pretty fresh for all of us. Apart from a Star Bourn-style memorial—whiskey wrapped with a ribbon that was shot off into space—we hadn't had a lot of time to deal with it.

A part of me felt bad about picking another commando to join us. For the longest time, myself, Loudmouth, Fixer, M.A.D., Flyby, and Oracle—The Wolf Pack—weren't just a team of bad asses who killed anyone that needed killing. We were a family. And picking some other Star Bourn to join our family? It didn't feel right.

As soon as we entered the hangar bay, we were greeted by two engineers. We ignored them and headed for the Hercules dropship stationed at the nearest hangar pad.

"All systems are ready to go, Legion," the pilot in the lower seat said.

Miller acknowledged the pilot, then promptly walked through the sliding doors into the Hercules. The rest of us followed suit. Miller slammed his fist down twice onto the door separating the pilots from the troop bay, which told them it was time to go.

The spacecraft doors closed, temporarily engulfing us in darkness before the interior lights came on. All of us, minus Miller, sat in the seats lined up in the center of the vessel while the Hercules lifted off. Miller kept his eyes on a terminal for a few moments, watching to make sure the takeoff went smoothly. The dropships were exceptionally built and flown by usually well-qualified pilots, but there was no harm in making sure the liftoff went well.

Miller finally turned to face us. "Alright commandos, let's go over the operation. Drones spotted an old Destiny-class freighter just outside the Newton System and reported it to local authorities. They reported it to Star Command, and Command is sending us to check it out," Miller said. With a push of a button, the terminal next to him showed a layout of the freighter. "We'll split up into teams of two to cover more ground. M.A.D. and Loudmouth will check out the cargo docks near the back of the ship. Captain Severre and Fixer will check the individual rooms on the lower decks. Flyby and I will check the decks on the upper deck and the bridge.

"From what the drones have shown, the freighter hasn't been functioning for at least a decade, so it should be safe to enter through the engines. Everything, and I mean everything, needs to be checked. I don't care how small it is, if something looks out of place, you tell me. I don't want some rookie scavengers to get blown to hell cause of our mistake, understood?"

"Yes, sir," we all said in unison.

"Good," Miller said, "If any of you have questions, now's the time to ask 'em."

"Should we expect any hostiles?" Loudmouth asked.

"I would say so. This class of freighter should be rotting away in some junkyard. The fact it's out here is suspicious enough for Command to send us to check it out."

The pilot's voice chimed in over the comm, "There's a lot of debris in the area. You'll have to disembark here and head to the ship on your own. We'll stay put and wait for your return."

Miller nodded as if the pilot was there next to him. "Understood."

A second later, the hatch slid open, exposing us to the zero-gravity of space. We activated our gravboots and took off our safety harnesses. One by one, we readied the magnehooks on our forearms and awaited Miller's signal.

"Alright, follow my lead and try not to get lost. The freighter's thermal detectors may not be functioning, but they put a hell of a lot of portholes in these things back in the day. So, if there *is* anyone in there, they'll be able to see you fumbling around like idiots," Miller said. "And use the debris as cover. Better safe than sorry."

With the order given, Miller deactivated his gravboots, and shot his magnehook at the nearest large piece of debris, pulling himself toward it. One by one, the rest of us followed after him. I went last, as is standard for commanding officers. Darting from left to right, Miller and my squad mates zigzagged through the debris field, using the alien wreckage as cover.

As we neared the old Destiny-class freighter, I couldn't help but get distracted for a moment by the space around us. Instead of the bleak blackness that normally surrounds the stars, the environment was filled with reds and blues and purples and, yes, black too. While we were too close to make out the nebula, I remember from advanced school that all the interstellar gasses around us swirled together to form a double helix shape.

It always amazed me as a kid how all the celestial imagery came together into pictures we could understand. Whatever higher power was out there must be an artist.

As fast as it came, I snapped out of my little daydream and got on with the mission, not missing a beat. Sightseeing could come later.

We reached the ship's four thrusters in record time and made our way to the top left thruster. Fixer took the lead, using a cutting torch to heat the hatch. Who knows how long this freighter had been out there for, but with no power, the hatch was guaranteed to be frozen to some degree. Through a private communications net we Star Bourn dubbed 'The Back Door,' Fixer told us how badly frozen the hatch was.

"Judging by the amount of frost, it looks like this ship's been out here for two months. I should have the hatch open in one minute."

With our gravboots activated, we covered Fixer while he did his thing. While scanning the space ahead of us, I began to observe the debris more closely. Between the shield-like bow of the ships, the singular thruster, and the red and silver color scheme, there was no doubt in my mind. At least a portion of the debris belonged to Anthrum Ascendancy ships. The other debris though, I couldn't quite recognize. M.A.D. must've been thinking the same as me.

"So, what's all this scrap from? Looks like anthrum mixed with something else. You got any idea, Legion?" she asked.

"It's ancient zauhlon. Must be left from the War of Devils," Miller said.

Now that I thought about it, the previously unknown debris did have that rough, thrown-together look zauhlon ships had. Still do, if the holo-vids are to be believed.

"What's this ship doing out here then?" Loudmouth asked, gripping his PR3 Punisher assault rifle tighter.

"Maybe they were scavengers," I said, though it came out as more of a mumble.

Fixer opened the hatch with a pop, then stepped aside for the rest of the Wolves to enter.

Miller grunted in response while the others climbed the stairs up to the engineering deck. I knew what that grunt meant: *I don't buy it*. Truth be told, I didn't either. This case already didn't make sense. The drones reported the ship hadn't been active for a decade, but the frost showed it had been out here for only two months with no power. It didn't add up.

Once the other Wolves entered the hatch, I was up next. Miller went in last, and within a few seconds, we reached the rectangular engineering deck where the rest were waiting. I could barely see anything, so I switched on my night vision. I was greeted by a grisly sight. Dried-up human blood was splattered across what was left of the bulkhead, and the hatch was barely attached to its hinges. The rest of the deck was pretty rusty, which backed up the theory that had been inactive for a decade.

"Uh, Legion? I see a few things out of place," Loudmouth commented, though nobody laughed.

"Cut the chatter," Miller said while moving his left fist behind him. Without hesitation we formed up on him, Fixer and I on his left, Loudmouth, M.A.D. and Flyby on his right.

We moved through the short corridor and entered the cargo dock. My eyes scanned the deck below us. Whatever wasn't strapped down was floating aimlessly. We didn't stick around long enough for me to look again, but it didn't seem like anything of value was missing. The big steel crates were still here, at least.

Miller gave a fraction of a nod, and we all split up into the predetermined groups. While the other two teams got to work on the search, Fixer followed me across the catwalk to the upper deck. Upon reaching the corridor leading to the bridge,

I spotted four hatches with small portholes in the center; two on the starboard side and two on the port side. I took the starboard rooms while Fixer took the port.

The hatches took some elbow grease to open. In the first room, there was nothing—no bed, no clothes, nothing. There were no signs of life anywhere.

While our search was underway, my mind drifted to Miller. Last we talked, he only had a year left of active duty. Even though command was likely to send him off to retirement, he mentioned wanting to pursue the role of commandant of the Reinhardt Schmidt Military Academy on Triton. He had no kids of his own, nor a wife. As far as he was concerned, civilian life was meaningless to him.

To this day, the thought of him as a commandant made me smile. He'd be perfect at the job.

Since the invention of machine enhancements a hundred years ago, the age of retirement had grown progressively higher. With a diminished population resulting from the First Contact War and fewer people enlisting, the service contained a large number of older veterans. There was some criticism in the media regarding a third of the military being made up of over-sixty-year-olds. At the end of the day, though, beggars can't be choosers.

With the individual rooms out of the way, we made way for the bridge. Fixer went to check the compartments and minor terminals while I went straight for the control panel. Almost immediately I noticed the recording chip was removed.

"Looks like we're dealing with either pirates or scavengers. The recording chip's been taken out," I said.

This was a common trick of the outlaws of the galaxy; remove the recording chip so Republic spies don't listen in on you. Now, whether the Republic Intelligence Division did such things, I didn't know. Wouldn't surprise me, in all honesty. Beneath those suits and ties were snakes who would do anything to get what they wanted.

The Wolves' Back Door channel chimed to life, "Hey, Cap? We found the crew ... or what's left of them," Flyby said.

This time it was Miller who spoke, "There are four skeletons here. Hard to say what killed them, but there's a lot of blood. Broken bones too."

Fixer and I exchanged looks.

"Are the escape pods still there?" I asked.

"Yeah. Unless M.A.D. and Loudmouth have found any other bodies, this is the entire crew," Miller said.

There was a brief pause where all of us waited to see if Loudmouth or M.A.D. would interject and confirm what Miller said. The Back Door remained silent, however.

"Well, what have you got, Loudmouth?" I asked. M.A.D. was known to get absorbed with whatever her task was, so I didn't think much of her radio silence. Loudmouth, though, was always talking, for better or worse. So, when I got nothing back from him, panic started to set in.

I shifted my eyes to the Squad Mates Vitals option on my heads-up display and enlarged it with a wink. Both M.A.D.'s and Loudmouth's vitals read "Unknown." This only popped up when the user was away from their helmet. Miller must have already been looking at the vitals though, because no sooner had I looked at the HUD's grayed-out silhouettes, he began taking charge.

"Captain Severre, Fixer, circle back and form up on us. You see any movement on your map that's not our tags, shoot to kill. Got it?" Miller ordered.

"Yes, sir," both of us said. Fixer hesitated for a brief second though. It was pretty easy for him to get skittish, so I could only imagine how he was reacting to all this. Not that I had to imagine, actually; I could see his heart beat increase.

"Keep cool, Jack. We've been through worse. Remember Yukov II?" I asked, hoping the fond memory calmed him down.

It seemed to work, as his heart rate went back to normal. "Don't remind me. Those buggers were the most annoying little things I've seen," Fixer said.

Both Fixer and I deactivated our gravboots and used the hems and bent shards of bulkheads to propel ourselves forward. We wouldn't have much tactical maneuverability, but we were able to be much quieter and move throughout the freighter faster. While moving to their location, Miller tried hailing the Hercules.

"Echo Nine, you read me? We need backup from the *Triumphant*. We've got missing marines here." He didn't get a response. Instead, he was greeted by static. "Echo Nine, do you copy? ... Dammit."

This whole op was looking like a disaster. My gut told me this was a trap, but who set it? This wasn't something Bloodhound would do. Those terrorists would rather build a measly fleet and try to take one of our colonies.

When we were twenty meters from the other Star Bourn, we reactivated our gravboots and jogged the rest of the way. Miller and Flyby still had their guns aimed down the corridor, but Fixer at least relaxed a little when we were united.

"Fixer, get one of these escape pod hatches opened. We're leaving," Miller said.

"What? What about M.A.D. and Loudmouth?" Fixer protested, "C'mon Cap, back me up!"

My gaze fell. It's not that I didn't agree with the sentiment—hell, I've spent more holidays with them than back home. But the fact of the matter was that the longer we stayed here, the sooner we would be MIA like M.A.D. and Loudmouth.

"Do as he says, Fixer," I said.

He looked at me with what I imagined was disbelief for a brief second, then turned to a nearby terminal. Fixer cursed under his breath before starting a small-scale reboot.

"The terminal in charge of maintaining the escape pods should be up and running in a minute. Hard to tell for certain though, these systems are—" Fixer said just before an ax lodged into his helmet. If it weren't for his gravboots, he would have gone flying. My eyes stared at his limp body for a moment before turning to look where the weapon came from.

Down the corridor were three hulking aliens in what looked like gold armor. Each had four arms that held swords, axes, and guns. Without hesitation, we opened fire on each other. There wasn't much cover in the corridor, but we made do. Instinctively, I dove behind the mechanical pillar connected to the terminal. Flyby wedged himself behind some of the exposed bulkhead, and Miller turned off his gravboots and used a part of the ceiling as cover.

With combined firepower, we took down one alien, followed by another. We didn't come prepped for a firefight; our ammo was running low.

"Are these who I think they are?" I asked Miller. I'd seen these aliens in the old vids, but I had to make sure.

"Fracking zauhlons," Miller replied with a bitter tone usually reserved for when he told war stories.

A rush of adrenaline pumped through me. These are the aliens who nearly wiped out humanity. Killed countless men, women and children. Thanks to these creatures, I grew up without a father. The third zauhlon fell to our combined might, its blood drifting upwards until it finally connected to the ceiling.

This kill felt different though. Now, I felt pride—and a pinch of joy—upon taking these brutes down. Not wanting to take my eyes off the corridor for too long, I glanced down at the terminal. The screen read, "Sixty percent until completion." Almost there.

For a moment I thought that would be it. Just a ragtag group of zauhlons looking to itch their legendary blood lust. Not even a second later I was proven wrong. Another zauhlon stepped into sight, but stayed behind the corpses of his allies.

Smart. He knew if he took one more step he'd be joining them. This one looked different though. On top of the well-constructed zauhlon armor, which sported a deep red color unlike the other golden sets, were pieces of what looked to be a mixture of basic marine and the more advanced Star Bourn armor, along with anthrum armor; clearly trophies from past victories.

The zauhlon wore a cape that'd seen better days. To finish off his grand look, he held a sword that looked different from the other zauhlons' swords. This one looked ancient, and had gems placed along the guard.

Seconds after this new zauhlon showed himself, two more aliens joined him. These were wearing black armor. Even with night vision it was hard to see them. For what felt like an eternity, the six of us stood there, staring at one another. The three of us humans took this time to reload what little ammo we had left. To be honest, I doubted it would be enough. Instinctively, I checked my hip. My military-issued machete was still there. I didn't know if that bad boy could hold up to their swords if it came down to it, but at least I stood somewhat of a chance.

Then, slowly, the caped zauhlon raised his sword and pointed it at us, "Kill the apes. Bring their remains to me," he said.

The dark zauhlons started shooting a millisecond faster than we did. As it turned out, their weapons were different than their golden buddies. One had two guns—a pistol and a shotgun—while the other carried a huge firearm. This gigantic weapon turned out to be some sort of cannon which fired a metal-spiked ball that hit Flyby square in the face. The cannonball smashed Flyby's helmet. As if by some miracle, the cannon didn't kill Flyby, though he was very clearly unconscious. His vitals were fading however. If I wanted to get him out of this alive, he would need medical attention ASAP.

Turning off my gravboots, I leapt over to Flyby and pinned him to where he was previously taking cover so as to make sure he wasn't further injured. Finally, one of the black-clad zauhlons fell. The one left was the bastard with two guns.

Briefly, I thought he would be easier to take out since, after all, how much good would a shotgun or a pistol do at this range? Turns out quite a bit. That handgun of his ended up connecting with me. While my shields took the brunt of the damage, what little I felt was different. Instead of the stinging sensation that normally came with getting shot, this felt like more of a jolt of electricity.

This caught me off guard long enough for him to shoot something out of his shotgun. It wasn't a bullet though; no, this was a magnehook that attached itself to my arm. I still had my gravboots off, so when it began to pull me toward the zauhlon, I wasn't prepared. As best I could, I held onto the piece of bulkhead that I was previously using as cover. Thankfully, Miller had my back and threw his machete at the magnehook cord, cutting it and freeing me in return.

Once again I glanced at the terminal. "Ninety percent until completion."

Miller and I put down the last dark zauhlon. All that remained was the caped enemy, their leader. With his sword in hand, he charged at us, letting out a guttural war cry as he did so. We opened fire on him, but he was taking it in stride. On top of that, luck wasn't on our side. Miller ran out of ammo, as did I. Taking out his machete, Miller prepared himself for the oncoming attack.

Unsheathing my blade, I pulled the trigger to heat up the edges of my weapon, prepared to join my surrogate father in what was likely to be a hellish fight. Boot camp had taught me what hand-to-hand battles with zauhlons were like. Half of those who survived ended up crippled.

The zauhlon was closer to Miller, so he engaged with him first. Miller held his own well, but the zauhlon laid into him with ferocious punches, denting Miller's armor in the process. Leaping in to help, I managed to cut through some of the zauhlon's armor. Unfortunately, he twisted to face me before my blade could pierce him. Tossing his sword to his lower right arm, the zauhlon used his now free upper right arm to grab me by the helmet and smash my head into Miller's. The attack had my head spinning, but as soon as I flipped back around to face the zauhlon, something caught my eye. The terminal read "Reboot complete."

Miller must have noticed this too, because he shoved me over to where Flyby was and resumed his fight with the zauhlon. I took the hint and turned my attention to the panel connected to the nearest escape pod. The system was way out of date, but I managed to get the escape pod door open and carefully pushed Flyby inside. As soon as he was in, I beckoned Miller to get in as well. He pushed himself off the portside bulkhead toward the escape pod, but instead of entering, Miller pushed me in. Before I could figure out what he was getting at, the escape pod door shut, cutting us off.

"What the hell are you doing?" I shouted.

"What needs to be done. Sorry, son, you're going to have to do this one without me."

Miller shifted his focus to the panel, frantically working away at it. Shortly after, a feminine, robotic voice greeted me and told me the pod would leave shortly. Banging on the door, I yelled for Miller to stop. The next thing I saw would stick with me for as long as I lived. The zauhlon, now behind Miller, grabbed him by the neck and lifted him up. He followed that by driving his sword through Miller's chest.

Moments later, the escape pod shot off, leaving Miller, the zauhlon, and my dead friends behind. In the span of five minutes, my world had crumbled down. Everyone I spent the better part of five years with was gone,

No, not everyone. I could still save Flyby.

Forcing the pain and grief aside, I moved to Flyby and strapped him in. That done, I turned my attention to the controls. If I remembered correctly, these old pods didn't provide much in the way of control, but I could at least steer this thing in the *Triumphant*'s direction. Familiarizing myself with the controls, I sent out a distress signal that would continually repeat. Leaning back in the leather seat, I felt a weight was lifted off my shoulders. I'd done everything I could. Now all I could do was wait.

My eyes constantly darted between Flyby's still-unconscious body and his vitals. They were faint, but still there. Flyby always was a fighter in situations like these. Now that things have calmed down, I noticed blood was seeping from under his helmet. Where specifically he was bleeding, I didn't know. Forcing myself to my feet, I walked over to my friend. The blood was dark red, which told me the severity of the injury. Still, I didn't want to attempt to remove his helmet and make matters worse.

Minutes after our narrow retreat, our escape pod was bathed in a blindingly bright light. Moving to the front of the small pod, I saw it was an Odin heavy dropship ten meters out. With the amount of space that was inside those bad boys, there was room for a medic and plenty of equipment as well.

Instantly, I let out a shaky, breathless laugh. Finally, we were in the clear.

02

[En route to Milara, Tria's Keep System.]

[Local system time: 1630.]

The Honeybee Military Personnel Transport Shuttle—or the honeybee bus, as most people in the service called it—was empty except for myself. Upon hearing my report, Captain Dannaver put me on the bus and sent me to Milara with barely enough time to change and pack my armor. Didn't even get to say goodbye to Flyby ... not that he could've heard me. I wasn't able to stick around and hear what exactly his injury was, only that he was stable and that the "best doctors in Star Command were seeing to him." That's what they always say.

I looked out the small window at the planet ahead. Milara was quite the sight to behold, as one would expect from the capital world of a galactic government. The space around it was busy—and I mean busy. Thousands of shuttles entering and leaving the atmosphere, starships of all different kinds, and more space stations in one place than I'd ever seen before.

As pretty as the bright lights from the ships and planet below were, they didn't do much to distract me from recent events. I would have to write letters to their families. What would I even say? No amount of words could make the pain go away. Nothing I could say would convey how much their fallen loved ones meant to me. M.A.D. would be the toughest. Unlike the rest of us, she had kids: one four years old and the other six.

Resting my forehead in my palm, I fought back tears. What was the point in that though? It's not like anyone was here to mock or belittle me. *Miller would*, I thought to myself. I could picture in my head what he would say in a situation like this.

You don't have it easy here, son, and I don't envy you. But you need to toughen up. There's still a job to do.

That last sentence echoed in my head.

There's still a job to do.

That line rung true. So long as one of us still lived to fight another day, the Wolf Pack lived on. And someone needed to avenge the fallen.

"Entering atmosphere. For those who would like a view at the glorious city of Panalith, please form a single file line and see the capital of Milara. When you're finished, return to your seat and allow the next passenger to look," the bot who piloted the bus said.

Pushing aside the dreadful event that weighed on me, I grabbed my luggage and decided to take a look. When I reached the front of the bus, I found out the bot wasn't lying when it described the city as glorious. The city was massive—biggest I've ever seen. It had two massive walls; one that separated the city and the wildlife, and one that likely separated the elites and the normal civilians. As it turned out, I was heading to where the rich and powerful lived. Wonderful.

We passed by enormous buildings and effortlessly entered into a line of traffic. Thankfully, we weren't waiting too long before the bot pulled away and docked at some station.

The bot thanked me for my company, but I didn't pay attention to it. I was too busy getting a sense of my surroundings. The station was packed to the brim with people of all races, colors, and sizes. Captain Dannaver told me to meet with an SC officer who would escort me to Senate Hall, but in hindsight that was the least helpful description he could have provided. Ultimately, I decided to move past the crowd and head to the edge of the station where it was less crowded. Hopefully there I could spot my escort.

I reached my destination, but it didn't prove to help much. Right when I was about to give up and try and hail a taxi,

I felt a tap on the shoulder. When I turned around, I nearly dropped my luggage off the ledge and to the slums below. In front of me was Fleet Admiral William Drake of the First Fleet. Before today I'd never met the man, but his victories in the First Contact War were known by all who served in Star Command.

"Sir!" I saluted. "I didn't expect to see you down here."

Admiral Drake smiled and waved away the formality. "At ease, commando. I wouldn't expect to find someone of my rank down here, either. You wouldn't happen to know where I could find a Star Bourn, would you? I'm to bring him to the Senate."

I was about to reply to the admiral, but he laughed softly and once again waved me off, "I'm joking, son. I got the dossier from Captain Dannaver. Come with me."

More than a little surprised, I followed Drake to a G12 Galloway hover car. I only recognized the model from one of Loudmouth's magazines; I wasn't much of a car man myself. We got in and entered the traffic line. Unlike the honeybee bus ride, it didn't look like we would get out of the traffic anytime soon.

"I'm surprised Captain Dannaver was able to convince you to escort me," I said, trying my hand at small talk. *Small talking an admiral*. The thought made me smile for a second.

"Oh, he didn't. The brass over at Fort Leonidas were going to send some poor sap who was about to end his shift, but I volunteered in his place. I was on my way to Senate Hall anyway, so I figured I would bring you with me, seeing how important your report was," Drake said. "Not many people survive a zauhlon ambush. I'm sorry about your team."

I nodded. "Thank you, sir."

The rest of the ride went on without a word.

In five minutes time, we docked at the massive building in the center of Panalith—Senate Hall. Immediately we were greeted by four security bots who escorted the two of us to where the Senate were located. The corridors leading to the room were wide and spacious, with an opening to the outside world to the right of us. Aesthetically it was nice, but tactically speaking it was stupid. Anyone could climb the wall, get in, and gun down plenty of very rich and very influential people.

Looking to the left, the wall was littered with Republic flags and holo-screens. The sound for the vid-news was off, but the headline read, "Tensions grow between GRSR and Valoran leaders: War imminent?" I shook my head. That's just what we needed.

We must have gotten there early, because the Senate was still in session. Whatever they were talking about though was clearly a heated topic, because Drake and I could hear them clearly despite the thick steel door separating us.

"Absolutely not! Humanity has already been granted enough royalties since they joined the Republic. We granted them a spot on the Senate, a city on Milara, and allowed them to have high-ranking government jobs. But if they want access to Milara's energy generator they need to *earn* it—"

"Oh, and the klex did?"

"Yes! We worked day in and day out for fifty years before we gained access to the energy generator. I know you and the Anthrum are biased in favor of your apes, but please—"

"Now wait just a minute—"

"Who are you calling *ape*, gray-head?"

"Order! This hall will not condone slurs on any side of the aisle. Cast your votes."

A small period of silence passed.

"Very well. A fifteen-minute break will be held, then the next matter will be discussed. The results for the vote will be revealed tomorrow."

Some members of the Senate walked, while some stayed in their seats looking at something on their data-pads. One of the senators who walked out happened to be Humanity's senator, Senator Joseph Bennett. When he saw me and Admiral Drake, he put on a tired smile and shook our hands.

"Admiral, captain, it's good to see you," he said, "I hope we weren't too loud in there."

"Don't worry about it. Is it always that heated in there?" I asked.

"Not always, but that seems to be becoming the norm recently. I apologize for my language in there, sometimes things just ... slip out," Senator Bennett said.

It seemed like Senator Bennett matched his reputation perfectly; polite and collected in person, fierce and relentless in Senate Hall. That's what you'd expect from someone who was born on Ishtar Prime.

"You think the Senate will listen to what we have to say?" I asked Bennett. The Senate was notorious for waving off issues, especially military-related ones.

"I think they have no choice," Bennett said, "You may not realize this, captain, but this is huge. If they don't do anything about this, they'd be blasted fools."

"If the Republic won't do anything about this, Star Command will," Drake said, clearly aggravated at the thought of inaction. I didn't blame him.

The Republic typically had a policy of "If you have a problem with it, deal with it yourself." That was fine in most cases, but with something as dangerous as the zauhlons, I'd feel much better with the Republic backing us.

"Yes, well, hopefully it doesn't come to that," Bennett said. "Now if you would excuse me, I'd like to get a cup of coffee before I have to go back in there. I'll see you gentlemen in a few." With that, he turned and walked to where the refreshments were, a security bot on either side of him.

The rest of the waiting time passed quickly, and the next session began. Admiral Drake and I stood next to Senator Bennett in humanity's corner. The Senate Hall itself reminded me of an old cathedral, housing the same style of architecture.

Truth be told, I wasn't all too familiar with the senators and their names, so I took the time we had before the session started to read the names on each of their plaques. The senator closest to us was the anthrum senator, Orthin Din. Next to him was the sahngrun senator, Sorvin Lesh. Next was klex senator Larr Sul, rah' salaruun senator Quinn Verum, grovinian senator Rusah Iruna and the Predecessor senator, Icaar.

Unlike all the other senators, Senator Icaar appeared in hologram form. From what I've heard about the Predecessors, they were quite the isolationists. It was hard to tell, but it felt like he was staring at me with that singular eye of his. Looking away, I secretly hoped he would do the same.

A female who matched the description of a grovinian—hammerhead-shaped skull, big white eyes, long neck, and large cheek bones—walked to the center of the room, and spoke confidently. "The Senate is in session to discuss a matter involving the human military. For this, we call the eyewitness to speak."

Taking that as my cue, I walked to the center of the room where the woman was. Clearing my throat, I stood up straight and put on a brave face. Public speaking was never my specialty.

"I'm Star Bourn Captain James Severre of the team known as the Wolf Pack. Hours ago, my team—accompanied by Colonel John Miller of the Star Bourn—investigated an abandoned freighter outside of the Newton System in the Einstein Cluster. Shortly after we entered the freighter, we were ambushed by zauhlons."

There was a brief pause where the senators whispered among themselves.

"How do you know it was the zauhlons?" Senator Sul questioned.

"Star Bourn helmets have built in cameras, senator," I said.

"Do you have the footage with you?" Sul asked.

I looked between Drake and Bennett. While I'd given a copy of the footage to Captain Dannaver, I didn't know what he had done with it. Something told me the senators wouldn't appreciate me running to grab my helmet so I could get the original.

Admiral Drake spoke up. "I have the footage. Shall I send it to all of you?"

"You shall," the woman next to me said.

With a tap of a button by Drake, the cam footage from my helmet appeared on screens in front of the senators. When it reached the part where the caped zauhlon appeared at the end of the corridor, Drake paused it.

Senator Din cursed, "Korruk! I knew he wouldn't go down quietly!"

Korruk.

As if a light bulb lit above me, everything clicked. The past two hours have been so filled with adrenaline and emotion that I didn't even realize. The zauhlon who led the ambush against my team was Lord Admiral Korruk. *The* Korruk.

"What's Lord Admiral Korruk doing leading small-scale attacks like this? It doesn't make sense," Senator Sul said.

I'll admit, hearing him refer to the deaths of my friends as "small scale" pissed me off.

"He may be the leader of the Zauhlon Legion, but he's still a zauhlon. He's probably using bait such as that freighter to sharpen his skills," Senator Din said. Unlike the klex senator, Din at least appeared uncomfortable to refer to my team in such a manner.

"The fact that this attack was so close to Milara is concerning," the woman next to me said. I hadn't even thought about that.

Senator Lesh scoffed. "What did you expect, Nyra? The zauhlons are barbarians. A couple of sanctions and a slap on the wrist isn't going to stop them. They're a ticking time bomb that should have been dealt with a hundred years ago."

"Agreed." Senator Verum nodded. "They've gone against our commands one too many times. I say we put them down for good. Give the word and I can have United Front fleets in their systems within the week."

"No. The Galactic Republic of Spacefaring Races cannot go around wiping out entire species we deem problematic. The best thing we can do is place more sanctions on them and do a better job at enforcing them," Senator Sul said. If he felt any compassion for me or my team, he did well at hiding it.

"What's wrong, Larr? Don't want your zauhlon friends to out the klex as the traitors you are?" Senator Din said with crossed arms.

For the first time since the session began, I saw Senator Sul show emotion, "How dare you—"

"That's enough!" The grovinian woman, Nyra, said, "The Galactic Republic will *not* commit genocide simply because the zauhlons have broken the law! That's beyond extreme."

This time it was Senator Bennett's turn to raise his voice. "They've murdered good servicemen, Nyra! People!"

"That doesn't give us the right to kill a thousand times as many people," Senator Iruna finally said, "I agree with Senator Sul, more sanctions is the way to go."

"There is another way," Senator Icaar said, his calm voice a stark contrast to the rising tensions of the rest of the politicians.

Everyone stopped arguing to hear what he had to say. While I didn't care all that much about politics, it was amazing how much respect for this man everyone had that they would stop everything to listen. That was a rare and powerful trait to have in the political world no doubt.

"The zauhlons respect strength above all else, do they not?" Icaar said. "They yielded when the anthrum defeated them hundreds of years ago. They yielded when the Republic stepped in and prevented humanity's extinction. And they will almost certainly yield now.

"I agree: total war is not the way to go. I've seen enough of that to know nothing good can come of that. But if we send someone in to assassinate 'Korruk the Immortal,' the rest of their Legion would submit to our sanctions."

"Or they would seek revenge," Senator Sul muttered.

"Or they would seek revenge," Icaar echoed, "I understand your desire to avoid the potential of a large-scale conflict, but look at things clearly. Our sanctions and laws obviously haven't deterred them. What makes you think that will change? Regardless of what restrictions we set in place, they will continue to disobey. Violence isn't always the answer, but sometimes it is."

Silence followed Icaar's words.

"I ... could see how that would work," Senator Iruna said.

"I still would rather fight them head on and be done with it, but that's a good middle ground. I agree," Senator Verum said.

The other senators nodded in agreement.

"No one objects?" Nyra asked. The senators remained silent. "Very well. Our course of action has been unanimously decided. Now we need to find candidates for the mission and vote on them."

Much to my surprise, Icaar lifted his finger and singled me out. "I vote for him."

While the senators were arguing over the topic of Korruk, I had slipped back over to Admiral Drake and Senator Bennett. It seems like I wasn't the only one shocked either.

"Him?" Senator Sul asked.

"I can vouch for his skills," Admiral Drake said, standing up. "Captain Severre is one of the best commandos we have to offer. If anyone could take Korruk down, it's him."

Senator Verum looked me up and down, then nodded. "The man survived a surprise attack from Korruk. If he can achieve that, then he's a worthy contender for this mission."

Nyra, still as surprised as I was, spoke up. "Are you sure you want to put your name forward, captain? This won't be an easy task."

I didn't hesitate. "Yes, ma'am."

Honestly, I didn't think there would be a chance to avenge my friends. Figured they'd rule me out as unfit; that they would rather use their own favorites than pick a human. Now that I was actually being considered, there was no way I wasn't going to pass this up. My Wolves will not be forgotten.

Nyra nodded. "Okay then. Senators, please put forth your own candidates. Once I receive the candidates, voting will begin."

There were a few moments of silence while everyone cast their votes. Senator Sul was the last one to vote.

"Good. The decision will be announced tomorrow morning. A fifteen-minute break will be held, then the final matter for today will be discussed," Nyra said, which prompted everyone to leave the hall.

Upon exiting the massive doors of the hall, Bennett placed a hand on my shoulder and smiled. "Good job in there, captain. Looks like the Senate finally grew a pair and will do something about this."

"You should be thanking that Predecessor, Icaar. He's the one who gave them the idea," I said.

"Regardless, you chose to accept this responsibility, assuming you do get chosen," Senator Bennett said. "Speaking of which, I'd say there's two votes set in stone for you, those two being myself and Icaar. The rest are hard to read, but I have faith they'll make the right decision."

"Make that three."

The three of us turned around to see Senator Din standing at the doorway.

Senator Din reached out his hand, which I shook. "I don't believe we've properly met. My name is Orthin Din. It's a pleasure to finally meet you, James."

My confusion at his last sentence must have been evident, because Orthin further explained, "I was friends with your father and John. They were the first humans I ever met, and I was the first anthrum they met. Your father told me about you and your mother but, unfortunately, I never got to meet you until now."

Despite the attempted explanation, I was even more confused. Miller never talked about his past all too much, and Mom never told me about Dad's time in the war. Thinking about it, it wasn't all too surprising that they knew some anthrum, seeing how they helped out humanity halfway through the First Contact War. But friends?

"I didn't know my father was friends with any anthrum. John, either."

Orthin nodded. "I'm not surprised. They had plenty of secrets that they held close to their hearts, many of which they've taken to the grave." Orthin paused, as if momentarily losing himself in the past. "If you have time, join me after the next vote. I may not know everything about your father or John, but maybe I can help you better understand them. After all they did for me, it's the least I could do."

I looked to Admiral Drake, who nodded, "We're off duty, captain. Consider the rest of the day your shore leave."

———◆○◆———

Orthin and I had taken a hover train over to New Motula, the anthrum city on Milara. The novelty mode of transportation was relatively empty, though whether that was because of a lack of interest or because Orthin had special senator privi-leges, I couldn't tell. Honestly, I was leaning towards the latter.

The city was beautiful. This was the first time I'd been to an anthrum location, so the stone-inspired architecture and glowing gems lighting up the streets took my breath away. I wasn't much of an architect guy, but I could appreciate the fine details of alien culture.

Orthin must have picked up my amazement because he smiled and looked at the rocky skyscrapers as well. "Beautiful, isn't it? As much as I miss Dravina, living here is the next best thing, in my humble opinion."

Some silence formed between us as we stepped off the train and wandered aimlessly through the streets, the glowing blue lights shining high above us.

"What was my dad like?" The question came as a surprise to me. I hadn't meant to ask it out loud, but it just came out. On the way there we had talked about Miller, his short temper and the fact that deep down he was a softy—and I'm still not sure I believe that. But we hadn't spoken much about my father.

Orthin pondered the question for a while. "When I first met your father, above all else he was tired. I could hear it in his breathing. From what the crew on my ship could tell, he and his commandos were fighting for days." Orthin chuckled. "I'm surprised he didn't blow us all to pieces, quite honestly.

"When the language barrier was broken, however, and I got to know him, the one thing that stuck out to me the most was that he was kind. Kind and brave. While I don't know too much about the origin of your war with the zauhlons, I remember how brutal it was. Kill or be killed. This sometimes meant that civilians would be forgotten about, with the warriors too focused on killing their enemies and avenging the dead. Not your father, though. He would always make sure the innocent got away safely, even if that meant disobeying orders."

"Were you in the military?" I asked.

"Oh, Surgus, no. I was actually a medic as a part of the Nylandal, a non-governmental organization. More often than not I'd find myself in the middle of grand battles, and it would be your father and John who rescued me. If I didn't know any better, I'd say that was their one mission throughout the entire war." Orthin laughed, but it was followed by a sorrowful, and possibly bitter tone, "No, if I'm being honest, I hate wars. I hate unnecessary death."

We were quiet for a moment. The alien city lights were even more beautiful now that it was night.

"What do you know about Korruk?" I asked.

It was out of left field, but it was in the back of my mind since the senate hearing. Even though I wasn't on the mission yet, I wanted to find out as much as I could about Korruk. Figure out his tactics, his weaknesses, his history, everything. I could find some of this out via a codex search, but seeing as how I was with a high-ranking official, I was hoping I could get something I couldn't get in a codex entry.

"Surely, you've heard him referred to as 'Korruk the Immortal?' There's a reason for that. Zauhlons can take some punishment, but Korruk is on a whole other level. Hundreds have tried to kill him, but none have succeeded. Many believe he'll be the first zauhlon to die of old age in centuries, not that he's all that close to that age yet.

"He's one of the best strategic minds in zauhlon history. Even though we defeated the zauhlons hundreds of years ago, they decimated our cities, killed tens of millions of civilians, and won more than a few battles, all thanks to Korruk. You must be very careful, James. Korruk isn't the type of leader to sit around and do nothing. He's up to something. I can feel it in my bones."

I let those words sink in. It would be a lie to say it didn't make me nervous. Seeing firsthand what Korruk was capable of was one thing, but to hear of all his past atrocities was intimidating. Still, I couldn't—no, *wouldn't*—back down. It was time someone cut him down to size and give him the ass-whooping he deserved. I prayed to whatever god was out there that I would be the one who delivered that to him.

With Milara's two moons looming high above us, Orthin hailed a taxi, and upon one stopping, he turned to face me. "You should head to back to Panalith and get some rest. No matter who the rest of the senators choose, you'll need to be up early in the morning."

"Thank you, Senator Din. I appreciate you taking the time to tell me about my dad. My mom never told me much about him, and John always avoided the topic. So it means a lot to finally hear about him," I said.

"Of course. And please, call me Orthin," the anthrum said. "If you ever wish to talk further, I'm but a comm call away."

<hr />

As soon as I reached Churchill Memorial Hotel, I began digging into the zauhlon codex entries. The knowledge I gained from them was useful, but I was after info on Korruk specifically. Unfortunately, there wasn't much to be seen. Or at least, I didn't have access to the useful info. After an hour of staring at my data-pad, I finally laid down on the bed and shut my eyes.

It'd been months since I've been in a comfy bed. Even though the bigger starships had quarters for each of its crew members, they weren't all that comfortable. The bunks were the worst though. I swore they just disguised steel planks as mattresses to save some money.

Just as I was drifting off to sleep, my data-pad buzzed next to me. The sudden noise jolted me out of my tired haze. Annoyed, I checked the message. Upon seeing the notification, I sat straight up and gave it my full attention.

It was from the Genova Military Hospital in the Newton System.

The message was from a Dr. Mara Trent regarding Flyby. A lot of the message was filled with medical babble that I didn't understand, but I got the gist of it. One of the spikes on the cannonball caught Flyby's eye, rendering it useless. On top of that, he had a serious concussion, and the lack of oxygen thanks to his oxygen supply failing didn't help that by any means. The message ended by saying there was no guarantee he'd be able to get back in the field, and that she would update me as time went by.

Frankly, I was just relieved he wasn't dead. At least one other Wolf survived that shit show. On the other hand, I was worried. Flyby's parents are very success driven. In other words, if you failed, you were nothing to them. If he has to go home because of an injury, that would surely be seen as a failure to his parents. I wrote a quick message to Dr. Trent to let me know when he was conscious and ready for visitors, then laid back down.

I didn't know how busy these next few months would be, but I was determined to visit him at least once. To let him know the others would be avenged. That was the last thought on my mind before I fell asleep. Justice was coming for Korruk, whether he knew it or not.

03

[SC Fort Leonidas, outskirts of Utopia.]

[Local system time: 0800.]

The hearing to decide who would go after Korruk finally ended. As it turns out, I was chosen for the job. The vote was four to three in my favor. I didn't get to see who I was going up against, and frankly I didn't care. No matter who they were, it didn't matter. I was going to kill that bastard, and I couldn't be happier.

Nyra, who was Speaker of the People as I later found out from Admiral Drake, gave a speech about the importance of the mission, but I already knew that. I already knew that if Korruk was left unchecked that more good men and women would die, just like my Wolves, and more families would be torn apart.

As soon as we left the hearing, we were picked up by an Odin dropship. This model was larger than the Hercules. It had more armor, could carry more troops, and had bigger and badder weapons. With its military license and registration tag, it got to bypass all the air traffic and go wherever the hell it wanted to, for which I was grateful. Within ten minutes, we were near the edge of Utopia—humanity's city on Milara—and were headed straight for SC Fort Leonidas.

The fort was a sight to behold, that was for sure. Anti-air turrets mounted on its high and mighty walls, multitudes of marines and troopers were out and about, and it all looked brand new. Looking at it, you couldn't tell if it was built ten years ago or last month.

We touched down on the landing pad closest to the city wall and entered the fort. Over the roaring engines of the Odin lifting off, Admiral Drake shouted, "If you're going to be tracking and killing Korruk, you'll need a ship."

"Sir, I'm a Star Bourn, not a sailor. I don't know a thing about captaining a ship," I protested.

"Oh, you won't be the captain of the ship. You may be a tough SOB, Severre, but that doesn't mean I trust you to command an entire starship," Drake said. "I do, however, have a ship in mind that has a good captain and that's small, fast and nimble enough to get you where you need to go."

We reached a viewing port that overlooked a hangar bay with perhaps the smallest military-grade ship I've seen. In front of me was a chrome vessel that looked more like a winged bullet than anything up to battle standards. From where I stood, I couldn't see many weapons, but what I could see were two Mark-Eighty Machine Guns poking out from the bow of the ship. They may not look it, but those guns could tear through a starship's hull without any trouble once the shields on an enemy ship were down.

"Captain, I'd like to introduce you to the *Sparrow*. She's a MK-III Assassin Class ship. Only three other ships of this class are in service," Drake said.

"She's beautiful," I said. It wasn't a lie either. For as few weapons as I could find, it really was a beautifully made ship. How well it could do in a fight remained to be seen.

"Thank you, sir," a man with a Scottish accent said behind me. "Her crew's even better."

I turned to see a bald man in his mid-forties standing at attention. He wore the signature white and black naval officer uniform, with the stripes of a captain.

"Captain Severre, I'd like to introduce you to the captain of the *Sparrow*, Duncan McCabe," Drake said.

"Pleasure to meet you," I said, offering my hand.

"The pleasure's all mine," McCabe replied, accepting the offer and shaking my hand firmly. "And please, call me Arty."

"Captain McCabe is an old friend of mine. As soon as you were assigned the mission, I sent him a message and asked if he was willing to help. Luck must've been on our side, because he just so happened to be on Milara for shore leave," Drake explained.

"Should you accept my help, captain, we'll take you to anywhere in the galaxy you need to go to," McCabe said.

Looking back at the *Sparrow*, I gave the offer some thought. That ship would be my home for the foreseeable future, assuming I say yes.

Home... I haven't had one of those in a long time. It might be nice to have somewhere I could go back to for a little while.

I turned around and gave McCabe a nod. "It would be my honor."

"Wonderful," Duncan smiled. "I'll have my crew back on the *Sparrow* by the end of the day."

With that, McCabe headed back to the chrome ship, leaving Admiral Drake and myself alone.

"On top of that, captain, I needed to tell you something," Drake started. "This mission you're embarking on is far too dangerous to be done on your own. As such, you'll be assigned new members for your squad, the Wolf Pack."

I knew it was coming, but it was still a punch in the gut.

My knee-jerk reaction was to tell the admiral to screw off, but I knew better than that. Instead, I swallowed the anger that came from that statement and pushed my emotions away. I hated it—hell, I resented it—but that was the way the system worked. If I needed a couple of new commandos by my side to avenge my family, so be it. Push comes to shove, I'd leave the team after the mission is complete and run lone wolf for a while. Those types of ops were few and far between, but they were available for the Star Bourn who couldn't work with their fellow commandos.

"Fine," I finally said. "But I get to pick my team."

Admiral Drake thought about this before nodding. "You have a deal."

***

I spent the rest of the day cooped up in one of Fort Leonidas's meeting rooms going through the list of all active commandos. After what must have been hours, I'd finally put together my new team.

First up was Second Lieutenant Charles Smith, call sign "Tenner." Tenner and I actually have some history. We were in the same training company back in boot camp, and both our teams had worked together on more than one occasion. After double checking to see if he had left the Wolverines, I found out I could pick anyone, regardless of whether they were a part of a squad. I hesitated picking him and pulling him out of his team, but I needed someone I could trust, now more than ever. His specialty had always been negotiation. Or, as the old Wolves and I would say, "he was loaded with credits."

Second was Corporal Elizabeth Carter, call sign "Boomer." Among the Star Bourn, there were two paths to getting to where you were. One was to be a prodigy in boot camp and the academy, where they would then advance to another year of intensive training. The other path was for a marine to receive a recommendation into the program. The latter was the path Corporal Carter took. From what her record said, she was pretty fresh as a Star Bourn, but she knew how to kill enemies better than some of our veterans. On top of that, she had been part of a marine bomb squad, so she knew her way around explosives.

Up next was Sergeant Robert Grayson, call sign "Grampa." He was a veteran from the First Contact War, which piqued my interest. He'd been a Star Bourn for almost thirty years, and despite his low rank considering his time, he was the best of the best. An expert in heavy weaponry, and apparently an expert in close quarters combat too. I don't know if that meant I'd be seeing a sixty-year-old engaging in sword fights, but it seemed like a good quality, especially when going up against zauhlons.

Lastly was Warrant Officer Jeanpaul Watson, call sign "Bullseye." He was an expert marksman who reportedly never missed. Surprisingly, there wasn't much to this guy's record. Upon further examination, I found out why—at the bottom of his data file I read "lone wolf." That nearly made me pass on him. I've worked with lone wolves before, and they were a pain. At the end of the day though, it wasn't about all of us getting along. So long as he could do his job, that was all that mattered. *After this, you'll be one of those pains in the ass too.*

I looked and looked for a sixth member to round it out, but I couldn't find anybody good enough. That wasn't fair to all the Star Bourn on the list though. It wasn't that they weren't skilled—if this was any other mission, there were more than a few I'd have picked—it's just that for taking down Korruk, I needed the best of the best, and I felt the Star Bourn I picked were exactly that: the best humanity had to offer.

With the new roster for the Wolf Pack to my liking, I sent the list to Admiral Drake, who had gone back to the Sol System. Looking out the bulletproof windows of the meeting room, I found out it had been more than a few hours; the sun was already setting. I checked the time on the data pad and found out it was already 1700 hours. A moment later, I got a message from Captain McCabe. It read, "The crew is gathered at the docking bay. Meet me at the airlock and I'll introduce you to everyone."

I was less than enthusiastic about the grand introduction Arty had apparently set up, but I understood it. The mission we were about to take part in was huge, so it would be better to get familiar with everyone I'd be working with.

On my way to the hangar bay, I got a message from Admiral Drake reading, "Give me until the end of tomorrow and I'll have them in Tria's Keep." Good. The sooner we can get this op started, the better.

Upon reaching the hangar bay, I found Captain McCabe waiting for me near the airlock, just as he said in the message. We said our hellos and entered the *Sparrow*. Keeping to the ongoing themes of the ship, the interior was unlike any SC starship I'd been in before. The corridors were clean—almost shiny—and were shades of white and gray, a contrast to the typical gunmetal-colored corridors of typical military starships.

In no time we were at the *Sparrow*'s cargo bay. In front of Arty and I were three hundred men and women, nearly all of them in similar white and black naval uniforms. The only ones who looked different were the engineers, who wore gray coveralls. As you can imagine there was plenty of chatter, most likely regarding what this was about. As soon as Captain McCabe stepped into sight, however, they all piped down.

"I won't waste any time here. We've been given a mission not only by Admiral Drake, but also the Galactic Senate. That mission is to kill Lord Admiral Korruk. For those young folk who skipped history class, this is the man who sought the extinction of the anthrum. This is the man who sought *our* extinction during the First Contact War. And this is the man who went against the laws set in place by the Senate and murdered more of our own.

"Four good men and women recently lost their lives because of his bloodlust. For this and for the lives of all the others he's murdered, we are going to track him to the ends of the galaxy and put a bullet in his head. The leader of this mission is the man next to me, Captain James Severre. He and a team of Star Bourn will be joining us until the mission is complete. You'll treat him with the same amount of respect as you would me. I expect all of you to work to the best of your abilities to get this done. Everyone but the senior officers are dismissed."

I'll admit, I was impressed.

As nearly all three hundred of the crew left to go back to their stations, I took the opportunity to observe the senior officers who stayed. As much as I was unfamiliar with all the different ship roles, I was able to guess that the woman in the engineering coveralls was chief engineer and the older man in the white coat was the doctor.

After five minutes, the only people left in the bay were Arty, myself, and the *Sparrow*'s senior officers.

"Captain Severre, let me introduce you to the senior officers," McCabe said. "To your left is chief engineer Lieutenant Rebecca Walker."

"Nice to meet you," she said with a grin before I could get anything out. "I've never actually met a commando. You'll have to tell me how accurate the holo-vids are. Actually, speaking of which, is it true each piece of armor is tailored specifically to your body? You know what, hold that thought, we can talk about that later. Anyway, I'm sure it'll be fun working with you and the others."

"Here's hoping," I said. Note to self, don't start a conversation with her unless I'm ready to be there for a long time.

"Next is master-at-arms, Lieutenant Commander Tim Williams."

The man wore a uniform similar to the normal white and black, but he had more blue in his sleeves. Despite the intimidating scar across his nose, Tim gave me a warm smile.

"Good to meet you, Chief Williams," I said, matching his smile.

"Same to you, captain. I'll make sure you and your team are unharmed while on this vessel," Williams said.

"To your right is Lieutenant Commander Amanda Lynn."

Despite wearing a tired expression, she maintained a straight posture. "Don't worry, captain, we'll have your back."

"Good to hear, LC. We'll need that attitude for the mission," I replied.

"Next up is Doctor John Holiday. Outside of myself he's our most experienced officer."

"Oh, please, Captain Arty, let's not sugarcoat it. That's just another way of saying I'm old," Dr. Holiday laughed, "Regardless, it'll be my pleasure to work with you and no doubt patch you up, Captain Severre."

I smiled. "That's a guarantee. I hope you're good at that sort of thing."

"Captain Severre, do you think I could've gotten this far as a Star Command doctor if I wasn't?" Dr. Holiday joked.

"Lastly, we have the *Sparrow*'s chief helmsmen, Norman Richards," Arty finished flatly.

Norman stood taller than the rest of the senior officers, including myself. Despite being thin and rather weak looking, his voice was low and booming, like one of those old boxing announcers.

"Thanks for putting in a good word for me, captain," he said sarcastically, "The *Sparrow* is a good ship, Captain Severre. But a good ship is nothing without a good pilot. And lucky for you, you're looking at a great pilot."

"Alright, all of you are dismissed," Arty said. He waited for all the officers to leave before he turned to me. "Come on, I have somewhere I'd like to show you."

My curiosity piqued, I followed Arty through the ship, now filled with officers going about their day. A minute later, we entered the bridge. The command deck was straight ahead and was raised higher above the rest of the bridge. At the edge of the command deck was the captain's chair. Beyond that on the main level was a machine that projected a map of the Milky Way, allowing Arty to set the *Sparrow*'s destinations. On either side of the command deck were two curved staircases that allowed access to the main level, where there was a plethora of terminals.

With us next to the captain's chair, Arty spoke in a lower tone so that no one else heard us. "Listen, Severre. I understand this mission is important, and you have my word we'll do what needs to be done. That said, the safety of my crew is of the utmost importance to me. If it comes to it, I'm putting their lives above the mission."

"Understood, sir."

Arty smiled, then took a seat at his chair. "Get her up in the sky, Richie."

"Aye-aye," Helmsmen Richards said.

Before I had time to protest, the engines were roaring to life, and we were airborne. We flew through the evening sky and out of atmosphere, the stars becoming our new backdrop.

"Captain Arty, my team won't be here until tomorrow," I said.

"Don't worry, Severre, we're not leaving the system. Just warming her up and getting you used to her," Arty said, "I'll inform Admiral Drake to have your team ready for pickup at Genesis Station. For now, enjoy the ride."

[The next day.]

[Local system time: 1520.]

As it turned out, the new Wolves arrived earlier than I expected. The *Sparrow* was on her way to Genesis Station to pick them up. Meanwhile, I was waiting by the airlock in my fatigues. I wanted to pick them up and get this started as fast as possible. Despite that, I wasn't all too eager to meet them.

It would be nice to see Tenner, sure, but I still wasn't keen on a new set of Wolves.

Next to me were ship security officers, Ensigns Tom Valentine and Walter Hitchcock, who were telling me about a recent adventure the *Sparrow* went on. It was hard to get the clear story with the two of them talking over each other, but it was something about a test run for a new set of engines the grovinians were developing. On their way to Evonar's Wings, they were caught in one of the fabled slip-space storms. I wasn't sure I believed that, but I went along with it.

"The scientists on board said the odds of going through one of those storms was one in a million," Valentine said, "Of course it's our luck we ride into one."

"Worst of all, we went all that way, went through all that crap, just for those blasted grovinians to say, 'Oh never mind, we decided to test it out ourselves,'" Walter said. "You know those storms give you hallucinations too? I was throwing up for a week afterward."

"Yeah, that sounds like something they'd do," I said.

Just then, Richie's voice chimed in over the public comms. "Arriving at Genesis Station in one minute." Then through the comms above the airlock only, Richie added, "Your guys will be in Hangar Bay Forty, bullet brain."

"Thanks, airhead," I said. For the short time I'd been on ship, Richie and I had developed a competition to see who can come up with the best insults for one another.

"Alright, well we'll see you around, captain. Wouldn't wanna get in the way of Star Bourn business," Valentine said.

"Sure thing. Maybe next time you can tell me more fairy tales, like about the time you guys ran into the space dragons in the Orion's Dove sector," I said.

Despite smiling, Hitchcock tried to answer in a serious tone. "Listen, sir, next time you're puking your guts out because you went through one of those storms, just know I'll be laughing the entire time."

In no time, I felt the slight shake of the docking magnets attach themselves to the *Sparrow*, and after giving the crew in the station a second to connect the walkway, I opened the airlock and made my way to Hangar Bay Forty.

Pushing past all the officers, engineers, and marines, no doubt desperate for their shore leave to begin, I finally made it to the elevator. Not five seconds later, I was at Hangar Bay Forty. Fifteen meters in front of me stood all four commandos I'd picked out. They looked like they'd been waiting there for a few minutes already, so I didn't waste any more time and walked up to them. Upon seeing me, all four of them stood to attention and greeted me with salutes.

"It's good to finally meet all of you. I'm not sure what Admiral Drake told you, but I needed the best of the best for a mission most would say is impossible. I'll brief you all officially when we're somewhere less public," I said, "The ship we'll be serving on is in Deck thirty-eight. It's the smallest one in the docks. Ironically, it's not hard to miss. Dismissed."

Boomer, Grampa, and Bullseye left for the elevator. Tenner, however, stayed behind. The two of us smiled at each other and went for a handshake before bringing it in for a hug.

"Good to see you again, Cap," Tenner said.

"Same goes for you," I replied, "I hope this wasn't too much of a problem, separating you from the Wolverines."

"It wasn't, trust me. Truth be told, I was getting ready to step down. As much as I love those bastards, I can't go a day without wanting to kill them," Tenner laughed. Just as we were about to enter the elevator, Tenner stopped me, "Hey, James. I just want you to know I'm sorry about the Wolf Pack. The higher-ups gave me, and I assume the others, a rundown on the mission, and I heard what happened. We're going to give them hell for what they did."

"Damn right we are."

04

[Vorka System, Anubis Nebula.]

[Local system time: 1500.]

Deep in the heart of the Badlands was what had to be the most good-for-nothing system in the galaxy; the Vorka System.

Its sun was a tiny little thing. Its planets were nothing but small icy rocks which had been mined hundreds of years ago. To top it off, it was filled to the brim with asteroids, making it a pain to traverse through.

Little did the galactic citizens know, this system housed the heart of the black market.

Among the many asteroids orbiting Vorka IX was a hidden factory by the name of Serpent's Hole. Concealed within one of the asteroids, Serpent's Hole was massive, being twelve hundred kilometers wide and sixteen hundred kilometers tall.

While big, there were many asteroids nearly the same size orbiting the dead planet.

Ten kilometers away from Serpent's Hole sat an old yet fearsome flagship. The ship looked like the barrel of a gun, with two fins on each side and two on the top and bottom. Etched into the steel hull was the word *Zenavalor*. The closest translation for this was *Vengeance*.

Scattered across the system were thirteen other gun-barrel-shaped ships of all different sizes, yet none were as old or as seasoned as the *Vengeance*. Together they formed the small flotilla dubbed Gorr's Wrath, whose purpose only a select few knew.

Inside all these ships were thousands of zauhlons training for the combat that was sure to come. They were preparing their stations in case they needed to fight sooner than expected, and planning for actions that would soon be played out. Each and every one of them was thirsty for blood. For war.

But none was more thirsty than Lord Admiral Korruk, who sat on his throne inside the *Vengeance*.

He couldn't keep luring humans in and killing them for sport anymore. It satisfied him only temporarily. He could see it in his men as well. It'd been so long since they saw true combat. Deep down he knew this waiting and hiding was making them lose respect for their leader. They didn't know the truth, however. They couldn't see the big picture as he could.

Korruk looked around at his bridge. Much like the ship itself, it was long and rectangular. His captain's chair sat in the center of the bridge. All around him the bridge crew worked tirelessly. Even though he never showed it, he was proud of these men. They were truly the best the Legion had to offer.

While there were some new faces, the majority of the bridge crew were the same officers he'd served with for decades. Those veteran officers were there with him during the war with the apes and bore witness to the battle which earned the *Vengeance* her mighty scar on her starboard side.

Yes, that battle over the planet they called Mars was awesome. Even though his forces had lost, and it served to further hurt his pride, Korruk could admit that battle was one to remember.

The *Vengeance* wasn't the only thing to get scarred from that battle, however. Without realizing it, Korruk gently touched the burned skin on his neck. Images of the fight flashed before him. The death, the destruction, all of it. He slaughtered dozens of apes that day, but his arrogance blinded him long enough for a nearby grenade to burn him. He was lucky to be alive, but that wound would serve as a reminder of the lost battle.

His communications officer turned to look at him. "Transmission from Overlord Gorr."

Korruk nodded. "Put him through."

An image of a zauhlon appeared in front of him, the lights of the bridge dimming so the picture was clear. The large holographic zauhlon was littered with scars, and wore prestigious-looking armor.

While it was impossible to tell from just looking at the hologram, Korruk knew that Gorr's armor was crimson red and wore its indents and scratches with pride. Like himself, Gorr had a cape attached to his armor, signifying that he was above all other zauhlons. Apart from Korruk, that is. They stood side by side as equals, as they always had.

"I take it everything is well, Lord Admiral?" Gorr asked in his rough, raspy voice.

"Yes, my lord. I returned not long ago from a hunt, but the men who accompanied me were weak and died. Two humans escaped, but the rest were butchered," Korruk said.

"You let two apes escape your clutches? That is unlike you, old friend."

He was right. Korruk prided himself on his thorough hunting trips. When he was on the hunt, none of his prey escaped. This time was different though. After going on so many little hunts like these, Korruk had gotten cocky and slipped up. Regardless, a couple of apes managing to run away didn't concern him.

"Fear not. They're insignificant in the grand scheme, my lord. As we speak, a corvette is on its way to Tsello to make sure the bug doesn't talk," Korruk reassured.

This seemed to put Gorr at ease. "Good. What of the Rahalah?"

"Development is going exactly as planned. As it stands, it will be complete in thirty days."

"Good, good. And has our contractor kept his word? He hasn't pulled any tricks?" Gorr asked.

"No, my lord. He's been nothing but professional," Korruk sighed. "I still don't trust him. Yonguns are conniving little lizards. He's just waiting for his chance to strike."

"Let him play his cards first, Korruk. Then, when he thinks he has the upper hand, impale him. With or without him, our Rahalah will be unleashed," Gorr said.

Korruk nodded and leaned back into his chair. He waited for the transmission to cut, but it never did. Instead, Gorr looked at him, waiting. The lord admiral almost smiled. His friend knew him well, that was for sure. "How is Luram?"

"Cold, as usual. The people are getting restless. They know war is coming, but the secrecy is eating them away. If this takes any longer, I wouldn't be surprised if civil war broke out."

"It's the same with my flotilla. Everywhere I go, I can feel their resentment. It's only a matter of time before they attempt a coup," Korruk said. After a pause, he spoke up. "Is this secrecy really needed, Gorr? I understand wanting to limit any leaks, but at this rate we'll be fighting the Republic *and* ourselves."

"You know the answer to that. If our plan is outed, we'll be crushed within the week. Everything we've built—our armies, our ships, our weapons—would be for nothing. I may have agreed to let your senior officers in on the plan—a decision I'm still against, mind you—but our entire race? No." Gorr sighed. "We're almost there, Korruk. Stay strong."

The transmission cut, and the lights reverted back to normal. Korruk sighed. He always said that. *We're almost there, Korruk. Stay strong.* Ever since they were fledglings, Gorr would tell him that. As comforting as those words had been time and time again, they did nothing but frustrate him now. Shaking his head, Korruk pushed the conversation aside. There was nothing he could do about it.

His mind wandered to the humans who escaped. He had faith that General Orrim and the *Wraith* would make short work of them if they dared to show themselves at Tsello. A part of him however—a very small part that lurked deep within his soul—hoped they failed, and that the apes would track him here. His blade yearned for their blood. To right the wrong of letting them get away.

Yes, let them come, Korruk thought. *If they wish to die so badly, I will show them no mercy.*

———◆○◆———

[On route to Echoes Reach, *Sparrow*.]

[Local ship time: 110.]

After receiving a lead from Admiral Drake about an info broker named Zavi, we set course for a planet named Tsello in Echoes Reach. Some quick research told me all I needed to know about Tsello. It was a city world filled to the brim with druggies, wannabe gangsters, and people like this Zavi fellow. I've personally never worked with intel gatherers, but I've heard enough about them to know they'll nickle and dime you to death.

I tried to look deeper into Zavi, but he was good at staying low. All I was able to find out was that he owned a bar called Guar Killo in the Des'gnat District. Apparently, this area of the planet was going through some reconstruction, which was a double-edged sword for us. On the one hand, it meant there wouldn't be a lot of people on the streets, so we would be more exposed. On the other hand, if we were to run into trouble, it meant there would be fewer civilian casualties. It was a tough situation, but we would have to make do with it.

Resting my data-pad on the counter in front of me, I looked out the observation deck window at the swirling reds, blues, and yellows that made up the gravity tunnels we traveled through. Even though I only had a rough grasp on how slip-space travel worked, there was no denying it was a pretty sight to any who laid eyes on it. We still had seven hours before we arrived at Tsello, so I took this little bit of time to relax.

After everything that's happened, this was actually the first time I was able to sit down and have a drink. I was careful to only have a small glass of Quinlin red wine. Last thing I needed was to get drunk on my first mission with the new team. Still, it was nice to enjoy a glass. Quinlin was Fixer's favorite brand of wine, so I suppose this was my way of saying goodbye to him. The night after the incident, I'd decided I would say goodbye to each of the dead in different ways. This would be my sendoff to Fixer.

Miller's would be reacquiring his Doom Bringer sawed-off shotgun and killing some hell hounds on Hera's Fall with it. He always hated those things. M.A.D.'s would be to dig up an old picture of the team together and send it to her kids. They never saw much of her, so I think that's what she would have wanted. And Loudmouth's would be to get piss drunk. I may not be able to down as many drinks as he could, but I'd be damned if I wouldn't try.

[Zeena Station, Tsello.]

[Local system time: 1840.]

So far, so good. After being questioned a lot by the local authorities, we were given the go-ahead to land. Tsello—and the entirety of the Trident's Verge region for that matter—weren't big fans of the Republic. The condition for us being allowed on the planet was to leave any and all rifles on the *Sparrow*. I wasn't happy with the arrangement at all, but there wasn't much I could do. To make up for the disadvantage, I had all of the Wolves bring Fury hand cannons.

They were notorious for their recoil, which meant they weren't used in combat zones often. That said, it was perfect for a situation like this. While heavy, they packed a hell of a punch. Depending on who you asked, they rivaled the power of some shotguns on the market.

With all of us by the airlock, I gave them the rundown on the mission. "Our target is a torr named Zavi. He should be in his bar, Guar Killo. If not, we'll ask around. We only want information from him, so don't do anything to annoy him. In fact, try to be friendly with him. If we can make an ally of this guy, he could prove useful down the road.

"As for Tsello, it's a crime-ridden world, but most of the crimes are gang and drug-related. As long as we don't stick our noses in other people's business, they'll leave us alone." I pressed a few buttons on the wall-mounted terminal next to me and brought up the schematics for a seventy-story building still under construction. "If things get hot and we can't make it back here, this is our LZ. Intel says break time for the workers is between 1900 and 1930 hours, so we shouldn't run into any resistance in the building. Any questions?"

Bullseye raised his hand, "What if the torr won't talk?"

Grampa chuckled and cracked his knuckles. "Oh, don't worry, he'll talk."

"If he won't talk willingly, we'll distract him and search his computers." I turned to Grampa, "Whatever you do, don't do any permanent damage. Just a quick knockout would do."

Boomer spoke up next. "What's the plan on getting to the LZ?"

"There's an elevator in the center that'll take us all the way to the top. If that breaks down for one reason or another, we can use some nearby stairs or use our magnehooks," I said. "Anything else? Good. Helmets on, commandos. Let's move out."

Almost instantly we felt like fish out of water. There were no humans in sight. There weren't any Republic races here for that matter. It was all natives to Trident's Verge. From the alluring averians with their sleek builds and horned heads, to the krin, their six tentacle-like arms being unlike anything I'd seen before. All of that was to say, whenever we passed someone, they stared at us until we were out of their sight. It was only when we reached the slums that people seemed to stop caring.

The lower parts of the city were not only dense and closed in, but old too. The ground below us was made of concrete. Advertising signs were scattered all over the place and there were more shops than I could count. The more you looked up however, the more current-day Tsello looked. Holo-signs, stylish buildings with sharp, unusual edges. It was like they hadn't bothered with tearing down the old and instead just built on top of it.

As if this place wasn't bad enough, it was pitch black out and pouring rain. I heard about Tsello's dark nights, but this was unbelievable. If the brightly lit signs weren't there, we'd have to turn on our night vision.

In ten minutes, we reached the entrance to Guar Killo. The windows were completely blacked out, and it looked like it was put together with a bunch of small pieces of metal.

Switching to the Back Door, I spoke to the Wolves. "Remember, play it cool. This is Tenner's bread and butter, so he'll do most of the talking for us."

With that, I entered the bar first, followed by the rest of the team. For a brief second, everyone stopped to look at us before going back to their respective conversations. In fairness, the bar looked much nicer than the exterior would lead you to believe.

It was round in shape, with the bar itself as the centerpiece. Behind the bar stood a torr dressed in expensive-looking clothes. After the helmet's identification system confirmed his identity was indeed Zavi, I turned to Tenner. "Do your thing."

Tenner simply nodded. He walked over to the bar and took a seat, with Grampa and myself sitting on either side of him. Bullseye and Boomer sat in an empty booth.

"Welcome to Guar Killo. What can I get ya?" Zavi asked, trying to mask his tiredness.

"Actually, I was hoping to find a person. Do you know where I can find Zavi?" Tenner asked, playing dumb. Let the torr introduce himself. Smart.

Zavi opened his arms, as if welcoming him. "Today's your lucky day. You found him! Now whaddya want? I ain't got all day."

Tenner leaned in. "I need some information, and I was told you were the best of the best in that regard."

Zavi placed a hand on his heart. "Stop, you're making me blush," he said sarcastically. He looked at Tenner, then to me and finally Grampa. He let out a deep sigh before nodding. "Alright, come on back."

The info broker led Tenner, Grampa and me into his back office. It was small, but surprisingly cozy. Zavi took a seat in the giant leather chair behind his desk and gestured to the chairs in front of him. Tenner and I sat; reluctantly Grampa did as well.

On the way there, I told Boomer and Bullseye to keep an eye out through the team's comm line. I didn't like leaving them behind but seeing a squad of Star Bourn strolling towards you, well armed or not, is more than a little intimidating.

"So, what is it you need? A Bloodhound base? Corrupt politician's name? It must be something important to come all this way to this glarkhole."

"We need to find a zauhlon," Tenner said.

Zavi appeared to have stopped breathing for a split second. Looks like we struck a chord. "Who do you need specifically? There's plenty of zauhlons out there."

"Does the name Lord Admiral Korruk ring a bell to you?" Tenner asked.

"'Course it does. I ain't stupid."

"Never meant to say otherwise," Tenner said. "Do you know where he is?"

"I might."

"Would some credits help refresh your memory?"

Zavi smiled. "Possibly."

Tenner tapped a couple buttons on the device built into his left forearm armor. "You'll find fifteen thousand credits have been added to your account now."

Zavi checked to make sure, and all four of his eyes widened in surprise. "Impressive, human. Very impressive."

I silently thanked God that Tenner came from a rich family.

"So? How's your memory doing?" Tenner asked.

Looking at his data-pad, Zavi began to speak. "I've heard he's in the Vorka system, over in the Anubis Nebula. Must have something to do with Serpent's Hole. That's the only reason anybody would go there."

Tenner and I exchanged looks.

"What's Serpent's Hole?" I asked.

Zavi paused, then began rubbing his temples, "Y'know, it was on the tip of my tongue. Old age is a killer, I'll tell ya."

I could tell Grampa was itching to sock this bug in the jaw. Tenner forwarded another fifteen thousand credits.

"Oh, I remember now! It's a factory. 'Heart of the black market,' they call it. You ever wonder where terrorists and pirates get their weapons from? It's all thanks to Serpent's Hole," Zavi explained.

"Thanks for the information, Zavi. I hope we can talk again sometime," I said.

"Yeah, me too," the info broker replied, still looking at his data-pad.

Grampa, Tenner, and I got up and let ourselves out. *Serpent's Hole*. Assuming Zavi was telling the truth, this could be big in more ways than one. Sure, it was a good lead on Korruk, but if we could confirm this place existed, the Republic could launch an attack on the factory and deal a huge blow against terrorists and the scum of the galaxy.

Halfway to the main bar, we heard a series of explosions and gunfire. Pulling out our hand cannons, we raced to the door to see what was going on. Upon entering the room, we saw Boomer and Bullseye using the circular bar as cover while four zauhlons laid heavy firepower into them, preventing them from getting any shots in.

Before the attackers had time to register our presence, we opened fire on them. This pause in gunfire from the zauhlons allowed Boomer and Bullseye to fire at the aliens as well. Our combined firepower took out two of the zauhlons. One of the brutes flipped one of the tables on its side and used it as cover while its brother in arms shot a cannonball our way. We dodged the cannon and joined Bullseye and Boomer behind the bar.

Using this time to reload our guns, all of us patiently waited for the zauhlons to run dry and have to reload themselves. When the time came, we popped out of cover and opened fire. The zauhlon with the cannon had found cover with his ally behind the table. Unfortunately, the table was steel, so our bullets, as heavy hitting as they were, weren't getting past the piece of furniture.

Grampa pulled a frag out of one of his pouches. "Shall I?"

"Do it," I said.

With the command given, Grampa activated the grenade and tossed it overhand. The frag landed with a *tink*, followed by a moment of silence. Right when one of the zauhlons began to yell, the grenade went off. The dark red blood of the zauhlons splattered across the walls, and what little remained of the windows shattered. With no red dots on the map anymore, I hesitantly rose from our cover. No one was left alive but us.

Zavi raced out, eyes wide and mouth agape. His bar was a wreck. The liquor had almost entirely been destroyed, the majority of the patrons were dead, and blood was everywhere, "What the *hell* is going on here?"

"We were ambushed by zauhlons," I said. "What were they doing on Tsello?"

Zavi hesitated, then sighed. "I ... might have been more involved than I let on."

Grampa cracked his knuckles. "Go on."

"Years ago, Korruk contacted me and asked if I knew a place where weapons could be made in secret. I told him about Serpent's Hole. I thought that was the end of it," Zavi explained. "I ain't a history major or nothin', but I knew enough about Korruk to know I shouldn't ask questions. Apparently, he didn't like me having a clue about what he was doin'.

"Some zauhlons came in one day with a gun to my head. Long story short, I convinced them not to blow my head off, but every now and then they pay me visits. They never did anything like this though ..."

Tenner turned to me. "You think they knew we were coming?"

"I don't know, but I got a bad feeling about this. Let's head back to the *Sparrow*," I said.

Before we left, Tenner said, "I'll be sure to send enough credits to cover the repair cost."

"Yeah, yeah," Zavi waved us off. "Before you go, take my comm info. I don't wanna see your faces in my bar again."

I punched in his comm number and set it as a contact. I felt bad about what we did to his business, but I was thankful for the contact info. Hopefully next time we need his information it won't end in a shootout.

While we hustled down the street and toward the *Sparrow*, Zavi called after us. "When you see Korruk, tell him he can kiss my ass!"

Whoever was on the streets had disappeared, no doubt scared off by the firefight. The sudden emptiness put me on edge. I'd been through a few abandoned sections of colonies before, and I always hated it. It always felt like an ambush was around the corner.

In this case, it was. Upon turning a corner, a jagged grenade bounced its way to us. On instinct, I grabbed the explosive and tossed it back where it came from. Thankfully the rest of the Wolves hadn't turned the corner, so the only one who got scraped by the shrapnel that shot out of the grenade was me. Nothing vital was hit, just a few cuts on the arms.

Heavy gunfire came from where I tossed the grenade. I couldn't tell how many, but my map indicated at least three.

"Looks like we're going to the LZ," I said. "Follow me. Double time it, Wolves!"

We ran through a few alleyways. Thanks to the audio receptors in my helmet, I heard heavy clanking not too far behind us. *More zauhlons*, I thought. While sprinting, I pulled up a map of the district. It looked like there was a part of the city in ruins that we could cut through. It was dangerous since we didn't know how stable the ruins were, but it was worth a shot.

I took a sharp right and squeezed through some claustrophobic buildings. A minute later, we found ourselves at a crumbling block of the city. The buildings were falling apart, hover cars were burnt to crisps, and skeletons were littered throughout the place. Whatever happened here wasn't good.

I led the Wolves to the nearest building where we hid under some debris. After waiting a few minutes to see if we'd been followed, we got out and headed back to the streets. It looked like we lost them for now.

"Alright, looks like we can get to the LZ by cutting through here. Let's get off this shithole," I said.

[Des'gnat District, Tsello.]

.

[Local system time: 1855.]

A zauhlon in silver armor smashed his fist through the window of a nearby building, shouting in anger. No one dared to speak a peep in his presence, because no one dared to face General Orrim's wrath.

The route the apes took was just small enough that they couldn't fit through, so they'd effectively lost their prey. Taking a moment to calm himself, Orrim thought hard about where they could be going. They could be heading back toward Zeena Station, but were they foolish enough to try that again? They may be weak, but these apes were at least somewhat intelligent.

Nearly all of the buildings here were the same height, so an extract from their vessel would be difficult. Knowing how humans were, they wouldn't want to risk any of these pathetic aliens getting hurt, either. *So where would they go to get extracted?* Orrim thought, *Where would I go?*

He looked up, and it hit him. Even from where they stood, the enormous Luminus Corp Tower could be seen. It was a gamble, but Orrim decided to play his cards.

"Captain Borrvik! Send a gunship to the tower under construction in the Des'gnat District. I believe that's where our prey is running to. If I'm wrong, stay near the slip-space highway and prepare to meet the human ship in combat," Orrim barked through the comms.

He knew getting shouted at like this angered the captain of the *Wraith*, but he didn't care. He needed some heavy firepower at the tower in case they didn't reach the apes.

After a tense moment, Captain Borrvik replied, "Fine. Speak to me like that again though, and I'll kill you. I don't care how much Korruk favors you."

Orrim huffed, "You can try."

05

[Fifty meters outside of the Luminus Corp Tower, Tsello.]

[Local system time: 1910.]

Getting inside the tower wasn't difficult at all. A small lock buster was all it took, and we were in. Our C-Scramblers kept us from being caught on any security cameras. It didn't do much, but it at least made us fuzzy on any camera we appeared on. Next stop was the elevator.

I tapped the button to open the lift. Grampa and Boomer had their guns pointed at the elevator while Bullseye and Tenner watched our backs. The circular elevator opened with a *ding*, revealing itself to be empty. Good. Last thing we needed was to come face to face with workers who decided to skip their break. All of us entered the lift with some room to spare.

While the elevator swiftly brought us to the seventieth floor, I checked the time. The *Sparrow* should be here in five minutes. From what Arty said, local authorities were giving them trouble for the sudden need to lift off. I'm sure our stunt at Guar Killo had some role to play in their suspicion. Regardless, there was nothing we could do about it except stay put.

With another *ding*, the doors slid open. Like the main lobby below, it was devoid of life. We took the stairs leading to the roof and waited by the door. Switching my audio receptors to high, I leaned my helmet against the door, straining to hear any noise indicating there was anyone waiting out there. When I heard nothing, I set up another lock buster, backed up a bit, and leveled my Fury hand cannon.

A second later, sparks flew from the door, and it slid open. Quietly, we poured out onto the roof, making sure to take cover as we did. Our maps reported zero enemies or unidentified life signs, and a quick scan of the roof confirmed that.

Ahead of us was a hangar pad where the *Sparrow* would pick us up. Apart from that area, the walls overlapped the roof by four feet. Behind us was the peak of the wall, which was ten feet above us. We moved to the west of the roof, as that was blanketed in darkness. Boomer and Bullseye kept their sights on the elevator in case those zauhlons joined us, while Tenner and Grampa watched the hangar pad.

Four more minutes to go. All things considered, this was going well. My first mission with the old Wolves was ten times as crazy as this, ending up with us pinned down by one of Bloodhound's automated turrets. If it weren't for Oracle's tech skills, we would've been torn apart.

"Shit! Gunship inbound!" Tenner called out.

All of us sunk into the shadows and hugged the cover we were using.

"Did it look like it belonged to the zauhlons?" I asked.

"Yeah, it was theirs alright," Grampa said.

I nodded, then opened a comm channel with Arty. "We've got a zauhlon gunship here. They haven't spotted us but be ready to shoot it down."

"Got it. Hang tight, Severre," Arty said.

Instinctively I looked at the elevator. If those zauhlons sent a gunship here, chances are they're on their way here too. The lift was painted with the bright spotlight emitting from the gunship. If that hit us, it wouldn't matter how dark it was here. This kept getting worse ...

"Stick close to cover. If it sees us, we're screwed," I said.

All of us laid down and leaned against the piece of metal, almost trying to become one with it. The blinding search light flashed above us, sweeping past our cover but never hitting us. Seconds after searching our corner of the roof, it moved to another part.

It was then that the zauhlons arrived.

Silently, I cursed our luck. Staying out of a gunship's sight was one thing, but add a squad of zauhlons to avoid? This wasn't looking good.

A quick peek showed that the gunship's spotlight remained at the opposite end of the roof while the zauhlons searched it. They were using the spotlight to make it easier to look for us. Smart. With my Fury in one hand, I unsheathed my machete. If I had to kill a zauhlon I'd rather it be done quietly, but I wasn't going to give up my hand cannon for that either.

Suddenly, the spotlight lit up the area around us, indicating that the zauhlons were coming our way. Two zauhlons moved next to Boomer and Bullseye, looking around the area. We were out of sight for now, but if they looked our way ...

Two more minutes. I prayed the *Sparrow* wouldn't be held up by the authorities any longer than they have already.

As if everything went in slow motion, I watched the zauhlon closest to us turn his head towards us. Before he could get a word in, Boomer jabbed her heated blade between his chest plate and through his heart. At the same time, Bullseye swung his machete at the other zauhlon's hoof before digging his vibro-knife into the fallen zauhlon's head. The silent kill was all for naught though. The gunship saw it all, and opened fire on us. Boomer was able to get her arm back to safety, but even from that short time in the danger zone I saw some skid marks left by the oncoming storm of gunfire.

The constant rain of bullets scoured the floor around us. The machine gun fire hitting the cover behind us felt like a massage against my back. I was worried if this kept up the bullets would just tear through the metal. The remaining four zauhlons dared to enter the gunship's line of fire and try to kill us themselves. We all fired at the zauhlons, hoping our Fury hand cannons would be enough to hold them back.

Our shields were drained from the attack, and my HUD showed Boomer and Grampa had been shot, but we were all still alive. One of the zauhlons, however, was not. His body fell on top of Boomer, who used it as a shield while her shields recharged. Eventually the zauhlons retreated to some nearby cover and let the gunship do its work. Unfortunately for them, while gunships are deadly, they need to recharge.

The hellfire of bullets ceased, and I took this time to pull out one of my two condensed bombs and chucked it at the gunship. It exploded upon impact, but the blast wasn't enough to bring it down. The three zauhlons resumed firing at us, which kept us in cover long enough for the gunship to fully cool down and begin its stream of bullets.

"Think a destabilizer would work on the gunship pilot?" Tenner asked.

Destabilizer grenades took away the target's hearing and vision for a certain amount of time, depending on how close you were to it. Truth be told, I didn't know the answer to that. If it was a civilian vehicle I'd say yes, but a military vehicle was a gamble.

"It's worth a shot," I said. "Try and get it as close to the gunship as you can but be careful."

Taking out the small blue ball, Tenner hesitantly poked his head out from the side he was closest to. When he realized the fire was directed more towards the other side, he pressed the activation button and tossed it at the cockpit as best he could.

The destabilizer ignited a little more than halfway to its destination. When the gunship stopped firing, we knew it worked. Not a moment later, a blue beam shot through the zauhlon gunship, blowing it to pieces. Before the debris even had time to hit the roof, the *Sparrow* came soaring in, making a sharp one-eighty as it did. The cargo bay door was already opened, so all we had to do was wait for it to get close enough for us to jump in. When it did, none of us hesitated and sprinted toward the human-made ship.

One by one each of us leapt onto the extended ramp. When we were well into the cargo bay, the doors closed, and the *Sparrow* raced out of atmosphere.

"Arty, set a course for the Vorka system. That's our next destination," I said, not wanting to waste time. If they had a gunship, there was no telling what else was here.

"Aye aye. You might want to hold on," Arty said.

Leaving my helmet in the docking bay, I sprinted to the bridge. On my way there, the *Sparrow* shifted right then left, as if dodging something. Whether those are civilian ships or missiles, I didn't know yet.

When I entered the bridge, things were surprisingly calm. It reminded me of the relaxed attitudes of dropship pilots. I walked over to the XO station but stayed on my feet. Twenty kilometers out was the Slip-Space Highway.

"Captain! Radar's picking up an enemy signature. Says here it's a zauhlon corvette classified as the *Wraith*," Lynn said.

"We don't have the weapons to take it in a head-on fight. Richie, dodge it as best you can and get us through the Highway," Arty said.

"Already on it, captain," Richie said, "Just need to get close enough to input the coordinates."

When the *Sparrow* was eight kilometers away from the *Wraith*, the corvette began firing its missiles. Richie effectively dodged the missiles and flew dangerously close to the enemy ship. The missiles, which were locked onto us, crashed along the belly of the *Wraith*, wounding but not destroying the zauhlon vessel.

"Alright, coordinates are in! Hang onto your seats," Richie said.

Without slowing down, the *Sparrow* raced headfirst into the highway, which warped us into the gravity tunnels. I let out a sigh of relief and leaned my head back.

"So, what's at this Vorka system, captain?" Arty asked.

"A factory called Serpent's Hole, and if luck has it, Korruk."

[Luminus Corp Tower, Tsello.]

[Local system time: 1920.]

Orrim shouted at the night sky in anger. This mission, which should have been simple, was a colossal failure. The humans not only escaped his and his men's grasps, but the *Wraith*'s as well. With his helmet off, Orrim blinked away the lingering effects of the destabilizer grenade. A dropship was already on its way to bring them back to the ship, but Orrim feared by the time they entered the Vorka system, the humans would already be inside the Serpent's Hole. The only saving grace was how well hidden the factory was.

With his vision fully restored, he was able to see one of the zauhlon's signature Archon dropships heading their way. Orrim looked at his surviving zauhlons, who carried one dead warrior each. He moved to the last remaining body and threw it over his shoulder. They may be dead, but they deserved better than rotting on an alien world. He only wished they could go back and get the other fallen zauhlons as well.

The Archon didn't even land before the thick sliding doors heaved open. The living zauhlons tossed the dead bodies into the dropship before lifting themselves into the vessel. When the doors shut, they left for the *Wraith*.

His helmet back on, Orrim moved to the back of the Archon, already securing a comm channel with Lord Admiral Korruk. Not two seconds later, a holographic image of Korruk appeared on Orrim's wrist, visible to himself only.

"Lord Admiral Korruk, I have an update on the situation," Orrim said. When Korruk nodded for him to continue, he spoke again, "Before they were killed, my scouts confirmed the presence of armored apes in the bug's bar, so it would be wise assume they know of Serpent's Hole. They've left the system, so they should be expected in two days. I'm on my way back to the *Wraith*. As soon as I'm on board, we're heading to the Vorka system to intercept the humans."

Korruk stayed silent for a moment. After the brief pause, he turned his focus to Orrim. "Very well. Try to lead them toward Vorka X. The frost demons should be enough to destroy them. Failure will not be tolerated a second time, Orrim."

With that, the transmission was cut, leaving Orrim alone with his men. He swore under his breath at his terrible luck. Up until now, everything was going to plan...

He couldn't fail now. Not when he was so close. Orrim had spent years climbing the ranks of the Legion, all to get close to Korruk and stab him in the back. He would murder Korruk and take his place as Lord Admiral. This would be his ultimate revenge, and he wasn't about to let some apes ruin it.

◆○◆

[Comm Room, inside the *Sparrow*.]

[Local ship time: 1930.]

After making sure everyone received the proper medical attention they needed, I took a quick shower and put on my fatigues. The shots Grampa and Boomer took weren't serious, and were treated fairly quickly. Dr. Holiday said they would need some physical therapy the next day just to make sure everything was working fine, but that was okay with me. Better safe than sorry.

As soon as I was dressed, I headed to the comm room to update Admiral Drake. As soon as the line was secured, I informed him of everything. Serpent's Hole, our run ins with the zauhlons, and our fight on top of the in-progress tower.

"I see. Your trick with the scramblers won't fool anybody with a brain, but since there's no clear footage that it was you in the building, it looks like we were able to avoid a war with the Coalition of Independent Races. Good work, captain, but I think Zavi had the right idea in keeping you away from there. Anything else like that happens again and we're screwed.

"That aside, this Serpent's Hole has me intrigued. Drones have a tendency to be unreliable in the Badlands, but I always figured that sector of space was where pirates and the like got their equipment. If you can confirm the existence of that place, that would be huge in creating a more accurate map of the inner workings of the Badlands," Drake said.

He was right. Command always figured something like Serpent's Hole must exist, but a confirmation would do wonders for the war on crime.

"There's also Korruk to factor in," I added.

"That too," Drake said, his voice trailing off. "Korruk spending years around a secret weapons factory is a giant red flag. You need to get to the bottom of this, Severre. Even if you can't kill him there, find out what he's up to. The Badlands is free game, so do whatever it takes."

"Yes, sir," I said.

The comm line ended, and I leaned forward on the railing. This mission could have gone a lot better, but at least no civilians were harmed and none of the Wolves died. Checking the time, I realized it was only 1933 hours. My body was exhausted, but there was more work to do. There may not be a lot on Serpent's Hole, but it was my job to gather as much intel as possible.

I pushed myself off the railing and headed to the portside observation deck. At this rate, that might as well be my office.

On my way there, my mind wandered to Korruk. What kind of weapon would a warlord make? Would he go for the destructive kind—nukes, planet crackers, that sort of thing—or would he go for a chemical-based weapon? Based off what's known about him, destructive weapons seem to be in his ballpark, but I wasn't about to rule anything out. The next question would naturally be, who or what was his target?

I shook my head clear. One thing at a time. First things first, let's see what I can find on Serpent's Hole. Then I can focus on that bastard.

06

[Serpent's Hole.]

[Local system time: 1455.]

The sound of a heavy body collapsing onto old metal echoed throughout the area. Sounds of machinery at work masked the noise of the corpse, leaving no one the wiser. A well-armored anthrum stepped over the lifeless zauhlon, the barrel of his gun still smoking. He looked down at his handiwork before looking back at the trail of bodies he left behind.

Why are there so many zauhlons on patrol? He asked himself. Throughout his time in the Hole, there were never this many zauhlons out and about. *Something's about to happen.*

He got to work disposing of the bodies, hiding them in crates, pushing their corpses off the ledge, whatever was easiest before continuing his hunt. His contact said the resources for the zauhlons were being shipped to a lower level of Serpent's

Hole. According to rumor, it was being delivered to Zone Two. If that's the case, his best chance at finding his target would be to hitch a ride with the cargo and get off before they arrive at their destination.

No matter what it took, he would find Korruk and kill him. He may have escaped justice before, but it would catch up to him soon. No matter how far he ran, he would pay for all the war crimes he committed. Releck would make sure of it.

[Vorka System, Anubis Nebula.]

[Local system time: 1530.]

We dropped out of the Highway right as I entered the bridge. The sight was ... plain, to put it mildly. That matched with the description of the Vorka System to a tee; a star system full of asteroids and dead planets. I knew its secret though. I knew what was really there. The trick was in how to find it.

"Richie, bring up a map of the system and start a scan for any asteroids that are hollow," Arty ordered.

"Got it, cap'n. It could take a while though, given how many there are," Richie said.

A holographic recreation of the system unrolled itself in front of Arty. I couldn't see it all too well from where I stood, but in the bottom left corner was a list of how many asteroids were in the system that the scanners registered; a whopping sixty thousand. Richie was right in that it would take a long time.

We moved out of the way of the highway and latched onto an asteroid, the bow of the ship facing the way we entered.

With nothing else to do, it felt like hours passed. Looking at the clock, I wasn't too far off. It'd been two hours since we arrived. I found myself fooling around with the zipper of the skinsuit I wore under my fatigues, looking around the bridge. A quick glance at the holo-map told me the scan was at sixty percent completed. *Thank God I didn't sign up for the navy.*

From one of the nearby terminals, I heard the indication of a ship exiting the Highway. It didn't take me long to recognize the ship as the zauhlon corvette from Echoes Reach—the *Wraith*.

Before we could take any evasive maneuvers to get out of the *Wraith*'s radar range, the corvette began to turn our way and fired off three missiles. Thanks to Richie's quick reflexes, we dodged two of the three missiles, but the third slammed into us. Our shields took the brunt of the damage, but we were still rocked by the blow.

"Fire two missiles and put some distance between us, Richie. When we're a good ways off, turn around, lock onto the corvette and fire the rest of the first volley," Arty said.

Richie didn't reply; instead he set right to it. The two missiles shot off as ordered, though the *Wraith*'s shields absorbed the damage. We flew past the enemy ship and past a few asteroids. The sheer number of space rocks made it difficult to maneuver very fast without risk of bumping into them, but Richie managed well.

When we were two kilometers away, Richie turned the Bird around and locked onto the *Wraith*. The corvette turned to face us and was making a beeline to where we were, asteroids be damned. As soon as we locked on, Richie fired the next three missiles, which danced around the rocks and to their target. Thanks to a combination of low shields, bumping into an asteroid and our missiles, we managed to damage the *Wraith*, setting fire to the bow. This didn't stop the zauhlon ship, however. The *Wraith* fired off six missiles, all of which raced toward us.

"They've locked onto us," Lynn called out, "Based on the way they are maneuvering, it looks like they're being manually controlled too."

"Try to lose them in the asteroid field, Richie," Arty said.

"Aye aye."

Looking down at Lynn's terminal, I saw an image of the missile's arc and mentally confirmed her claim. The way they sped towards us came off as organically influenced. Not the way computer targeting systems perfectly arced their shots. *Curious.* Why would they give up the effectiveness of CTSs? It didn't make sense.

As odd as the decision was, they ended up landing a hit on us, followed by another. At this point our shields were low, and with all the asteroids chipping it away further, we weren't able to regain them. Thanks to Richie's moves, we got one of the missiles to collide with an asteroid. Another missile rammed into one of its allies in the chaos, leaving one left.

The lone missile made a wide turn, aiming to hit the port side of the *Sparrow*. Richie responded by turning to starboard. With the missile inching closer, everybody held their breath. One more hit and our shields were toast. Thinking on his toes, Richie banked up. The missile—or more accurately the missile's controller—couldn't keep up and smashed into the ice-coated asteroid in front of us.

To be safe, Richie kept flying until he felt we were at a safe distance. We stopped just short of the nearby planet's orbit. A look at the radars showed the *Wraith* was nowhere to be seen. Everybody collectively let out a sigh of relief. I was still on edge though. Apart from the last turn, we didn't make any crazy moves, so it wouldn't have been hard for the zauhlon ship to keep track of us.

Arty must have felt my tension, because he spoke up, "What's wrong, captain?"

"Zauhlons don't give up. They wouldn't let a few rocks get in their way, even if it meant damaging their hull," I said.

"To be fair, it's more than a few," Richie piped in.

While my concern was heard, we still took this time to regain our shields and put out any minor fires that started during the chaos. My eyes wandered to the planet next to us. It had an icy blue hue to it, with no signs of land—or clouds for that matter.

Everything about this planet screamed "ambush" to me. The way the zauhlons gave up their hunt for us, the manually controlled missiles, and the fact it all led us here. Maybe it was all a coincidence, but nonetheless it didn't sit well with me.

A moment later, the ship groaned and showed signs of damage. Images showed a clean, dagger-like cut across the *Sparrow*'s hull. Out of the viewport across the bridge I caught a glimpse of an icy, snake-like creature as it slashed our hull again.

"What the hell was that?" Richie asked, already firing the thrusters up to get out of here.

Arty swore under his breath. "It's a trap! Get us out of here, Richie."

"Aw, and here I was planning on staying," Richie retorted.

Another whip rocked us forward. A transmission from Engineer Walker confirmed where we were hit. "Fire in engineering! We have a casualty."

Master-at-arms Williams was immediately on it. "I'll have officers down there to put out the fires ASAP."

"Why aren't our shields working?" I asked, to no one in particular.

"Looks like they're moving too fast. They're not registering in our shield systems," Richie said.

Our helmsman drifted from left to right, desperately trying to dodge our attacker. As good as Richie was, it was hard to respond to an enemy that you barely knew. A few more of its snake-like buddies joined him, cutting away at the hull.

"Hull integrity down to seventy percent," Lynn called out.

"Get a lock on those things and fire the missiles. I want them dead!" Arty ordered.

"Aye aye, captain," Richie said, his hands dancing around the missile controls.

For those five dreadful seconds, everything felt tense. I had no idea if this ship would hold up against the onslaught of attacks. The *Sparrow* might have been fast, but now it was time to see if it could take a punch.

Richie didn't have to wait for Arty's word. As soon as he got a lock on the creatures, he fired the missiles. I watched the missiles fire out of a compartment near the bow of the ship and arc overhead. The first one was a direct hit, shattering its icy target to pieces. The second missile missed but destroyed an asteroid which knocked the second creature away. The third and final missile was another hit, killing the last of our attackers.

With the immediate danger out of the way, I let out a breath I didn't know I was holding. Once again I found myself thankful I never joined the navy, but this time for different reasons. Having to sit by and watch the action play out was nerve racking beyond belief. I much preferred being in direct control of what was going on.

The asteroids started to clear up, which allowed us to put more space between the monsters and ourselves. As it turned out, we weren't out of the fire just yet. A kilometer ahead of us was the *Wraith*, her back turned to us. Looked like those zauhlons expected us to be killed by those ice creatures. They had a surprise in store for them.

"Richie, fire the rail gun along the spine of the *Wraith* and knock out their power," Arty said.

"Aye aye."

As soon as the weapon was charged and loaded, Richie did as he was told and fired the rail gun. The kinetic warhead went up the spine of the corvette, causing plenty of minor explosions in the process. The *Sparrow*'s rail gun was nowhere near as powerful as most rail guns that were built into ships, but it still got the job done.

The thrusters of the *Wraith* failed, leaving her dead in space. While it wasn't destroyed, at least the zauhlons couldn't contact their pals.

With the corvette taken out of the picture, we sped off to a remote part of the system. Wherever we stopped, I prayed there wouldn't be something else that wanted to kill us.

When we arrived at a sector of space that Richie deemed safe, he swirled his seat around to face Arty. "By the way, captain, the scans are finished. There's a completely hollow asteroid in orbit of a planet called Vorka IX. On top of that, it has a helluva lot of metal in it."

"Sounds like we've found our factory. As soon as the engineering deck is in good shape, take us there nice and slow," Arty said.

I got up and looked at Arty. "I'm going to head to engineering myself, see if they need any help." I figured I'd be more useful down there than be cooped up on the bridge.

Arty nodded, then went back to working away at the panel in front of him. I certainly didn't envy his position. Looking out for a squad of Star Bourn was one thing, but an entire ship full of people?

As soon as I got up, Chief Williams turned to me. "Captain Severre, speak with Mister Bridger. He'll tell you what needs to be done."

I nodded and left the bridge. As I made my way to engineering, crew members buzzed past me frantically. I wouldn't go as far to say as it was utter chaos, but it was clear they hadn't been in many battles. Before long, I made my way to the engineering deck. All that was left of the fire was smoke. Some engineering personnel were being helped to the med-bay. In the corner was a body with a blanket draped over him; the casualty Walker mentioned.

I quickly spotted a man giving orders to the left of me and walked up to him, "Mister Bridger?"

The man looked to be in his fifties and had a confidence to him that only experienced officers had. "That's me."

"I came by to see if you needed any help," I said.

He jabbed his thumb over at an area hidden behind some stations. "There's a beam that fell on Ensign Jenner. We're trying to lift it, but it's heavy as all hell. More hands would be appreciated."

With a nod, I jogged to where the sailors were located. Just like he said, a beam had fallen on the poor soul and dug into the girl's leg. Gathering around those who were trying to lift it, we raised it just enough for someone to pull Jenner out from under it. The men nodded thanks and preceded to get her to the Medical Bay.

"Crazy, isn't it?" I turned around to see Walker standing there awkwardly. She looked completely lost, "They always warned us stuff like this could happen, but to actually watch someone die …"

Tentatively, I placed a hand on her shoulder. Comforting people wasn't my specialty, but I knew how she felt. "I know it's hard, but I have no doubt you did the best you could. As terrible as it is, sometimes things happen that are out of our control."

Walker swallowed and nodded. "Yeah."

"What was his name?" I asked.

"Gregor. Van Gregor."

"After this mission is over, we'll drink to him," I said. It wasn't the healthiest remedy, but it worked.

She smiled, though I could tell it was far from genuine. "Sounds like a plan, Severre."

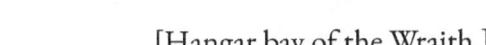

[Hangar bay of the Wraith.]

[Local system time: 1750.]

Orrim slammed his fist into the dropship, seething with anger. The *Wraith* was running on its backup generator, but that only provided interior lighting and life support. Their weapons and engines were effectively useless thanks to those humans. Even getting the hangar bay doors open was a struggle.

His best soldiers were piling up into the Archon next to him, ready to enter Serpent's Hole as soon as the hangar doors were functional. As they lined up, ready to kill the apes that were causing them so much trouble, Orrim stopped to think.

Surviving multiple ambushes, the ice demons, and incapacitating a corvette ... these humans were proving to be capable warriors. Perhaps they could be useful.

Orrim wasn't fooling himself. As crafty as they were, they stood no chance against Korruk. If they could weaken him though, that would allow Orrim to strike and take over as leader of the Legion. Given their skills, the humans might be able to pull this off.

With his plan set in stone, he moved to another Archon and told the pilot to be ready to land on the *Vengeance*. The pilot knew better than to ask questions, so he did as he was told.

Next, Orrim pulled one of his captains to the side and told him if Korruk made contact with the dropship, to tell him Orrim died in the attack.

The captain agreed to this, proving his loyalty to Orrim. As much as Korruk liked to think otherwise, he didn't know his warriors. Not really. He was too busy inside that blasted rock. He hunts every now and then to raise morale for the warriors, but it never lasted. Orrim was the one who took them on consistent raids, who raised their spirits, and who kept them in line. He was the one who took the time to learn their names, who trained them when their skills were getting rusty.

So when the captain—Turrik—agreed to lie for him, he wasn't surprised. Because these were *his* men, not Korruk's.

The hangar bay doors finally creaked open, allowing the Archons to pass through the one-way shield protecting everyone from the vacuum of space. Orrim parted ways with his captain and entered the empty Archon. The doors sealed shut, and his upcoming fight became all the more real. For the first time in his life, he found himself hoping a bunch of humans succeeded in their mission. What had the galaxy come to?

[Bridge of the *Sparrow*.]

[Local system time: 1810.]

Arty sat in his captain's chair, watching what was almost certainly Serpent's Hole grow closer. Engineering was still a mess, but the fires were out, everyone who was injured was getting patched up, and there were enough people down there to keep everything working, so that would have to do. Truth be told, he wasn't keen on sitting around in space. Not with what happened less than an hour ago.

Severre and his men were waiting by the airlock, armored up and ready to get out and find out what Korruk was doing in this factory. As important as this mission was, Arty's mind began to trail off to a different risk when they entered the massive asteroid.

The *Sparrow* was a unique gal. Fast, durable, and small. A lot of people would kill for a ship like her. People who had crews, a large supply of weapons, and most importantly, the drive. He hadn't been in the Badlands much, but he knew that the lowlifes there were on a whole different level than the kind found in Republic space. If they had their mind set on doing something, they'd do it, even if it meant getting themselves killed.

When he shook away the paranoid thoughts, Arty noticed he was tapping his finger and stopped. An old tic from when he was younger that he could never shake. *Let them try*, Arty thought.

Over the past few years, the *Sparrow* had become a home to him. Multiple opportunities showed themselves that would have allowed him to captain a larger, more prominent ship, but he declined all of them. This was where he belonged, and if the universe let him, this would be the last ship he would captain on. So, if some pirates wanted to try to take his ship, they'd have to fight for it.

Just when Arty calmed himself entirely, Richie nearly fell out of his seat, "Captain, we have a zauhlon dreadnought in our sights!"

Arty jumped out of his chair and all but raced down to where Richie sat. He was right, just barely visible to the naked eye was a massive kilometer-and-a-half-long zauhlon starship. The ship looked old and had many scars etched into its hull. Like with all zauhlon dreadnoughts, the ship was essentially one massive gun.

Lucky for them, it looked dormant, clinging to one of the asteroids.

"Bring us into Serpent's Hole nice and slow. Do your best to stay away from the ship. We don't want to garner any attention," Arty commanded.

Richie did as he was told, his nervousness obvious to any who paid attention. Arty couldn't blame the man even if he wanted to. No matter how much training you had for this, nothing could truly prepare you to face an enemy dreadnought, especially with a ship smaller than a corvette.

Captain Arty walked back over to his captain's chair and opened a comm channel with Severre. "Captain Severre, we have a zauhlon dreadnought in our sights. Doesn't even look like she knows we're here. But if I were a betting man, I'd say that's confirmation Korruk is here."

There was a pause.

"Got it," Severre said.

He could sense a certain amount of tension in the commando's voice. Arty couldn't imagine what his mindset was. Space combat, while difficult, was in a completely different ballpark from boots-on-the-ground combat. Add to that the experience their target had, and this was sure to be a stressful mission.

"Captain, we're entering Serpent's Hole now," Richie said.

They entered through a medium-sized hole, and for a moment were enveloped in darkness. After the thick airlock hatches allowed them entry, that was replaced by the sight of a poorly made city with factories scattered around the place.

Through the polluted smoke came a small ball-shaped droid. It scanned the *Sparrow* once, then twice. When it was satisfied, it whizzed off deeper into the asteroid. It looked back, as if it was waiting for them to follow.

"Follow it, but keep a distance," Arty said.

Richie did as ordered, and they began following the bot. It took them to a deeper level, which from what the holo-boards read was Zone Five. From there, it led them to a docking bay where other expensive looking ships were resting.

When the landing magnets locked onto the *Sparrow*, Arty once again opened a comm link with Severre, "Captain, we've landed. It's all on you now. Good hunting."

"Roger that. Keep her engines warm in case we need you," Severre said.

———◆○◆———

[Hangar Bay Three-One-Five, Zone Five.]

[Local system time: 1812.]

I, along with the rest of the Wolves, stood by the airlock, fitted with our armor and our weapons. Unlike on Tsello, we were able to bring whatever we wanted, so we stocked up on Punishers, Eclypse marksman rifles, a Leviathan sniper rifle for Bullseye and a Quaker rocket launcher for Grampa. "A little insurance in case they have those cannons again," as he put it. I wasn't complaining.

"Alright, our mission is to locate Korruk, and if the opportunity arises, kill him. Arty said a zauhlon dreadnought was spotted, so the odds of him being here have risen significantly. Serpent's Hole is a complete unknown for us, so there's no map on it. We'll need to pinpoint the bastard's location first, then secure a route.

"In major factories and shipyards, it's commonplace to keep a log of your customers, your projects, and where your supplies are sent to. Finding a terminal with this info is our first objective. Any questions? ... Good. Let's move out then."

With that, I opened the airlock and all of us walked down the ramp. Around us was the most expensive looking hangar bay I've ever seen. I thought Genesis Station looked grand, but this? It was on a different level entirely. The floors and walls were white with an impeccable shine to them, and all the other ships here were just as prestigious-looking. It was a stark contrast to what was just outside, which was an awful city with a green-tinted fog looming over it. Clearly, whoever ran this place thought we were important enough to be here.

From our right, a humanoid bot walked up to us and spoke with an artificially cheerful voice. "Greetings! I am B03-00, the administrator of this port. My scanners tell me this is a currently active Star Command ship. What may I ask brings you here?"

"This ... is an off-the-record visit. You're aware of the human terrorists Bloodhound, I assume? My bosses have told me to get rid of them, once and for all. And since this is the best place to get weapons, I figured you guys could help with that. For a price, of course."

"Who told you that?" the bot asked, not missing a beat.

"Zavi, an info-broker in Trident's Verge," I said. I didn't want to rat him out, but I couldn't think of anyone else. Whether it was on purpose or not, this bot was good.

B03 paused for a moment, before speaking up in his unwavering synthetic voice. "Ah! A friend of Mr. Ratullo is a friend of mine. This could get him in a lot of trouble. Regardless, I would gladly point you to our best weapon forgers."

"That won't be necessary. Is there any mode of transportation we could use? I trust my ship will be in good hands," I said.

"Why, yes! Around the corner to my left are some hover cars, both with and without roofs," B03 said, pointing in the direction. "And don't you worry about your ship, good sir. We haven't had an incident here in five hundred and twenty days."

Through the Back Door channel, Bullseye spoke up. "Cap, this seems like a good place to find one of those terminals we need. If I were a betting man, I'd say this droid knows where one would be."

I glanced at the bronze bot who was now waddling away from us. "If you think you can get it to talk, go for it."

Bullseye nodded, and walked up to the bot. With quick reflexes, he stabbed the droid where the voice box was located and pulled it aside and into the shadows. B03 was still functional, but with Bullseye straddling it, it was completely helpless. The marksman opened a compartment located on the back of the droid's head and got to work. After a few seconds of this, B03 went limp, then reawakened.

"Okay, I found a terminal. We can't access it remotely, so we're gonna have to be escorted by the droid."

"Good work," I said.

Bullseye lifted B03 back to its feet, and the bot promptly led us further inside the docking bay. With its voice box taken out, things were silent. All we could hear were the droids working throughout the halls.

Before long, we stopped at a small terminal with a green screen. B03 unlocked it with a device in its finger, which allowed Bullseye to use it. After a minute or so of digging around, it looked like he found what he was looking for.

"Got it. Looks like Korruk's a long-time customer. He's been having something called 'Project 31' built for the past few years," Bullseye said. "This mainframe of theirs has everything registered too. How many people are here, what species they are, and what's in development. If this data is right, there are three hundred zauhlons in this rock. Get this though. There are only five in a place called Zone Two."

"That must be where Korruk is," I said. "Download a copy of all that data and send it to the *Sparrow*."

"Yes, sir. I've got a map of the place here too. It looks like it's only of Zones Six, Five and Four though," Bullseye said.

"It'll have to do. Download that and send it to me," I said.

"Yes, sir."

A second later I received the map. From there, I uploaded the data to everyone's HUDs. Taking a better look at it, this place looked like a maze. If we didn't have this map, we'd be screwed for sure.

"Alright, we got what we came for. Let's get in one of those hover cars and get to Zone Two."

We hustled outside to where the vehicles were. On the way there, something stuck with me. "Project 31." The fact it didn't give away anything about what it could be irritated me. Whatever it was, it couldn't be good.

07

[Serpent's Hole, Zone Two.]

[Local system time: 1816.]

Zone Two was almost devoid of organic life, save for Lord Admiral Korruk and his royal guards. All the workers there were machines. This area of the asteroid was reserved for the most expensive projects, and rightfully so.

The zauhlon leader currently stood in a circular hallway protected by glass, looking into a large room. In the center of this chamber was his prize. His revenge; the Rahalah.

It was a Frankenstein of all different kinds of technology. Yet at the same time, it was sleek. Beautiful, almost. It resembled a cocoon in the final stages of its form. In this shell were fifteen nuclear warheads. Like the technological outer hull, these warheads were of many different origins. Zauhlon, anthrum, yongun, even human.

The core of this weapon was the lithium shells coating the insides of the bomb. Taken from newborn stars, it was this element that would allow Korruk to strike judgment on his enemies. It was expensive and time consuming, but it would be worth every credit.

The veteran warrior allowed himself to close his eyes. For hundreds of years the Republic had embarrassed the zauhlons. No, not just the zauhlons. They embarrassed *him*. Loss after loss, his men began to question him. Look down upon him. Even if they never said it, he knew they thought of him as weak. The thought made him grit his teeth.

Korruk worked too hard to get to where he was. He wouldn't let all that blood, sweat and tears be for nothing. No one would think him weak ever again. Not Gorr, not his zauhlons, and most certainly not the galaxy. With the Rahalah, he would reaffirm his place as Lord Admiral and bring the Republic to its knees.

Lord Admiral Korruk: conqueror of the Republic, killer of worlds, lord of the stars.

A smile formed on his face. Not only would he be feared by the galaxy, he would be respected by Gorr. There could be no better reward than that.

His eyes shot open at the sound of the sliding door opening behind him. A reddish zauhlon whose name Korruk didn't know bowed before him, "Lord Admiral, there's been sightings of the apes who hunt you. They should be at the west entrance to Zone Four in under an hour."

"Have all nearby zauhlons regroup at the west entrance and be ready to shoot down anything that approaches," Korruk snarled.

"Your will be done."

Korruk was once again left alone. Orrim's failure at stopping these apes enraged him, but he would deal with that later. Right now, he needed to make sure these humans were stopped.

The idea of a group of humans traveling all this way to kill him amused the Lord Admiral. Hundreds had tried, yet these apes—no, more like cockroaches at this point—thought they could accomplish what so many others have failed at? He admired their determination, but it would be for nothing. He would kill them, and they would be forgotten. More numbers to his list.

"Is the great Korruk nervous?" a hiss of a voice said from behind him.

He didn't need to turn around to know who it was.

Phantom; the ruler of Serpent's Hole. Fitting that the leader of a place with such a name was a yongun, who themselves were the serpents of the galaxy.

"Don't fool yourself. They are mere vermin," Korruk said. "How goes the construction of Rahalah?"

"Well, assuming there is no interference," he let that last bit settle in before continuing, "it should be done within thirty night cycles."

"There will be no interruption," Korruk said. "I will see to it myself if need be."

"I trust that you will. Regardless, I will position my men alongside your soldiers. Think of it as an act of goodwill," Phantom said. He walked up to Korruk so they were side by side. "Humor me, though. What would happen if they weren't stopped, and they went running to their Republic about this?"

"Then we will accelerate production of the Rahalah."

"To speed up production time would cost twice as much."

"So be it," Korruk said, letting his anger seep through. "Get this done when I say, and you can have all the credits you desire."

Phantom feigned satisfaction and turned to leave Korruk. When he reached the door, however, he looked back at the zauhlon. "Don't make promises you cannot keep, Lord Admiral."

Korruk bit his tongue and watched as Phantom limped out of sight. When he was gone, Korruk connected with the dropship that just entered Serpent's Hole. "Orrim!" he barked.

A moment later, an unfamiliar voice spoke up. "My lord, General Orrim was killed in our battle with the human ship. I'm his successor, Captain Turrik."

Korruk growled. "The humans are in Serpent's Hole and are on their way to the west entrance of Zone Four. Get there before they do and kill them, or else you'll be joining Orrim in the afterlife."

"Yes, my lord."

With no more distractions, Korruk rested his upper arms against the glass and leaned forward, trying to calm his temper. While he was happy Orrim was one less problem to deal with, the fact he died while cooped up in a starship was disgraceful. He hoped this Captain Turrik would prove to be a worthy successor.

Lord Admiral Korruk shook the thoughts away and looked at the Rahalah. His weapon. His ultimate creation. So long as this nuclear bullet reached its target, Korruk didn't care how many of his men died. It would be worth the cost in the end.

[Thirty minutes away from Zone Four, west entrance.]

[Local system time: 1830.]

The car was cramped, but we made it work. I, along with Grampa and Boomer, sat in the back seat while Tenner and Bullseye sat in the front. From all the ops we did, I knew Tenner was a good driver, so that was his role. Bullseye got lucky in a game of rock-paper-scissors.

Looking at the incomplete map of Serpent's Hole, I went over our plan of action for the umpteenth time in my head. For each entrance, we'd stop a few kilometers out, see how many enemies there were, then either go through the intended entrance or find another way. Based on what's shown here, there should be a small sewer entrance that would work for us. As much as I hoped it didn't come for that, I knew the odds weren't in our favor.

Moving on, once we made it to Zone Two, we were to locate Korruk, find out what "Project 31" was, and if we could, kill him. If we couldn't, then we'd place a tracker on a piece of zauhlon equipment. Assuming it didn't get discovered, this would let us keep track of him from then on out.

I'd already gone over the plan with the others a dozen times, so I decided not to make them suffer through yet another debriefing. While I tried my best to iron out the details, I could hear Grampa talking about cars with Tenner. As it turns out, he was a motor head. I smiled under my helmet. Those two would get along just fine.

Boomer stayed quiet. Clearly the conversation about the car we were in didn't interest her. To be honest, I couldn't say it interested me either. When there was a pause in the discussion, she took the opportunity to change the topic.

"Hey, Grampa, you're an FCW vet, right?" she asked.

"Yeah, why?"

"If that's the case, why is your rank so low? Most of the servicemen from that war are colonels and generals by now," she said.

She was right. I meant to ask about that myself, but between intel gathering, Tsello and coming here, I hadn't had the time to.

Grampa shrugged his shoulders. "I can get more done out here than in some office up in a starship. Besides, the ladies love a fighting man."

"You still get ladies? I didn't think they went for men in their sixties," I said.

"Watch it, kid. I still got three years until I reach sixty," Grampa said.

"You got any good stories? We still got a little while until we reach the first entrance," Bullseye said.

"I got a few," Grampa said. After thinking it over, he spoke up again. "Would you believe me if I said I was in the Titanic Battle of Mars? I was out in the trenches with seven thousand marines, commandos, and anthrum. Let me tell you, seeing the zauhlons charge us with their war machines and tanks was enough to make the toughest man wet himself.

"We must have gone through hundreds of magazines that day. I was stationed near the docking bay, so I didn't get to see too much action, but I still got to kill my fair share of zauhlons. That all changed when one of those Ragnaroks came to our location. It was killing most of our guys there, so I took the marine next to me and we hid in the tunnels. Thought maybe if we played dead, we could get it from behind and knock it down. Turned out that marine wasn't playing.

"When it walked over us, it collapsed the tunnel. Luckily it got its foot stuck, which gave our tanks enough time to roll in and take it out, but I was buried for a few hours. Lucky for me, those marine helmets can give you oxygen for up to four hours," Grampa sighed, "They don't make 'em like they used to."

"Hold up, so you were a basic like Boomer?" Tenner asked.

"Damn right. They must've noticed how bad your aim was and wanted a real marine to teach you how it's done," Grampa said, no doubt a grin plastered on his face.

That comment got hollers from Tenner, Bullseye and me while Boomer and Grampa just laughed.

"The Star Bourn I worked with when I was a basic were okay shots, but they relied too much on their toys. I don't know what they'd do in a fistfight though," Boomer added.

"I'd like to say run, but they're too stupid to do that," Grampa said.

While the two turncoats laughed at their jokes, Tenner spoke up. "Yeah well, at least we know how to use our tech. Back when I was with the Wolverines, we were with a squad of basics that didn't know how to work a lock buster. We were there for five minutes until they finally did it right."

For the next few minutes we all went back and forth, trying to prove which were better, the turncoats or prodigies. In the back of my mind, I hope it wasn't lost on Grampa and Boomer that they'd become the very Star Bourn they were making fun of. Regardless, it was nice to have banter like this. Up until now, I hadn't interacted with the new Wolves all that much outside of the missions we went on. Skill was important but knowing the Star Bourn you were fighting with helped too.

If we made it out of Serpent's Hole, we'll all have to get a drink sometime.

The talk died down, and thirty minutes later, we were getting close to the west entrance. Even with the naked eye, I could see a lot of people at the entrance. I couldn't say for certain yet, but I'd bet they were looking for us.

Tenner pulled the car aside and landed it on a rooftop, out of sight from those at the entrance. Most of us stayed back by the car while Bullseye crawled to the edge of the building. It didn't take long for him to start calling out targets.

"I'm seeing lots of zauhlons, Cap. Some yonguns, morguls and chuzunns too. They're looking towards the gateway," Bullseye said.

Each time Bullseye spotted an enemy, he marked them on our maps. He wasn't even done and there were already forty. I acknowledged, "They're expecting us."

Grampa pulled out his Quaker and stroked it. "I say we don't disappoint them."

"How many rockets did you pack?" I asked.

"Four," Grampa said.

After thinking it over, I shook my head. "Save them. I don't want to waste the ammo on a distraction."

Grampa hung his head low and threw the Quaker back over his shoulder.

"Looks like we're taking the sewer entrance," I said, heading to the hover car. I could hear almost all of them groan. No matter what sewage system it was, the smell always clung onto a commando's skinsuit. I hoped being in a car would help prevent that, but I didn't cross my fingers.

With everyone back in the vehicle, Tenner started up the engine and got to flying. He immediately took us in low and hugged the lower streets to keep us out of view. From what I could see of the city, it was falling apart. Calling it a city was generous too; it looked more like a bunch of sloppily put together buildings.

We reached the sewer entrance in no time. Now that we were face to face with it, I was worried the car wouldn't fit. Thankfully though, Tenner was able to squeeze it through at the expense of the car's paint.

Luckily, the sewer tunnel wasn't as narrow as the entrance, so we carried on with our journey. Instead of relying on the headlights, Tenner decided to drive with night vision on. While seeing with night vision wasn't as clear, it allowed us to see just about everything instead of only what was in front of us.

It didn't take long for us to notice the anorexic chuzunns staring at us. They looked like they were thinking of all the different ways they could rip open the car and eat us. Everyone but Tenner readied their rifles in case the aliens decided to get ballsy.

Our map detected at least twenty of them so far. If they wanted to, they could jump us at any time. Looking at the map, we were just over halfway through. That was when they attacked.

They ran at us all at once. The car's frame held up well, but the glass broke early on in the assault. We unleashed a tornado of bullets onto our attackers, killing them with ease. These chuzunns weren't wearing any armor, so they were easy to kill. When they first lunged at us, Tenner picked up the pace as best he could. In doing so, he ended up smashing into a few of the aliens.

One of the chuzunns that latched onto the car grabbed my Punisher's barrel but ended up burning his hand. I took the opportunity to put a bullet in between his six beady eyes. We were right by the exit when a chuzunn leaped in front of us and landed on the windshield. We didn't have the time nor the space to shake it off, so we took the crazy alien with us when we smashed through the exit.

As soon as we were free from the confined space of the sewers, Bullseye opened his door with a Sentinel in hand and shot the chuzunn. The alien, now dead, fell to the streets below. Tenner activated the wipers briefly and got rid of its splattered blood.

"Well, that was fun," Grampa said. "Not as fun as killing all those zauhlons would've been, but still a good time."

I shook my head, chuckling. "Maybe you should spend your days in a battle-simulator. Seems like it'd be your cup of tea."

"Already tried it. They kicked me out," Grampa said, reloading his Punisher.

I looked at the map and zoomed into the Zone Three entrance. Its layout was the same as the one we just passed. "Alright, looks like we're working with the same setup for Zone Three's entrance, so our plan will be the same. If things are looking hot at the main gate, we'll take the sewer detour."

"I swear if we have to go through that again ..." Tenner commented.

"We'll do what we have to. We've come this far, a few chuzunns and a river of shit won't stop us," I said. "Besides, it's better than a gunship."

08

[Deep into Zone Three.]

.

[Local system time: 2030.]

Releck lay prone on an old hangar pad, a cronus speeder bike a few meters from him. The fact he had to steal that from some poor family tore at his heart, but it had to be done. A heavy conscience was worth the price of Korruk's life.

He'd heard some rumblings in the zauhlon's general comm channel. A whole lot of them were gathered at Zone Four's west entrance. Why, Releck didn't know. Maybe a riot that got out of hand? There was no point dwelling on it. That gathering meant there were fewer zauhlons here, which bode well for him.

The past day had been rough for the rogue anthrum. Releck hitched a ride like he originally planned, but it didn't take him as far as he wanted. When he tried to get into the next cargo shuttle, he was spotted and nearly killed thanks to his cockiness. He stopped the bleeding, but he used the last of his medi-foam in the process. From there, he stole the cronus speeder that was parked beside him and followed the shuttle to Zone Two's entrance. He knew better than to follow it in.

From his time in Serpent's Hole, Releck heard the rumors that if you went into Zone Two without authorization, you'd be shot on the spot. If he was going to get in there, he'd need to trick the system.

On either side of the massive gateway were two structures built into the wall. If he could break into one of them, he could steal a registration code and get in safely. From what he could see, most of the guards were either yonguns or security bots. He would park below the west building, climb the wall and sneak into the facility. Releck didn't know whether there would be a hatch on the belly of the building, so his plan was to get onto the hangar pad. It was only guarded by two bots, which wouldn't see him if he got on behind them. As good as bots were, their programming was limited to a fault.

Releck went over the plan in his head one more time before jumping on his cronus and flying to the town below. The deeper you go into Serpent's Hole, the less civilization there was, Releck found out. Originally it was packed with buildings—while they weren't tall, it was definitely a city. Now though, they were few and far between. It was mostly just rock and metal.

When he reached the bottom of the wall, he shot out his magnehook and began scaling the metal structure. While he did this, Releck's mind drifted to his old home in New Motula. It had been so long since he visited there, or his father for that matter. The thought of his old man made him smile. If he could see him now, he'd have a heart attack.

The next thing he knew, he was at the bottom of the building. As he expected, there were no hatches, so Releck began carefully walking upside down via his gravboots. The experience was nauseating and nerve racking, but he reached the hangar pad quicker than he expected.

A quick peek over the ledge told him he was just behind the bots. After putting some more distance between where he would climb up and the bots, Releck pulled himself up onto the pad. Phaeleron particle-powered assault rifle in hand, Releck entered the facility, keeping to the shadows as best he could, only killing the reptilian yonguns with his vibro-knife.

The control center—which would hold all the authorization codes of everyone who had access to Zone Two—was just ahead. It was guarded by four security bots. There was no other entrance to the control center, so Releck would have to engage the droids. Setting his rifle to high intensity, he emerged from the shadows and shot all four of the robots. All of them collapsed, the circuits in their heads smoking and fizzling. Fearing someone nearby heard the metal bodies falling, Releck raced into the control room. It was now or never.

While he was no tech wizard, the terminal was simple enough that Releck understood what he was doing. With the authorization code he got off the black market, he would be able to come and go as he pleased. The only caveat was that he had to reset the code to his biological signature. For the inner zones of Serpent's Hole, it was the DNA equivalent to a password. The task of resetting the code was normally a cumbersome one, but this was something Releck had been practicing for some time.

After a few seconds of tapping away and setting everything up, he took a few steps back and let himself get scanned. Shortly afterwards, a female synthetic voice spoke from the terminal, "Authorization code AO-937-02 redirected to current body. Welcome back, Mr. Undirth."

Releck had no idea who this Undirth guy was, but if he was already in Zone Two, he was in trouble. If the gate read his authorization code coming in twice without having left once, it could identify him as suspicious and fill him with lead.

Thankfully, no one had come to investigate the noise, and Releck was able to leave via the same route from which he entered. The trek down the wall was much easier than going up, and before long he reached his cronus, still in the same spot where he left it. Now was the moment of truth.

As he flew towards the gate, he prayed to the gods—if they really did exist—that this would work. He passed through the gate and held his breath. Soon he was thirty meters out, then a hundred, then five hundred. When he was a kilometer away from the entrance, he sighed in relief. It worked.

Now that he was through that obstacle, he looked around, taking in his surroundings. It followed the same pattern of having less and less life, only this time there was nothing. No buildings other than factories. He couldn't see anybody walking around. Drones buzzed around all over the place. All the lights were blue, which was a contrast to the green fog that filled most of the Hole so far. Overall, the whole place was eerie. It felt like Releck didn't belong here. Like no one did.

He pushed those thoughts aside. None of that mattered. What did matter was finding Korruk. Before the fighting started and he had to use his medi-foam, he heard some of the za-uhlons mention a place called "Warehouse Four-One-Nine." Whether this was where Korruk himself would be, Releck didn't know, but it was the only lead he had, so he began his search.

———◆◇◆———

[Nearing Zone Two's entrance.]

[Local system time: 2045.]

As we approached Zone Two's gateway, everyone went silent. Unlike the last entrance, no one was waiting for us. On one hand I was happy. I wasn't looking forward to another close encounter with chuzunns in a sewer, after all. On the other hand, something didn't feel right. Felt like we were walking into a trap. We were already fifty meters away from passing the entrance though. If we turned around now, it might raise suspicion to anyone in the buildings on either side of the gate.

At first nothing happened. I thought maybe I was just too used to things going wrong. Then my gut was proven right. Our car was scanned, and not two seconds later we got hit. TM80 Dragonsbreath machine guns ripped into our engines, sending us on a one way trip to the ground below.

"Hold on!" Tenner said, desperately trying to take control of the free-falling vehicle. Maybe "take control" wasn't the best phrasing. "Crash us gently" felt more fitting.

A quick glance at everyone's vitals told me they were still alive. Accelerated heart rates, but alive. I've been on a few airborne vehicles while they crashed, and I knew enough to know this was going to suck.

To Tenner's credit, he did a good job steering the falling car away from any factories or hard-to-get-out-of places. We first hit the edge of a trench-like street, then fell into said street. After bouncing and sliding across the metal road, we finally came to a stop. I took a few deep breaths. That went better than I hoped, all things considered.

"Everybody okay?" I asked.

They all gave an affirmative, and we got out of the destroyed car. Grampa patted the shell sadly before we all moved away from the crash site and into the shadows. As far as I could see, there was nobody here. No living people anyway. My radar backed up the sentiment too.

We stuck around for a minute to see if anybody would investigate the crash. See what kind of enemies we would either have to avoid or fight going forward. Sure enough, four drones packing twin assault rifles came flying to the scene. They didn't see us, but surely they saw there weren't any bodies. They flew off in different directions, no doubt searching for where we could be.

Turning to the others, I addressed them over the Back Door, "Alright, looks like we'll have to go with plan B."

"What's plan B?" Grampa asked.

Truth be told, I didn't know. The map we downloaded back at the hangar bay didn't cover Zone Two, so we were in the dark here. We knew a handful of zauhlons were in Zone Two, but we didn't know where. If only we could get a bird's eye view ...

"That's it!" I hadn't meant to say it aloud, but now that everyone had their eyes on me, I turned to Bullseye. "Did you pack the Eagle?"

"Eagle" was the nickname for Star Command's prototype drone they recently started issuing to us. It was limited in where it could go, but it was a remote-controlled camera that could identify enemies or places of interest.

"I wouldn't be a good commando if I didn't," Bullseye said. Taking the small drone out of his belt, he extended the wings and switched it on.

"When you get it up in the air, switch to radio signals," I said. "We won't be able to tell who it is, but with the radio signals we'll be able to see where the living beings are in this zone, which will make things a hell of a lot easier for us."

"Yes sir."

While Bullseye worked the Eagle, we covered every opening we saw. There were two main passageways to get to where we were—the path leading to the street which we came from, and a path behind us which led to an unknown location. While none showed up, it wouldn't surprise me if there were security bots here too.

"Alright, I got a few hits," Bullseye said. "There are two people south of here around two kilometers away, one to the east seven kilometers away, and five people to the north five kilometers from here."

"I reckon the zauhlons here would stick together, which means we're heading north," I said. "Mark the building on our map."

Bullseye did as I ordered, marking a Warehouse Four-One-Nine as our objective. It wasn't ideal, but we began walking to the location. Knowing these zauhlons, one of which was likely to be Korruk, were so close gave me some butterflies. It feels like a lifetime ago when I saw Korruk murder Miller before my eyes. It was finally time to make him pay.

[Warehouse Four-One-Nine, Zone Two.]

[Local system time: 2047.]

Things had taken an interesting turn. Lord Admiral Korruk was just made aware of a hover car that was shot down a few kilometers out. The sudden bit of action, along with the knowledge of the humans entering Serpent's Hole, told Korruk all he needed to know—his men at Zone Four had failed, and the people in this car were the apes hunting him. No bodies were found, so there was no confirmation, but deep down he knew it to be true.

The fact no one was in the crash told him they were still alive and searching for him. Credit where credit was due, they managed to sneak past his warriors and get this far. They may have taken the coward's way out, but they got here nonetheless. The best he could do was honor them with his presence and give them a worthy death. Perhaps then he could finally put this behind him and put his focus back on the Rahalah.

After calling his Centurions to him, he informed him of their new hunt: find and kill the apes. He told them of their craftiness, and that they were likely on their way here as they spoke. He also told them that failure wasn't an option. Either they kill the apes, or they die trying. Anything else would earn them death at Korruk's hands.

With that, Korruk and his black-clad killers exited the corridor overlooking the Rahalah. Moments later, the sound of metal clashing with metal echoed through the corridor.

Seconds after that, a figure dropped into the space that Korruk so often stood at while overlooking his bomb. This figure was Releck, who had listened to what Korruk said. *Humans, this far in Serpent's Hole? Did the Republic finally send a team to deal with Korruk? Took them long enough.*

That must have been what all the commotion was, too. He'd heard a crash outside the walls of the warehouse, but he didn't know what it was.

Releck wanted to follow after Korruk, but the object beyond the window to his left captured his attention. He could hear the machinery at work inside the object, the way its heaviness creaked against the metal floor, daring it to hold its weight. Whatever it was, Releck could see it was big and most certainly dangerous.

Tapping a small button on his helmet, Releck took a picture of the object. While neither he—nor any anthrum for that matter—had a need for pictures with their photographic memories, it was a feature implemented by the Republic. Until now, he didn't think he would ever use it. Despite the fact he certainly wasn't a friend of the Republic, this object gave him a bad feeling. The way it hummed, it reverberated throughout his very being.

Shaking away those nerves, he focused on the issue at hand. Korruk was in the main section of the warehouse, oblivious to the fact that an intruder was already inside looking to end his life. The problem was that the warehouse was a maze. Releck was lucky he was able to find an easy way around it via the vents.

Not wanting to waste any more time, Releck exited the hallway and began searching for Korruk for what he hoped was the final time. Victory was so close. All he had to do was reach out and grab it. Then not only would Korruk pay for his crimes in blood, but Releck would prove his worth as a soldier.

09

[Outside Warehouse Four-One-Nine.]

[Local system time: 2050.]

A couple dozen meters in front of us lay our destination, Warehouse Four-One-Nine, where our target, Korruk, supposedly was. My mouth grew dry. This was it. If for whatever reason Korruk wasn't here, we would be back to square one.

The building was massive. Bigger than any warehouse I've seen before. More so, there was no entrance in sight. This would be a problem.

"Alright, let's look for a way in," I said. With that, we fanned out and searched for anything that could help us.

It didn't take long until Boomer spoke up. "There's an open window a hundred meters up on the east side."

I looked up, and sure enough she was right. We all piled underneath the opening and one by one climbed up to the window using our magnehooks. Carefully we descended into the warehouse, making sure to cover those who were still reeling down. Mine were the last pair of boots to hit the metal floor.

Upon further examination of the interior, I swore to myself. The blasted place was a maze. I strained my memory, desperate to remember if I saw anything noteworthy before I lowered myself into the warehouse. I remembered seeing a catwalk toward the west side of the building, but not a way to get to it.

"Alright, well, we're not going to get anywhere by standing around. Let's—" I was cut off by gunfire grazing my helmet. Not a second later all of us were in cover. That was too close.

We returned fire, dropping the drone that almost hit me. Two more drones flew into the battle, then another two. Luckily, similar to the drones that investigated our crashed car, these were equipped with assault rifles, so their fire wasn't accurate.

We took down another drone, which crashed into a ball of flame. Not long after that, another of the flying bots went down. That was when the bipedal bots showed up. Four of them came from the east and were wielding Vandall II scout rifles. It was a common weapon for pirates and the like. More accurate weapons were in play, so we had to be more careful.

With practiced accuracy, I tossed an EMP grenade towards a group of bots. It knocked out the droids long enough for us to destroy three of them. All that were left were the two flying bots and the one bipedal.

Before we could act further, they stopped abruptly. Not a second later, the lights were cut. I had a bad feeling about this, but I wasn't going to wait to find out if that feeling had any substance.

Over the Back Door, I began dishing out orders. "There's a catwalk west of here. When we get there, we'll use the high ground to identify any targets. If you see them, you're authorized to shoot on sight."

They all acknowledged the command, and we began moving. A minute into our walk, a faint *creak* was picked up by my audio receptors. I stopped and pointed my gun in the direction it came from. That soft noise turned into a loud one, and it dawned on me what it was. One of the tall shelves was in the process of collapsing—on top of us.

"Move!" I said.

Leaping forward into a somersault, I just barely avoided the shelf and its large crates. What followed was a series of loud bangs and clanks that lasted ten seconds. When everything went back to being quiet, on instinct I spoke through the Back Door. "Status report."

"I'm here with Bullseye, Cap. We're good, but we're on the other side," Grampa said.

"I'm with Boomer," Tenner said, his voice sounding tense. "We're pinned down by some of the crates. Nothing's broken on my end."

"I'm all good too, just a bad headache," Boomer said.

Thank God. Before I could come up with a plan B—or were we on plan C by now?— Tenner spoke up. "I can see a gap between the crates behind us. Looks like it's big enough for us to pass through."

"Good. Bullseye and Grampa, you two go look for the power switch. Tenner, Boomer, see if you can find a shelf easy enough to climb and help me find my way to the catwalk."

As we all went about our tasks, that bad feeling only grew. These shelves were heavy; just looking at them caused serious concern. For one to conveniently fall over along the path we were taking ... it couldn't be a coincidence. Someone must have pushed it over. *The zauhlons!*

In that moment, a sense of déjà vu washed over me. My team was split up into twos in a dark location with danger around the corner. Things weren't going to turn out the same though. I was determined to make sure of that.

"Keep your eyes out," I said. "This is what happened when the old Wolves were killed."

The warning from Cap had put Bullseye on edge even more so than he already was. He wasn't good with closed-in spaces—which was pretty much the entirety of this mission so far—and the prospect of zauhlons watching their every move made him jittery. *He* was supposed to be the hunter, the man who stalked his targets, not the other way around.

He held his Eclypse scout rifle close to him, ready to shoot anything that moved that wasn't Grampa. The electrical box would be towards the north, according to the grizzled commando. "Most warehouses have the same layout, no matter the size," Grampa told him.

A faint, almost nonexistent *clank* sent them hiding behind a nearby shelf. Peaking through the shelves and past the crates, Bullseye spotted a zauhlon twenty meters away. He told Grampa as much, and the two climbed the shelves till they were just under ten feet above the ground. Staying as quiet as they could, they watched the zauhlon walk past them. This one was different from the ones they've fought in the past, however. Instead of gold armor, their stalker's armor was black, making him hard to see, even with night vision.

"You ever see that kind of zauhlon before, Grampa?" Bullseye asked through the safety of the Back Door.

Grampa grunted. "Yeah. They're called Centurions. Think of them as the zauhlons' version of commandos. They're a pain in the ass to kill too."

Bullseye nodded, the cogs in his mind shifting. "You think an armor-piercing round to the head would do the trick?" Technically speaking all modern-day bullets were made with armor-piercing tech. The type Bullseye was referring to was the Mark Two-grade rounds. The kind that could make a head explode upon contact.

"Yeah, that would work," Grampa said. "Or ... a well-placed rocket could work too."

"They would hear it from a mile away." Bullseye shook his head. "Sorry, Grampa, looks like you'll have to wait another day to use that bad boy."

After some grumbling on Grampa's part, they began stalking their stalker. *This is more like it*, Bullseye thought.

They reached the north wall of the warehouse, and with it, a long walkway that stretched two hundred meters. The zauhlon must have been self-conscious about how open he was, because he began to pick up the pace. Before Bullseye could pull the trigger, the zauhlon rounded the corner.

"Blast it," Bullseye said. "Hey Grampa, you think you could bring him back into view?"

Grampa nodded. "I can try." Taking a mag from his pouch, he threw it overhead. The small object bounced a few times before it slid near the corner where the Centurion turned.

Must have been a ball player, Bullseye thought.

Sure enough, the black-clad zauhlon cautiously approached the mag. Bullseye lined up the shot. He watched as the zauhlon picked up the object and looked it over. Right when he turned to look their way, the marksman fired.

A second later, the alien's head was no more.

His body fell forward, blood pouring on the metal floor.

With the imminent danger out of the way they walked towards the electrical box and got the power working. The sudden bright lights took some getting used to, but their helmets helped with that.

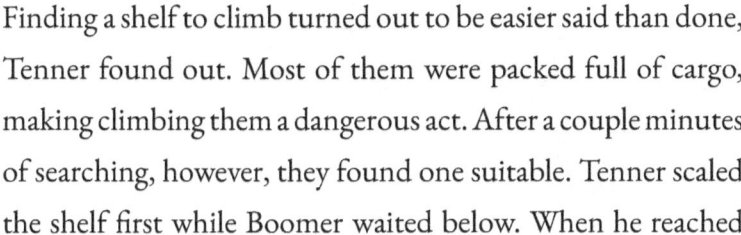

Finding a shelf to climb turned out to be easier said than done, Tenner found out. Most of them were packed full of cargo, making climbing them a dangerous act. After a couple minutes of searching, however, they found one suitable. Tenner scaled the shelf first while Boomer waited below. When he reached thirty feet though, something caught his eye. Hiding around the corner fifty meters to the north was a zauhlon, watching them. The alien hadn't figured out he had been seen.

"Don't look now, but there's a zauhlon fifty meters behind you," he said to the former basic.

"Got it," Boomer said. With that, she feigned ignorance and began looking at the items on the shelf. When she saw a smaller object, she reached out for it and pretended to knock it over.

Wedging himself further onto the shelf, Tenner caught sight of another zauhlon to the south. Again, he updated Boomer on the situation.

"You think there's room up there for me?" she asked.

After surveying the small space, Tenner answered, "Maybe, but we won't have much space to work with."

"Alright, get ready to drop a smoker on my word. And make sure the timer is set to two seconds," Boomer said.

"Holy shit," Cap muttered.

Tenner tried to see what Severre was looking at but couldn't from his position. "What is it?"

"There's an unlocked crate here. It's full of bomb parts," Cap said, "High explosives, rykor cocoons ... Whatever Korruk's doing here, it's big."

The next few moments happened in a flash. Boomer activated a smoker, and not a second after, the two zauhlons opened fire with their high-powered assault rifles.

"Now!" Boomer said.

Tenner activated his own smoker, and in two seconds time, the grenade ignited. Tenner put the pieces together on what her plan was. Boomer climbed up the shelf as fast as she could through the smoke, the black-armored zauhlons oblivious to her disappearing act. The two attackers moved on her last known position. Little did they know all they would find was a condensed bomb.

As soon as Boomer reached Tenner and the zauhlons were enveloped by the smoke, she detonated the CB. As the explosion ripped through the now lit warehouse, Tenner was worried they might have damaged the tall shelf they were on. He couldn't figure what was worse: almost getting crushed by one of these or being on one while they fell. *Definitely almost getting crushed*, Tenner thought.

Things didn't get much better from there. Gunfire rang out where Bullseye and Grampa were located, and the flying bots came back, this time with a new entourage of ten. Because of how little space they had to work with, Boomer and Tenner had a hard time shooting the little buggers. Enough was enough.

Tenner opened a private comm link with Captain Arty and told him of the situation, and that they needed backup. Sure, they hadn't gotten to Korruk, but the crate full of explosives Severre found was more than enough to put two and two together. Arty told him they'd be on their way and to hang tight.

"I see him," Severre said, sounding almost transfixed.

The comment caught Tenner off guard. "What?" he demanded, as he shot down another drone.

"Korruk. I see him," Severre clarified, "I'm going after him."

Tenner tried to convince him otherwise, that they needed help with the drones, but it was no use. Severre was going after Lord Admiral Korruk even if it was the last thing he did. Maybe it would be.

In front of me was Lord Admiral Korruk. The man who not only killed my friends—no, my *family*—including Miller, the closest person I had to a father. I'd planned for this moment in my head. Told myself I wouldn't make it personal. That I wouldn't let my feelings get in the way of the mission. But now that I was here, all that preparation went out the window.

No words were spoken between us. He raised his sword—the same one that killed Miller, high above him and took a defensive stance. He was baiting me to strike first. Without realizing it, I unsheathed my machete.

I knew what I should have done. I should've filled the bastard with bullets. Ultimately, that's not how it went down. It was stupid—incredibly so—but I wanted to prove myself superior to him. To kill him the same way he killed Miller. My emotions got the better of me and I charged Korruk.

That was my first mistake.

Korruk effortlessly dodged my lunge and kicked me in the ribs. The move took the wind out of my lungs. I rose to my feet one second too late and was met with an uppercut. My back hit a crate behind me, the only thing that kept me from falling down again. I blacked out for a brief second. When I came to, I saw Korruk thrusting his sword my way and just barely moved aside.

I slashed upward, aiming at Korruk's upper left arm. The heated edge of my blade found an unprotected part of his arm and made my target bleed. I followed this up with an attempt to stab Korruk in the back, but he countered by grabbing my wrist and delivering a ruthless headbutt.

The blow sent me to my knees. If Korruk wasn't still holding onto my wrist I'd have fallen down completely. My HUD was scrambled for a few moments and my vision was blurry. When I could see clearly again, Korruk had raised me back to my feet and was punching me in the gut over and over again. By the time he was done I wanted to throw up. He finally let me go and took a few steps back, once again taking a high guard stance. The bastard was toying with me.

I struggled to stay on my feet, let alone pick my machete up. Mimicking his form, I chose to course correct and wait for him to attack. When he did, it took everything I had to keep up my guard. For an eight-foot brute, Korruk was fast. I tried to stay calm, take deep breaths, but every time I breathed in, I felt a sharp pain. It dawned on me that my ribs were more than likely bruised.

Desperate to put some distance between us, I tried to kick Korruk away. This was my last mistake.

Upon lifting my leg, I felt another bolt of pain in my ribs. This caused me to hesitate and lose my footing. Taking advantage of my sorry state, Korruk elbowed me in the head. This shut down my HUD. He followed this up by grabbing my throat and lifting me off my feet. The next thing I knew, he lunged his sword into my abdomen. Because of his grip on my throat and the pain in my ribs, I couldn't muster the strength to scream in pain. All I could do was gasp and fall to the floor when he let me go.

"Tell me, human, what is your name?" Korruk asked. "You've come a long way. You *will* die here, but I'll make sure you aren't completely forgotten."

He's mocking me, I thought. This is all a sick game to him. Still, there was some truth to what he said. I didn't need my HUD to tell me I didn't have much longer in this galaxy.

"Go to hell ..." I said using all the strength I could muster.

With a huff, Korruk raised his sword and prepared to bring it down into me one last time when something stopped him. The zauhlon looming over me shouted in pain and swung around to hit someone behind him. When he did, I saw blood trickling down a spot on his back. Not only that, but I saw who his attacker was.

It was ... an anthrum? What was he doing here? That was the last question I asked myself before I blacked out.

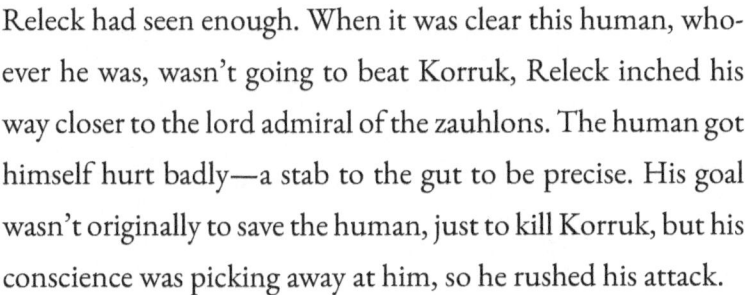

Releck had seen enough. When it was clear this human, who-ever he was, wasn't going to beat Korruk, Releck inched his way closer to the lord admiral of the zauhlons. The human got himself hurt badly—a stab to the gut to be precise. His goal wasn't originally to save the human, just to kill Korruk, but his conscience was picking away at him, so he rushed his attack.

Right when Korruk was about to end this man's life, Releck struck. Using a sword he'd taken from a dead zauhlon, he stabbed Korruk in the back. Well, as best he could at least. Thanks to the layers of armor Korruk wore and the general toughness of zauhlon skin, he only dug the sword an inch or two into the alien in front of him.

It was enough to hurt, and therefore anger, Korruk. The zauhlon swung around and hit Releck with the back of his fist. The blow sent Releck stumbling back, but he quickly recovered and took a defensive stance that protected his torso. Releck was by no means a swordsman, but codex entries on anthrum/zauhlon history taught him the basics.

This is it, Releck thought. *It's now or never.*

Korruk charged and sought to overwhelm the young anthrum, which he succeeded. Using a combination of blade and fists, he managed to get Releck off his feet. Before he could straddle him and further beat him senseless, Releck grabbed his vibro-knife and wedged it into Korruk's thigh between the plates of armor. Once again, Korruk voiced his pain. While Releck hoped this would slow the eight-foot beast, it seemed to only fuel him further.

With the knife still in his thigh, Korruk laid his fists into Releck's helmet, cracking it. Releck was only barely conscious. Still, despite the state he was in, he knew full well that he was beaten. The only chance he had at beating Korruk was with a surprise attack, and that was ruined because he wanted to save a stranger.

Images of his father flashed before his eyes. He would never know what happened to his son. No one would. He took a deep breath, accepting his fate. He wouldn't go out whimpering.

The sudden and very loud noise of thrusters working at full throttle, followed by a series of explosions changed that. If it weren't for the sound dampeners in his helmet, he would've lost his hearing from the sudden chaos. He felt Korruk run away. No, not run away. More likely he was finding cover. Cover from what? There was too much going on. Releck couldn't focus.

Once again, he took a deep breath, trying to calm himself. It was a trick his father taught him when he was a child. "When you're overwhelmed with noise, take deep breaths and focus on one sound at a time." Those were his exact words. So that's what Releck did.

The first sound he focused on was the gunfire. Machine guns from the ship that came in, bullets from other places in the warehouse, and bullets from a couple dozen meters south. That was where Korruk was. The second sound was the thrusters. Followed by the buzzing of drones, shouting, and creaking. What was that creaking?

Releck soon found out. One of the massive shelves fell down with a sudden and loud *thud*. If he had been a few more meters north, he would have been crushed. Pushing that morbid thought aside, he had to act fast. He failed his mission; that much was obvious. But he still had that picture of whatever that thing was further in the warehouse. The Senate needed to see that. On top of that, that human was still alive.

Crawling over to the injured human, he threw him over his shoulders and climbed over the fallen shelf. As best he could, he tried to stay low to avoid being hit. He'd never been in a war zone before, but being here right now, crawling with a wounded soldier while two sides unleashed hell upon one another, the risk of being shot oh so very high ... this was the closest Releck had ever gotten to actual combat.

Half way across the shelf, he heard a human male yelling at him. It took him a few moments to figure out what he was saying.

"Bring him over here! Come on!"

That's exactly what Releck did.

With the shelf crossed, he got to his feet and ran towards the ship and the other human combatants, the wounded man still atop his shoulders. As soon as his feet were on the lowered cargo bay ramp, said starship took off. With the help of one of the other humans, they brought the unconscious man further into the cargo bay. From there, medical professionals carried him to what Releck assumed was the med-bay.

As the cargo bay door closed, everyone who had been in the fight either stood, sat on a nearby crate, or lay on the floor, exhausted. It quickly dawned on Releck that he had no idea who these people were. For all he knew, they'd kill him once things calmed down.

Despite these concerns, he allowed himself to relax. If they wanted to kill him, all they had to do was take their friend and push him back into the warehouse. He just had to hope saving their friend was enough to warrant hospitality.

PART II

10

[*Sparrow* Med-Bay.]

[Local ship time: 1200.]

Upon opening my eyes, I was greeted by an absurdly bright light shining down onto me. I moved to shield myself from the light, but found I was hooked up to a tank of tecronim. While the green liquid medicine worked wonders on the body, its effects left a stinging sensation, one that I could now feel in my veins. As my vision adjusted to the lights above, I tried to think back and remember what happened. Before I could fully put the pieces together though, Dr. Holiday made himself known.

"You took quite the beating, Severre," Holiday said, leaning on a terminal. "You're lucky to be alive."

I tried to sit up, but I was stopped by a sharp pain in my midsection. Sighing through clenched teeth, I held my wound and relaxed onto the bed, "I don't feel lucky."

"I don't blame you. You were stabbed through the abdomen, have bruised ribs—along with bruises across your body I might add—and a minor concussion. To put it bluntly, if we didn't see to you as soon as you got here, you'd already be dead."

Dr. Holiday let that sink in for me. I have to admit, the thought did scare me, but not as much as it angered me. The only reason I got to that point was because of the brash and foolish decisions I made during the fight. I felt like an idiot.

"Well, I'm glad you guys got there when you did," I said.

"Thank Lieutenant Smith. He was the one that called the *Sparrow* in," said Dr. Holiday.

At the mention of Tenner, I remembered how he tried to convince me to not fight Korruk, and how I didn't listen. I was damned lucky he and the others survived. Actually ...

"Is everyone ..."

"Your team is fine, Severre. Cuts and bruises here and there, but no serious damage," Holiday said.

I let out a sigh of relief. If anyone had gotten hurt because of my bad choices, that would have been too much for me to handle. Once all this was said and done, I'd have to get Tenner a beer.

Dr. Holiday picked up a medical tool I didn't recognize from the counter, "Now that you're awake, I'm going to inject some tecronim directly into your abdomen. To make sure you'll be back on your feet sooner."

Great ...

As if he knew the pain I was about to go through and wished to save me, Captain Arty walked into the med-bay. Holiday saluted Arty, who nodded at the doctor and gestured to the bulkhead door. Dr. Holiday took the hint and left me and Arty alone.

"Good to see you're doing well, captain," Arty said, "Forgive me for getting right to the point, but what on god's green earth happened down there?"

After taking a moment to think everything over, I proceeded to tell Arty about everything. From our detour through the sewers all the way to my fight with Korruk. I made sure to point out the crate full of heavy duty explosives as well.

Arty held his chin between his index finger and thumb, "Were you able to place a tracker on the explosives?"

"Yeah, but it was one of the weaker models. If we're going to put it to use, we'll need to hone in on the feedback waves and increase the output tenfold," I said. After a period of silence, I sighed, "Whatever Korruk is doing with that many explosives, it's not good. I just wish we found something more concrete than that."

"You might be in luck. That anthrum that saved you is on board the Bird, down in the cargo bay. He hasn't spoken a word since he's gotten here though. If you can get him to talk he might have some useful info," Arty said.

I nodded, "Thanks for the tip."

Before Arty left the room, he turned to face me, "We're on our way to Crell. Figured the Senate would like to know about this."

I nodded again in thanks. The detour was an inconvenience, but Republic Core Worlds were the only planets with comm lines that have never been sliced before, and given the magnitude of what those explosives could mean, it was better safe than sorry.

Dr. Holiday walked back into the med-bay and picked up where he left off. As soon as the tecronim was injected into my wound, I felt a strong stinging in my abdomen. This was going to be a long day...

--------◆--------

The next time I woke up, all the stinging was gone. I tested how well the tecronim was working and tried to sit up, but the stinging came back. Looks like it was moving its way down. I could deal with that though. All I needed to do was stay still and relax. That felt like something I hadn't done in a long time.

Careful not to hurt myself, I picked up the data-pad on the nightstand next to me and checked my notifications. If anything, I could always put together my report on what happened at Serpent's Hole. As it turns out, I had one notification. Upon seeing who it was from, I froze. It was from Dr. Trent. The doctor caring for Flyby.

I was nervous to open the message. Afraid of what I might see. Pushing those fears aside, I finally tapped on the message. Like the last text from her, it was inflated with medical talk, but I was able to pick out the important details. When I did though, my heart dropped.

Due to the concussion he received, he would always struggle with dizziness and maintaining balance. He wouldn't be able to serve anymore.

She tried to end the message on a positive note, saying Flyby decided to accept weekly treatments to improve on the dizziness and balance. That's great and all, but the majority of servicemen who experience these issues were stuck with them for the rest of their lives, treatment or not.

I laid the data-pad on my chest and sighed. A part of me was holding out hope that maybe, just maybe, Flyby could come back and join back up with the Wolf Pack. This took that hope and threw it out the airlock.

The bulkhead doors slid open, and I half expected it to be Dr. Holiday ready to start his shift. To my surprise, it was Boomer.

"Hey, Cap, is this a good time?" she asked quietly.

"Yeah, sure. What can I do for you?" I said, trying to mask the mix of emotions I was feeling.

"I just wanted to check on you. When that anthrum brought you in, you looked like a corpse."

I laughed, but a mixture of the stinging in my abdomen and some still faintly bruised ribs made me stop. "To be honest, I still feel like one."

Boomer took notice of the data-pad still laying on my chest. "Back to work already?"

"Hmm? Oh, no this isn't related to the mission, it's ..." I hesitated, "It's about the teammate that survived the ambush. Flyby."

Understanding the sensitivity of the subject, her tone softened. "Is he okay?"

"He'll live, but he's being medically discharged," I said.

She gave me an apologetic look. "I know what it's like to see people leave. Back when I was a marine, my squad had a sergeant named Harry Tenson as our team leader. He'd been our TL for four years, so when it was time for him to retire, it was hard to say goodbye. I know the situation is different with Flyby, but at least you'll be able to visit him and tell him all your new stories."

I smiled. She had a point. We may not be serving together, but as long as we were alive, the old Wolf Pack would live on.

"Yeah, you're right," I said.

She returned the smile, then got up from the visitor's seat. "I'll let you be now. It's about time for training anyway."

"Tell everyone not to slack off just because the captain is bed bound," I said. "And hey, Boomer? Thanks."

She turned and flashed one more smile as Dr. Holiday walked in. "Don't mention it."

[The *Vengeance*, twenty minutes after the battle in Zone Two.]

[Local system time: 2130.]

He only had one opportunity at this. Orrim's life depended on it. The zauhlon general received word that Lord Admiral Korruk was returning to the ship. Captain Turrik had informed him that Korruk believed him to be dead, so Orrim would have the element of surprise. Furthermore, it seemed the humans might have proved themselves useful. Rumor had it Korruk was injured.

He took a separate Archon drop ship, but apparently his voice sounded strained. While this was merely a rumor, it was paramount Orrim locate where this injury was and exploit it.

Orrim was in his personal quarters, gathering everything he needed. A few extra pieces of armor from defeated enemies, two knives made of yuresh steel, and a souvenir from a raid in klex space, Khlevonian sand. Unlike sand from other planets, this type turns into ice upon contact.

While strapping on the additional armor, he mused how he likely deserved death for his missteps. He shook his head. None of that mattered right now. An encrypted message came in. It was from Furrak, a slave zauhlon who worked as an engineer. Lord Admiral Korruk landed in Hangar Bay Ten and was on his way to the bridge. Not only that, but his back was bleeding. *So, the rumors of his injury were true ...*

Orrim didn't bother sending a reply. Instead, he headed toward the portside passageway on Deck Three. From Hangar Bay Ten there was only one corridor leading to the bridge, and along that corridor was a damaged piece of bulkhead. If Orrim could hide there, he could get the jump on Korruk.

Using a shortcut, Orrim reached the passageway before Korruk did. He slipped into the damaged portion of the bulkhead and waited, peeping through the gap that separated himself and the corridor. For what felt like eternity, Orrim was nestled into the damaged piece of the ship, his yuresh knife in hand. While waiting for his target, his mind ran through the odds of success. Dozens, most likely hundreds of zauhlons had attempted to kill Korruk, just as he was trying to, yet all of them had failed. There was a reason he had been lord admiral for so long, after all. If Orrim wanted to be the one to finally take him down, he would need to be swift and strike in all the right places.

Footsteps echoed throughout the corridor, marching with an authority to them. It was Korruk. Now was the time.

Lord Admiral Korruk stomped by Orrim's hiding spot, accompanied by two other zauhlons; Centurions. The hidden general slipped out of the damaged bulkhead, careful to make as little sound as possible. When he was out, he dashed toward Korruk and stabbed him in the back where he was previously wounded. His repeated stabs deepened the wound, causing Korruk to shout in both surprise and anger.

One of the Centurions grabbed Orrim and attempted to pull him away, but the general knew every weak spot in a zauhlon's armor and where to swing to cut the Centurion's throat. Without missing a beat, he stabbed the other Centurion in the same part of the neck. Korruk, now facing his attacker, gritted his teeth. If he was surprised by Orrim being alive, he didn't show it.

"If it is death you want, I shall grant it to you," Korruk said.

The followingfight was brutal and bloody. Orrim used both his knives to cut Korruk along the arms and chest, though the lord admiral's extra armor pieces prevented those cuts from drawing blood. No matter how hard he tried, he couldn't get to Korruk's throat. Korruk knew his armor's weaknesses and knew to keep the blades away from there.

Korruk tackled the general to the ground and wrestled one of the yuresh blades away from Orrim. It took every ounce of strength in Orrim's body to keep the knife from being dug into his skull. He managed to push Korruk off of him, and when they both rose to their feet, they engaged in a knife fight that resulted in Orrim losing sight in both his left eyes.

The wound to his eyes allowed Korruk to wrestle the knife away from Orrim and once again get him to the ground. Following this, Korruk laid blow after blow on Orrim, breaking the general's nose.

Seeking to end the fight, Korruk raised the knife above him and prepared to bring it down into Orrim, but the silver-clad zauhlon pulled out his container of Khlevonian sand and tossed it in Korruk's eyes. Instantly the sand turned to ice, and Korruk was blinded. This allowed Orrim to turn over so he was on top and in control. Despite trying to wrestle the knife out of Korruk's hands, the lord admiral instead chose to toss it as far away as he could, making Orrim chose whether he wanted to stay in control or run for the knife. Ultimately, he chose to stay in control.

It was Orrim's turn to lay the beat down on Korruk. During the attack, Orrim knocked the canine tooth off of Korruk's mandible. Eventually Orrim wrapped his hands around Korruk's throat, trying to choke him out. Korruk first tried to pry the gloved hands off his neck but gave up and instead choked Orrim as well. It would come down to whoever had the stronger grip.

For a while Orrim was sure he would come out victorious, but as the choke-out continued, he found that, despite having been wounded in multiple spots, Korruk was putting everything he had into strangling Orrim. That rage and strength would be enough for Orrim's grip to loosen and allow Korruk to once again flip them so he was on top. When he felt the life slipping from Orrim's mouth, he released his grip and laid three more powerful punches into Orrim's face. Barely able to breathe, Orrim lay there, unable to move

He had been beaten.

Lord Admiral Korruk stumbled to his feet, still blinded by the ice and shouted, "Strip him of his armor and send him to the brig. Should anyone think it wise to try their hand at killing me, they will see what will happen if you do."

Two grunts emerged from the gathering crowd and did as they were told, leaving Orrim naked and humiliated in front of them all. They dragged him across the deck and through corridor after corridor until they reached the brig, leaving a trail of blood.

Without care for his wellbeing, they tossed Orrim into an open cell and activated the force field which would keep him there. Zauhlons who earlier would have died for him now treated Orrim like dirt, as was the way in zauhlon culture. Strength meant everything, and if you no longer had that strength, you were worthless. By leaving him alive and without his armor, Korruk was proving the general was exactly that.

———————◆O◆———————

[Cargo bay, *Sparrow*. Fin Kallus, Crell.]

[Local system time: 1015.]

Even though it had been only two days, I was feeling much better. Walking was still tough, and I'm sure I looked like Frankenstein's monster, but I could at least move around. We'd entered the Averus System a few hours before and docked in the city of Fin Kallus, Crell's capital city. Before I addressed the Senate, I wanted to talk to that anthrum. From what Engineer Walker told me, he loosened up a bit when he found out we were in a Republic system, which made sense. We may have appeared to be with the Republic, but looks could be deceiving.

As I approached him, he turned to acknowledge me. "I hope your stay here hasn't been too bad. I'm Star Bourn Captain Severre, team leader of the Wolf Pack."

Upon hearing my rank, the anthrum gave me a human-style salute. "Pleasure to meet you, captain. The name's Releck."

"Pleasure's all mine. Quite literally, too. I owe you my life. If it weren't for you, I'd be dead right now," I said.

"I was just doing the right thing, captain." Releck sounded almost humble. To be honest, I wasn't expecting that, considering we picked him up in the Badlands. Serpent's Hole, no less.

"So, what exactly were you doing in Serpent's Hole, if you don't mind my asking?" I leaned on one of the crates. "Were you sent by the Republic?"

"No, sir. In fact, it was the Republic's inaction that fueled me. It ..." Releck stopped himself. "Permission to speak freely?"

I shrugged my shoulders. "You don't serve under me, Releck. Say whatever you want."

He nodded. "It pissed me off. The fact they let a warlord like him go free with a slap on the wrist made my skin boil. Since they were too scared to do something about him, I took it upon myself to act."

"Well, you're lucky all this happened in the Badlands, or else you'd get arrested for vigilantism," I said. "How long were you in Serpent's Hole?"

"About a week. I have some friends who are slicers, and they told me there were sightings of Korruk there. After that, I was pretty much on my own, spare for some crooks with watchful eyes looking to make some credits," Releck said.

"Impressive. On your search for Korruk, did you find anything suspicious?" Here was the moment of truth. If Releck knew anything, now was the time to talk.

He hesitated, which gave me the answer. Now I just had to make him tell me.

"There's a lot of things in Serpent's Hole I found suspicious." Releck looked around. "Why would you want to know?"

I decided to play my cards here. If I wanted what he knew, I'd have to give a little something in return. "I'm hunting Korruk too, Releck. He killed my friends and the closest thing I had to a father. And I'm not going to stop until I kill him. But there's more going on here. He's planning something big, I just need to know how big. Our goals are the same, so if you saw anything connected to Korruk, I need you to tell me."

After no doubt thinking over his decision, Releck spoke up. "There was something. It's hard to describe the aura it is giving off. It was large and heavy, and it felt very dangerous. I took a picture of it with my helmet's camera, for what it's worth." Releck picked up his helmet. "If you have a terminal handy, we can download the image onto your computers."

This was better than I hoped for. Well, better may not be the right word. Considering the explosives I found, I had a good idea what it was. Regardless, I led him to the terminal in the cargo bay, and after a few seconds, the image popped up on the screen.

It was clearly some type of bomb, though I couldn't tell what kind. Releck was right in that it was large. It had to be over ten feet tall. The insides were exposed and glowed a bright white. Some panels were missing, so it was obviously still in development, though I had no clue how close it was to being complete.

"What did you plan on doing with this?" I asked him.

"I wanted to take it to the Senate. Not that they would listen to me. It's like you said, they'd look at me as a vigilante," Releck said.

"They'll listen to me. I'm going to be meeting with them in an hour. If you want, I can bring this with me, or you can come with me. They'll treat you with respect if I'm there with you," I said.

He shook his head. "It's probably best if you go alone."

I wanted to ask why he would think that, but I decided to let it go. I wanted to get there early, just in case my injuries slowed me down. Giving Releck a nod, I turn to leave the cargo bay, only to be stopped by an alien hand grabbing my wrist.

"Captain, wait," he said. "Like you said, our goals are the same. I know high stakes inter-species ops are a rarity, but please, let me join your team. I'll follow orders just as well as your human teammates."

The offer made me hesitate. I've never worked on the field with an alien before, and with the mission being as important as it is, that made me even more leery. That being said, I did owe him my life. Taking a deep breath, I nodded. "Alright. Welcome to the Wolf Pack, Releck."

11

Any minute now, the comm channel would switch on and I'd begin my report on the Serpent's Hole mission. The walk there was tough, but it was a beautiful day outside, so I didn't mind taking my time. Pushing that aside, the thought of that bomb weighed heavily on my mind. What was Korruk planning to do with that?

I didn't have time to think about that. The lights in the comm room dimmed, and real-time holo images of each senator appeared before me.

"Captain Severre," Nyra greeted me. "We've been told you have an update on the hunt for Korruk?"

I nodded, then proceeded to tell them everything, just as I did with Arty. Along with my report, I provided them with the image Releck showed me. When everything was said and done, all of them had wavering looks of concern on their faces, as they should have.

"This ... is a disturbing turn of events for sure," Nyra said. It was clear to me she didn't have much experience with situations like this. What should I have expected though? She's a politician.

"Agreed. Did you place a tracking device on the explosives, captain?" Senator Sul asked.

"Yes, senator. As soon as we regroup, we'll be planning our next course of action," I replied.

Senator Verum nodded. "Be careful, Severre. They've almost certainly figured out you know they're planning something. If I were them, I'd fortify this Serpent's Hole with the best defenses I could get ahold of."

"I agree with Senator Verum," Orthin said. "We need to go about this very carefully. They'll be expecting to see you again soon. Perhaps it would be best to wait and let the flames die down."

"Agreed. Should this bomb of his move anywhere though, you should jump in for the kill. We have no idea how far along in development it is, after all. For all we know, it's only days away from completion," Senator Lesh said.

The rest of the senators agreed with this. I, on the other hand, wasn't thrilled about it. I could see the logic in waiting, but it didn't sit well knowing Korruk would be getting away with building this bomb without any distractions.

"It seems the path forward has been decided. Ultimately, it's up to you, Severre," Nyra said.

Technically she was right, but if I did anything other than what they said, I knew they'd chew me out for it. I've worked with enough bureaucrats to know how this went.

Not long afterward, the meeting ended, and I was left alone. The guards outside escorted me out of the room and told me if I had any other calls to make, another comm room was around the corner. While I was originally going to head back to the *Sparrow*, I found myself walking to the other comm room. Once there, I punched in Admiral Drake's comm number. *Maybe he could give me advice on what to do.*

As soon as Drake's blue-tinted image appears in front of me, I give him a rundown on the situation, and about what happened in Serpent's Hole in general. The entire time he wore a hardened expression. In contrast to Senate Leader Nyra, Admiral Drake was no doubt processing all this with a tactical mindset.

"I see ..." Drake said. "I've heard whispers of Serpent's Hole before, but I was never able to confirm its existence. If that bomb Korruk is making is anything to go by, I'm tempted to send the fleet in and blow it to hell. The only downside to that is there would be a lot of vengeful factions looking for payback, let alone the zauhlons."

"What should I do, admiral? 'Sit around and let Korruk finish this bomb' doesn't feel right," I said.

Drake nodded. "I know what you mean." After thinking hard about what our next step should be, Drake spoke up. "Seeing as how we know Serpent's Hole is real, then maybe Phantom is too."

"Sir?"

"Drones haven't been the only way we've tried to verify Serpent's Hole's existence. Years ago, Star Command sent an undercover agent to work for the Eventide Vanguard Taskforce, an organization we believe are regular customers at Serpent's Hole, or a black-market factory similar to it. Our agent only heard talk about it before he was discovered and killed, but there was also talk about something—or *someone* else—Phantom.

"Based on what he reported, the EVT soldiers believed Phantom to be the head of Serpent's Hole. We didn't look further into it since all we had was a vague name, but this changes things. If we could confirm this Phantom exists and can get in touch with him, maybe we could get an edge on Korruk," Admiral Drake said.

I thought over what he said. It made sense that Serpent's Hole was run by someone, but how would we contact him? I voiced these exact concerns to Drake.

"That sounds great, but how do we even reach him? And how do we get information from him? Black market contractors aren't ones to sell out their customers," I said.

"To answer your first point, I suggest you use Zavi again. He turned out to be spot on last time, so it wouldn't hurt to check with him. As for your second point, you entice them with an offer they can't refuse. You're right in that they don't like to sell out customers, but these type of people will stab others in the back in a heartbeat if you give them enough reason to," Admiral Drake said.

I wish Tenner was with me, I thought.

After thanking Admiral Drake for the advice, I began the process of calling Zavi. Once I made sure the call was private and couldn't be tracked, I hit confirm.

Unlike Admiral Drake, Zavi took his sweet time in forming a comm line. When he did though, he was all smiles, just like he was when we first met him.

"Zavi Ratullo here, how can I—Ah shit, not you again. Whaddya want?"

"Thanks for the warm welcome," I said. "Listen, I know our last meeting didn't turn out well, but your information was solid, and I could use your talents again." I was hoping that little praise at the end would be enough to warm him up.

Zavi let out a long sigh and crossed his arms. "Alright, alright, what can I do for you?"

"Do you know someone named Phantom? Rumor has it he runs Serpent's Hole."

The info broker's irritated look quickly switched to one of fear and nervousness. In the short time I'd known him, Zavi never came off as someone quick to be afraid, so this sudden change in demeanor told me all I needed to know about this Phantom.

"Uh, listen pal, I got some calls to make. Remodeling the bar and all that, so I should really go."

Before he could cut the line, I quickly said, "I have credits. Name your price and you have a deal."

This made the bugman stop in his tracks. Despite his apparent discomfort at the topic of Phantom, he still thought over whether or not he should talk about him. All for some credits. Torrs really were something else.

"A million credits."

If I had a drink, I'd have spit it out at this point. "A million?"

"Take it or leave it. Your call," Zavi said.

Just about every fiber of my body was telling me "hell no," but I had to remind myself what was at stake here. With the amount of explosives Korruk had, this bomb could do some serious damage, which meant a lot of people could die. And people's lives were worth more than credits, even a million credits.

I sighed, then brought up my data-pad and got to texting Tenner. In my message, I told him I was dealing with Zavi and he needed credits. When he replied asking how much, I felt awful telling him the amount, like I was taking advantage of my friend. Despite that, he simply texted "Done, but you're gonna owe me. Remember that revolver I wanted?"

I nearly groaned. Of course I remembered. The Lone Defender RX50 revolver. Only a hundred were ever made. One of the most powerful handguns humanity ever made, being able to tear through shields with one bullet. Also, one of the most expensive guns on the market. It was the least I could do though.

Seconds later, Zavi began hollering and jumping. "Sweet Dara, I didn't think you'd actually do it! I'm kriggin' rich!"

I cleared my throat. "Phantom. What can you tell me?"

Reality quickly came back to Zavi. "Oh, uh, right." Taking a deep breath, Zavi started to sound like himself. "That rumor of yours is right. Phantom runs the place. Has for decades. Nobody knows who he really is, just that he's yongun. You seem like a good enough guy, Severre, so take my advice—don't get mixed up with him. He deals with credits, sure, but that ain't all. Word has it he wants something more."

"Like what?"

"I don't know, I've never talked to the guy. I've heard stories though, from friends who know some guys. Some say he demands loyalty, some say he wants a piece of his customer, whatever that means," Zavi said.

I didn't know what to think of the last part. While it seemed far-fetched, anything goes in the Badlands. Nothing that happens there would surprise me.

"Anything else?" I asked.

"Yeah, be careful what you say to him. From what I've heard, he's got an endless number of contacts. If you piss him off, he'll get you. No matter where you are in the galaxy." After a pause, Zavi glanced from side to side. "Hey, this isn't going to come back on me, yeah? Whatever it is you want with him, I don't want any part of it, and I don't want you dragging me down with you."

Raising my hands defensively, I reassured him. "Don't worry, Zavi, this is all on me. Now how do I get in touch with him?"

Zavi chuckled. "Don't worry, he'll get in contact with you."

With that, the torr info broker cut the line.

Zavi's last comment was ominous, and it didn't do much to help me. If he was right about Phantom's contacts though, maybe he wasn't lying. I felt a lot more paranoid while thinking about this.

Without any reason to stay at the ambassador's building, I decided to head back to the *Sparrow*. Not long after I left, I got the lingering feeling I was being watched. At first, I chalked that off to being a side effect of what Zavi told me, but I reminded myself: a good Star Bourn should trust his instincts, especially in cases like this. If I was being followed, I couldn't lead them back to the *Sparrow*.

Cutting through an alleyway, I listened carefully to see if I heard another set of footsteps. Sure enough, I did, though it was clear they were trying to be quiet. I couldn't walk any faster due to my injuries, and I didn't want to risk hurting myself and letting this person know I was wounded. With my heart racing, I thought over ways I could lose them, or take them out. I had no weapons, and I was too injured to fight head on. Looking around, I searched for something, anything. A loose pipe, a trashcan, even a bottle.

Finally, luck was on my side. I spotted an empty glass bottle next to a homeless man. Fight or flight mode was in full effect now as I reached for the bottle. As soon as I grabbed it, I turned around and prepared to swing it at whoever was behind me. My stalker was fast though. He grabbed my wrist and kneed me in the gut. I reacted more than I should have, opening myself up to a punch in the face. The next thing I know, a needle was stabbed into my neck. Whatever it was, it was strong. I felt the effects almost immediately.

I tried to fight back, but it was useless. None of my punches connected, leaving me looking like some amateur civilian. The man who drugged me didn't bother to fight back; he knew I'd be out in no time, and he was right. Within seconds, I fell into his arms, unconscious.

12

When I came to, I wasn't anywhere I recognized. Apart from a light that shined down on me, everything was pitch black. Upon trying to move around, I also found I was tied up with lacer rope. Lacer was a type of rope only top military organizations or powerful people had, which tightened and cut into the skin of the user the more they struggled. I knew enough not to resist, but alarm bells were ringing front and center in my mind. This was bad. Real bad. Every fighting bone in my body was calling for me to get out of this and kill the people responsible. Another part of my mind though reminded me of what Zavi said. "He'll get in contact with you."

Was this Phantom's way of getting in touch? Regardless, I couldn't do anything in the state I was in now, so I waited.

With no natural light coming into the area I was in, I couldn't tell what time it was. For all I knew hours could have passed. Despite not knowing the time however, I kept track of how long it had been since I woke up. After fifteen minutes, two men walked into sight. They were both sahngruns and held Grafta assault rifles. I'll admit, being tied up with two well-armed men in front of me made me nervous.

"What do you want with Phantom?" the sahngrun to my right said.

Confusion washed over me, but as soon as it came, it disappeared. *The bastard was listening in on me.* I knew the comm I called Zavi on wasn't as great as the one I used in my call with the Senate, but they weren't easy to hack either.

"You should know," I said.

My remark earned me a smack with the butt of a Grafta. Seconds later I tasted iron in my mouth.

"Phantom doesn't take new clients without an offering first," the man said.

I nodded. "I have a good sum of credits for him."

"No. Credits come later. He requires a blood offer."

Shooting a puzzled look at my captor, I waited for an explanation that I never got. So, this was what "a piece of his customer" meant. I wasn't thrilled about getting cut willingly, but I sucked it up and nodded. *Do it for the mission.*

"Well, what are you waiting for?"

The silent man pulled out a knife of yongun origin and walked behind me. While he did this, I was fully aware that if he wanted to, he could cut my throat and kill me. Giving this much power and trust to someone I don't know was uncomfortable, but luckily he didn't cut anything vital. Instead, he slit the palm of my left hand.

After squeezing out some blood, he walked back in front of me with a half-filled vial. Without saying another word, the two men walked away. Once again, I kept track of the time, the only sound that reached my ears being that of my blood dripping onto the metal floor.

To my surprise, only a minute passed before a blue hologram appeared before me. The man was hidden in robes, but I could make out his mouth, which instantly told me he was a yongun. This had to be Phantom.

"Captain Severre ..." he said slowly, emphasizing each syllable. "It's a pleasure to meet you. I apologize for the brutality that was used to bring you here. What can I do for you?"

"I assume you're Phantom?"

"You assume correctly. What is it you need? I'm a very busy man, captain."

A part of me was tempted to throw out another piece of sarcasm but I bit my tongue. The memories of how nervous Zavi and how dangerous he made Phantom out to be had come back to me. Instead, I chose to get straight to the point.

"Lord Admiral Korruk was in Serpent's Hole. What was he building?"

To his credit, Phantom didn't act surprised at all. "You're right in that he was here. However, it's unethical to release personal details on a client."

"That may be true, but I know when you're working in the Badlands, you have to do unethical things to be king of the hill. So, what would it take for you to tell me? Credits? Or something else?" I didn't know what "something else" would mean to Phantom, but I hoped it enticed him enough to make an offer.

After pondering my words, Phantom spoke up. "The ship you entered Serpent's Hole in was a model I'm only vaguely aware of. The Mark III Assassin Class corvette, correct? It's a thing of beauty. Fast, too. I could use ships like that for my business. I want the schematics."

Just as with Zavi's ridiculous price, my knee-jerk reaction was to say no. A ship like the *Sparrow* in the hands of someone like Phantom was a dangerous prospect, but I was once again reminded of the mission. How much was I willing to sacrifice to stay one step ahead of Korruk? If word spreads that I'm the one who leaked the blueprints of the *Sparrow*, my career would be over.

Phantom seemed to sense my hesitation, because he attempted to sooth me. "My methods are airtight, captain. If they weren't, I would have been discovered and killed a long time ago. Should you agree, this won't trace back to you or myself."

"And why would you care about my safety?"

"I care about all my clients, captain."

"Unless you're given a better deal."

Phantom smirked. "Touché. Regardless, I stand by my words. It's up to you whether or not you'll believe me."

Even though my heart was telling me not to do it, I decided to take a leap of faith. I needed to stop Korruk, no matter what.

"You've got a deal."

Phantom's smirk became a smile. "Good. I was beginning to worry you'd be as stubborn as I've heard most Star Bourn are."

The hooded alien snapped his fingers, and the two Sahngruns came back. One cut me loose, while the other held out a data-pad.

"Punch in the access code to your ship's computer," the Sahngrun with the data-pad said.

I looked at Phantom. "I only have the code for the holo-net, and that won't get you to the schematics."

"I already assumed as much. Fear not, captain. All parts of a ship's computers are connected in some form, much like the galaxy itself. Like one big spider web. I only need a point of entry, then my slicers will do the rest."

With only a second of hesitation, I took the data-pad and put in my access code. Seconds later, Star Command's insignia appeared on the screen followed by a welcome message.

"Thank you very much, captain. This will be more beneficial to my business than you could know," Phantom said. "Now, I'll uphold my end of the deal. As I'm sure you already know, thanks to your escapade in Zone Two, Korruk has commissioned me and my people to build him a bomb. The type of bomb, however, is one the galaxy hasn't seen in a long time. He's having us build a Category Ten bomb."

My entire body froze. Category Ten referred to the most destructive type of bombs: planet killers.

"The 'Rahalah', he calls it. It's Zurabic for 'revenge'. Bombs like these haven't been built for centuries, so construction has been rough. Much more difficult than your average bomb. It should take thirty more days to finish, but because of your little adventure and destruction of my property, Korruk is asking we complete it in half that time," Phantom said.

"He must be planning on attacking Milara," I muttered. *Or Earth.* "We have to stop him, fast."

"I don't have to do anything, captain. I have no desire to bring the wrath of the Zauhlon Legion down onto Serpent's Hole, nor do I care what happens to your Republic worlds."

"If you don't, you'll be facing the wrath of Star Command," I said. It was off the cuff, but I felt like I had to say *something*. It's like what Admiral Drake said earlier: heading back to Serpent's Hole anytime soon would be a risk, given that they'll be ready for us this time around. But we only had fifteen days till this planet killer was finished. I needed Phantom to help us out with this.

Phantom scoffed. "You're bluffing. Who are you to make such a threat? You're just a commando."

"True, but I've spoken with Admiral Drake, and he's already considering attacking Serpent's Hole. With this knowledge, he won't hesitate to blow you all to hell," I said.

"That's only if he finds out. If you're determined to go through with this, I could have you killed right now," Phantom said.

I was painfully aware of the two armed sahngruns, but I held my ground. "You think they won't notice if I go missing? Especially considering the mission I'm on? No matter which way you look at it, they'll trace it back to you, and you'll have hell to pay. It doesn't have to come to this. All I'm asking is that you make it easier for us to kill Korruk."

While the sahngruns looked ready to fill me with bullets, Phantom seemed to think over his options. Finally, the yongun spoke up. "Very well, Severre. I'll play your game. Korruk, his zauhlons, and the Rahalah will be moved to a facility on Klydoon, a planet in Diablos Corner. It's a flat world, so you should have an easy enough time taking him out. I'll need some insurance though, captain. In case the bomb gets damaged."

"What do you have in mind?" I asked, though I really didn't want to. I only hoped it wouldn't be anything like the *Sparrow*'s schematics again.

"Two things. One, I want to be paid back fully. The Rahalah was an expensive investment—fifty million credits, in fact," Phantom said.

Truth be told, I had no idea where I would get that kind of money. I certainly wasn't going to ask Tenner again. Regardless, I nodded. "And number two?"

"Never come back to Serpent's Hole."

Once again, I nodded. I wasn't planning on visiting again anyway.

"Good. You're a very agreeable man, Severre. Despite your little threat before, I like you," Phantom said. "Is there anything else I can help you with? I wouldn't want to leave a good client like you unsatisfied."

"One more thing, actually. Answer me this: Why are you so quick to betray Korruk? Assassin class ships will be useful, sure, but are they really more profitable than a fifty million credit investment?" Maybe I shouldn't have asked these questions, but my curiosity got the better of me.

Phantom smiled. "A good question, captain. Very good. You see, credits are very useful, yes. But what's just as useful to me are objects. Ship schematics, space stations, crews, so on and so forth. Korruk, while he gave me lots of credits, gave me no objects, unlike yourself, who will give me both."

I nodded, satisfied with the answer. In the back of my mind, I wondered if I could get away with not giving him the credits. *He'd probably kill me if I tried*, I thought.

"If this is all, then allow me to set this plan in motion. Be ready to attack Klydoon in five days. No more, no less," Phantom said. "I hope to do business again with you soon, captain."

With that, the hologram disappeared. Not a second later, I was hit in the back of the head with the butt of one of the sahngruns Graftas, my unconscious body falling to the floor. I should have figured they wouldn't let me walk out on my own.

13

It didn't take long for Orrim to lose track of time down in the brig. His nose had stopped bleeding, but the beating Korruk gave him left him feeling weak. But while his body was weakened, his fighting spirit remained steadfast. He wouldn't let this loss, as big as it was, deter him from his life mission. He would rise above this and get revenge on Korruk. Not just for enslaving him now, but also for humiliating him.

The guard who was watching over his cell left and was soon replaced by another guard. Orrim could tell this one was young just by the way he presented himself. Fledglings often had more of a bounce in their step, their confidence still over the roof, as if they thought they were the next general in the making. Elders, on the other hand, were more tense. They knew they could be ambushed and killed at any moment, whether by an enemy or by a hotshot zauhlon looking to rise in the ranks.

Fledglings were more easily manipulated too. As this zauhlon stood high and mighty over the former general, Orrim's mind began to work overtime, putting together his escape plan. It wouldn't be immediate—he was in no shape to fight anyway—but within days he would have this boy wrapped around his finger.

"I remember my first shift of guard duty," Orrim said with a voice weaker than he'd like. "It wasn't all too different from this. Some fool thought he could murder a commander. Didn't expect the old man to put up a fight."

The fledgling said nothing, but Orrim knew he could hear him.

"I'd like to reassure you that you'll be in the fight in no time, but I know that won't happen." The guard turned to look at Orrim, trying but failing to not to show interest. "Not for any lack of talent. I can tell you'll make a good warrior by the way you present yourself. Unfortunately, Korruk would rather have us hide in a backwater system instead of letting us fight."

"Why?" the zauhlon asked. It was a genuine question, one which Orrim often asked himself. Despite being Korruk's top general, he never told him why they were here, or for how long. Just to "be patient" and "have faith."

"I don't know. Korruk thinks he can get away with doing whatever he wants. He doesn't care about any of us. He certainly doesn't care about what we want." Orrim chuckled, but it came out as more of a cough. "Why do you think I tried to overthrow him?"

The young zauhlon shook his head. "I've heard rumors that it'll all change soon. That things will go back to the way they were."

This time, Orrim had no problem laughing. "I've heard those rumors for years. Look at us. We're still here. Tell me boy, what is your name?"

Orrim's guard, while he still had his helmet on, appeared to be shocked. The former general didn't blame him, of course. It's not often a zauhlon would ask for another's name. The only names that are important are the ones who are leaders. Captains, commanders, generals, etc.

After some hesitation, the zauhlon answered, "Niruuk."

"That's a good name. Plenty of excellent warriors and leaders share that name," Orrim said. "Allow me to pass down some wisdom, Niruuk. You can only get so far being a follower. Sooner or later, you'll need to be your own man and stand above the others. If you truly wish for things to change, you must be the change you desire."

Niruuk didn't say anything, but he nodded. The rest of his watch went on without a word. Orrim didn't want to push his luck. As he watched Niruuk leave and be replaced with someone else, he smiled to himself. He knew he had the young warrior hooked, and as long as he played his cards right, he would get his way in no time.

———◦———

[Comm Room, *Sparrow*.]

.

[Local system time: 1701.]

I had just finished telling Admiral Drake about what happened with Phantom—minus the part about me giving him my *Sparrow* access code. It ate at me to lie to Drake, but I couldn't risk him taking me off the mission for it, or worse—discharging me period. Being a Star Bourn was all I had. It was all I knew how to do.

Like he always does when I fill him in on what's going on, Admiral Drake listened carefully, making sure he heard every word I said. After thinking on my words, he spoke up. "First off, congratulations on making contact with Phantom and finding out what you did. I never would have expected this bomb to be a Category Ten. That being said, you made a big sacrifice to find that out. Eight figures is a lot of credits. I understand you did what you felt was right, but if you take it upon yourself to make another decision like that again, you'll be drummed out of the service. Understood?"

"Yes, sir," I said.

Drake nodded. "Back to the bomb. This raises the stakes immensely. Five days isn't a lot of time. Certainly not enough for the Senate to come together, make a decision, and hopefully at that point, gather an attack force."

"What do you suggest, sir?"

"We take matters in our own hands," Admiral Drake said. "Head to the Joro Nebula and regroup with the Eighth Fleet's Second Flotilla. They're spread thin, but the Second Flotilla is on standby, so they'll be able to help. From there, head to Klydoon and attack the facility. I'll leave it to the flotilla commander, Captain Adams to form a concrete plan."

"Yes, sir," I said, "Permission to speak freely?"

"Granted."

"What if this is all a trap? A flotilla is strong, but if they have a fleet waiting for us ..."

"It's a risk," Drake agreed, "but it's one we need to take. Worst case scenario, Captain Adams will send a code red distress beacon and you'll have to wait for reinforcements. Let's hope it doesn't come to that, though."

I nodded. The call ended shortly thereafter. Not wasting any time, I informed Arty of our next course of action, along with the knowledge of the Category Ten bomb. His eyes showed fear for the briefest of moments, but his voice was as confident and commanding as ever. As we left Crell's atmosphere, I decided to head to the portside observation deck. I needed to clear my mind of today's events.

When I entered the area, I found Releck sitting where I normally sat at the bar. As soon as he heard me enter, he put his hand over a comm device. We wordlessly acknowledged each other, and I took a seat next to him.

After a few moments of silence, I broke the ice. "Messaging your girlfriend?"

He laughed and shook his head. "No. My—" He hesitated before continuing. "I was going to call my father."

"Should I leave then? I don't want to interrupt," I said.

"No, you can stay. I'm not going to," said Releck.

I nodded and stayed silent for a while. Relationships, whether romantic or familial, have never been a specialty of mine. Whenever the old Wolves had problems, I listened to them, but I could never give them any worthwhile advice. While it's been awhile since I've had to be the one to initiate this sort of thing, I put on my best leadership voice and leaned on the bar.

"If you want to talk about it, I'm all ears. I can't promise I'll be helpful, but as your captain, I'm here for you."

That wasn't so bad.

Despite my little pat on the back, Releck stayed silent, leading me to believe my attempt at reaching out didn't work. Maybe these sorts of things worked differently in anthrum culture. Just when I was about to go around the bar and get a drink to try and forget this and everything else today, Releck spoke up.

"My father's a politician. He hates the military, and I want to be in the military. As you can imagine, we argue a lot about that," Releck said. He uncovered the comm device and pushed it aside. "I wanted to call him, but it's not worth the yelling."

"Are you sure?" I asked. "I won't sugar-coat it. This mission is looking darker and darker every day, and with how things are going now, we're looking at a final showdown. This might be your last chance to talk to him."

Releck tilted his head quizzically. I explained, "If all goes to plan, we're coaxing Korruk into making a last stand on some backwater world called Klydoon. I don't know how many ships he's working with, but putting that aside, the fight on the ground will be rough. He won't have much cover, but neither will we."

Releck stayed quiet, but he appeared to be more tense now. While I wasn't good at reading alien body language, if I had to guess, the weight of the mission was weighing down on him even more, which I'm sure didn't help with the situation with his dad.

"Look," I started, softening my tone. "You and your dad don't get along. I get that. And I'm not saying you'll die down there. As long as I can help it, I'm getting all my guys out of there alive. But you should talk to him now while you can. It doesn't have to be about the military or politics. Talk about sports, or a memory."

My words seemed to have calmed him down a little bit, so I decided to leave him be. Before I left the observation deck, I turned to face him. "Your father, is he ...?"

"Senator Din," Releck confirmed.

I nodded, not knowing what else to say. I couldn't imagine having a senator as a parent, what with them being away for so long. With that, I left the area, letting Releck do whatever he thought was best.

<hr>

With Releck once again alone, his hand hovered over the comm device. More specifically, the call button. Severre's words rung true, even more so now that he had an idea of what they were going to get into. Still, even with his encouragement, Releck was nervous to call his father. He knew he would ask where he's been, and Releck always had a hard time lying to his father. This would almost definitely lead to yet another yelling match, which Releck always hated.

Despite that, he forced himself to hit call. Even if it did come to that, at least he could hear his father's voice. That sense of familiarity was what he needed right now.

The comm device rang once, then twice. After the sixth ring, Releck heard his father's recorded voice asking him to leave a message. Knowing he wouldn't actually talk to him almost made Releck hang up and leave it at that. However, something inside of him kept him from doing so. Instead, he spoke what might be his final words to his father.

"Um, hello Father," Releck said awkwardly. "It's been a while. Too long. I'm sorry for that. I'm sorry the last time we talked was an argument too. The truth is, that finally egged me on in taking things into my own hands and learning how to fight. I spent the past couple of months in the Badlands, trying to find and kill Lord Admiral Korruk."

Releck laughed. "I can imagine you having a heart attack after hearing that. It's okay though. I did fight him, and I'm proud to say I injured him too. I lost, but during that fight, I got mixed up with some humans. Captain Severre and the ship he serves on, the *Sparrow*. You should know him. He's a good man, and I'll be joining him for the rest of his mission.

"I know you'll hate that, but this is my choice. It's always been my choice." He paused. "I'm sorry I'm not the son you wanted me to be. I wish I could be, but being a politician isn't me. I'm a warrior, Father.

"I don't know if I'll see you again. If I do, then why don't we go to the Flammera Diner? We haven't been there since I was a kid. It would be nice to spend some time together. If not, then ... I want you to know I'm proud of you. Being the son of the ambassador of our people ... it's not always easy, I'll admit, but it's something I take pride in. As much as this blasted galaxy is filled with corrupt politicians who only look out for themselves, I'm honored to be the son of one of the few honest ones out there. I love you, Dad."

14

[Klydoon, Diablos Corner. Four days from the assault.]

[Local system time: 0900.]

Klydoon was a frozen ocean world. With ice as thick as skyscrapers, there wasn't a single mountain on the planet. This left the planet completely flat, but for the odd facility here and there. As the morning sun rose in the east, there wasn't a cloud in the sky. To some, this would be a beautiful view.

Korruk was not one of those people. No, he detested the planet and all its icy glory.

As he was brought down to the factory Phantom told him about, flanked by four Centurions, he looked out at the surface, fresh snow hiding the thick ice. This planet provided zero cover. It was the equivalent of making camp in a desert, knowing that sand worms could see you and eat you alive.

Opening a comm channel with the *Vengeance*, Korruk shouted over the Archon's roaring engines. "Captain Merruk! Deploy gunships, Gorgons, cannon walkers and our Ragnarok to the factory and form a defensive perimeter."

Without hesitation, Merruk replied, "Your will be done. Shall I relay the order to the rest of the flotilla?"

"No, only to the *Insurgent*, *Oblivion*, *Havoc* and *Decimator*."

"Yes, my lord," the comm channel was shut off.

Korruk wasn't keen on placing all his assets out in the open. Regardless of what he did, however, they would be in the open. This whole planet irritated him.

The factory itself wasn't any better. It was old. Old enough to have dust and cobwebs. To its credit, everything was still functional, and the bots that ran it were working well enough. Upon reaching the control room—the lord admiral's soon-to-be command center—he found himself growing to hate the factory just as much as Klydoon itself.

What defensive weapons the factory had were decades out of date. They'd be lucky to take out the shields of an enemy ship, let alone destroy one. It was sturdy enough to have lasted this long, but Korruk feared how well it would hold up if they were attacked.

A nearby zauhlon interrupted his thoughts, telling him the Rahalah had arrived at the factory and was being carried to the lower levels. Korruk nodded and waved him away. While his men set up the command center, he would help escort the Rahalah.

Walking through the corridors, more and more zauhlons began filling the building. By the time he reached the Rahalah and its escort party, it looked like they'd always been there, working away to keep the facility functioning—or perhaps trying to get it functioning better than it has been. Korruk wished them luck with that. This place wasn't worth the effort, in his opinion.

The ten-foot-tall bomb was being moved via hover cart and nearly took up the entire corridor. Zauhlons were on either side of it, along with the front and back as well. Korruk led the way to the cargo lift, where it was then brought to a chamber not so different from the one in Serpent's Hole. Of course, it wasn't nearly as well kept, but the layout of the room was the same, minus the corridor that overlooked the room. Ten bots were waiting for them. As soon as they saw the Rahalah, they assisted the zauhlons with removing it from the cart and into the place they desired.

The power that was contained in the bomb always mesmerized him. Never in his many years of living did Korruk think he would wield a weapon this mighty. It was the stuff of legends. The kind of power the ancient zauhlons dreamed of grasping but never managed to.

With this power, he would make the galaxy tremble. This was only the first step though. This would start off the war in their favor, but it was up to Korruk to make sure it stayed that way. With the Republic scrambling to get back to its feet, the Zauhlon Legion would pillage the grovinian worlds. As advanced as they were, they knew nothing about war. With their tech, Korruk would upgrade his ships with the help of that klex. As much as he hated to admit it, that little gray head was a useful asset.

"By the gods, what is it?" a zauhlon next to him asked. When he realized who he was speaking to, he tried to stop himself, but it was too late.

Everyone but the bots froze, waiting for Korruk's reaction. More specifically, his punishment. Unless they were in the high council or his bridge crew, Korruk didn't take kindly to questions, much less ones from those who hadn't asked permission to do so first.

He turned to face the grunt who spoke. The warrior's eyes were wide, but he said nothing. He knew what he did and awaited his punishment. A respectable decision. There was nothing Korruk hated more than the type of people who cried at his feet begging for forgiveness.

His hand curling into a fist, Korruk contemplated a proper enough punishment. Given the grunt's following actions, he considered one good strike would be enough. Before he could act though, a thought came to him. He remembered his conversation with Gorr. *It's only a matter of time before they attempt a coup.*

This recent transfer to Klydoon would only accelerate that eventual coup. He needed to gain the full trust of his men, Gorr's opinion be damned.

Now facing the grunt, Korruk spoke. "A weapon capable of destroying planets. This is why we've been away from Luram for so long. In order to get revenge on the Republic, we need the weapons to do so."

While the silence that plagued the room still loomed over them, the atmosphere changed. Where before it was filled with a sense of fear, now ... now there was respect. A realization that all these years away from home weren't for nothing.

For the first time in a long time, Korruk felt nothing but respect emanating from his men. And it was glorious. Empowering, even.

Korruk turned his attention to the Rahalah, forgetting the rest of the grunts in the room. Sure enough, they got the message and left their leader alone after a salute. His thoughts were solely on what he just did. If Gorr found out ...

No, Korruk thought, *Gorr be damned. This is for the good of our people. To prevent a rebellion.*

That's what he told himself.

Deep down, he knew exactly why he did it. That rush of respect he felt after going so long without it. An understanding, a newfound trust in their leader. He needed to feel that again. Korruk nodded, his mind made up. When everyone who needed to be in the factory arrived, he would tell them all of the Rahalah.

His comm device chimed to life. It was Overlord Gorr.

He accepted the call and was greeted by his friend. "Korruk, how are things progressing?"

He didn't address me as Lord Admiral.

"There's been some changes to the development, my lord." When Gorr said nothing, he continued. "A hunting party of humans made it into Serpent's Hole. I wounded their pack leader, but Phantom fears they discovered the Rahalah. As such, he's moved production to a planet called Klydoon."

"Hrmm ..." Gorr grunted. Without even seeing the factory, Korruk could tell he didn't like this. "This new world, Klydoon, how is it?"

"Truthfully, it's detestable. It's entirely flat, leaving us out in the open. The factory isn't much better. It's decades old, and it shows. If we were to be attacked, we wouldn't stand a chance. I'm currently deploying tanks and cannons to serve as a better line of defense, but they can only do so much," said Korruk.

"This 'Phantom'... how much do you trust him?" Korruk knew what his overlord was asking. 'Do you think he's setting you up?'

"In the years I've worked with him, he's never tried to stab me in the back," Korruk said, "As for trust ... you know me. I don't trust anyone but you and my bridge crew."

"Very well. Be careful, old friend. This reeks of a trap. Should anyone non-zauhlon approach this factory, kill them on sight."

"Of course, my lord." For the briefest of moments, Korruk considered telling Gorr of what he did. He hated keeping things from his friend. That feeling subsided when he thought on what his reaction would be. Anger, and only anger. He wouldn't understand.

Gorr signed off, leaving Korruk alone with the Rahalah and the bots. As much as Korruk loved his friend, it was for the better that he be left out of this. His bomb would be complete soon enough, and this wouldn't be an issue anymore.

Orrim, former general of the Zauhlon Legion, was on his hundredth sit-up when Niruuk began his guard post. Since their first meeting, they'd talked multiple times to the point where, unless another guard passed by, Niruuk was completely relaxed around Orrim.

"Have you found out where we've jumped to?" Orrim asked in between sit-ups.

"I have. A planet called Klydoon," Niruuk said, shaking his head. "From what the other zauhlons have said, the planet is worthless. A flat wasteland with nothing but a factory, which is where we've set up camp."

This caught Orrim's attention. He stopped his sit-ups and faced Niruuk, "Then why are we here?"

Niruuk shrugged his shoulders, "I don't know. From what I've heard, it looks like we're here to stay."

"If what you told me is true, then this is suicide." Orrim stood up. "We'll be discovered by anybody looking."

"You're right. Why we would plant our hooves here is beyond me," Niruuk said.

"Damn him," Orrim cursed. "Korruk has sentenced us all to death. We need to stop him before it's too late."

"What you suggest is easier said than done. You tried doing this yourself, and look where that got you," Niruuk said.

Orrim slowly nodded, "You're right. On my own, I failed. If I had a team of warriors, though ... rebels willing to murder Korruk for the greater good, there's no doubt in my mind we would succeed."

"You think so?" Niruuk asked.

"I know so. Korruk is powerful, but he's only one man. Once more zauhlons see how foolish it was to bring us to this world, I have no doubt they'll see the light and help us."

Niruuk nodded, but said nothing. He didn't need to. The idea was placed in his mind, and that was all Orrim needed. He went back to his sit-ups. Despite him manipulating this fledgling to help him break out, it truly perplexed him why Korruk brought them all here. As much as he despised him, Orrim always knew Korruk to be strategically smarter than this. Even if he knew what he was doing, this secrecy would be his downfall. Unlike when he was general, he was hoping this wouldn't change. His rebellion hinged on Korruk keeping everything under wraps.

<hr />

[Haunted Reef System, Joro Nebula.]

.

[Local system time: 1310.]

With a light rattle of the ship, we entered the Joro Nebula's most lively system, the Haunted Reef. Connected by asteroids and debris of battles long before, the Haunted Reef was home of one of the largest marketplaces in the Badlands. Whereas Serpent's Hole was where everything was built, it was here where things were sold. The Haunted Reef was also home to a very large, very dangerous chuzunn cult.

We weren't here to deal with them though. The Eighth Fleet was already taking care of that. We were here for Captain Adams' ship, the *Poseidon*. Thankfully, it wasn't that hard to find an Alpha-class dreadnought.

As soon as we were two kilometers away from the ship, our comms lit up. We were being hailed. Arty gave the go ahead, and a second later a voice that oozed confidence began to speak. "*Sparrow,* this is Eden Leader. Command sent us to escort your shuttle to Small Craft Bay One."

"I appreciate it, Eden. We'll have our shuttle out in fifteen minutes," Arty said.

With that, Captain Arty and I made our way to the cargo bay, where the *Sparow's* shuttle was located. Our pilot was already getting its systems warmed up when we arrived, so once we were strapped and secured, we were off. From there, we followed the squadron of Valkyrie star fighters to the small craft bay.

Once we landed, Arty and I exited the shuttle and into the bay. For a brief moment, I looked around at the array of vehicles docked with us. There were dozens more shuttles here, engineers working on each and every one of them. The dull and hardened look of the small craft bay proved once again how unique the *Sparrow* was. *And now Phantom could make hundreds of them.*

Captain Adams stood ten meters in front of us on the catwalk, arms behind her back. I didn't know much about her, but she looked tough as nails. You had to be to do ops in the Badlands. Upon reaching her, we both saluted. She acknowledged and nodded for us to follow her.

"I'm sorry for the lack of proper introductions, but I'd rather get right to planning our course of action," she said. On our way to the bridge, she slowed down a bit, so we were all walking side by side. "When Admiral Drake told me about the op, I almost laughed. It seemed too unreal. Lord Admiral Korruk, a Category Ten bomb? I couldn't believe it."

"What convinced you?" I asked.

"The look in his eyes. He was dead serious," Adams said. When we entered the lift to the bridge, she leaned into me and asked, "I've read the files on your mission so far, but I have to ask: What's Korruk like? In combat I mean."

I took a moment to think back on what happened in Serpent's Hole. "Calculating, brutal, and unforgiving. I wouldn't wish a fight against him on my worst enemy."

The lift doors slid open, and we continued on to the bridge. Less than a minute later, we entered the large command center of the *Poseidon*. This bridge was very different to the *Sparrow*'s. As opposed to the captain's chair looming over the rest of the bridge, it was only a few steps higher. Ten feet in front of the captain's chair was a table with a holo-display of a planet illuminating from it. Captain Adams led us there and zoomed into the planet.

"This right here is Klydoon. Thanks to some drone footage we collected years ago, we're able to make an accurate map of the world. As you can see, it's flat all around, spare for some facilities here and there." She swiped at a screen on the table, which showed a different set of images, "When Admiral Drake told me of the mission, I decided to poke around, see what I could find. I reactivated the drone in this system and tried to get some more up-to-date photos. This is what we got."

The first image was a small flotilla of zauhlon ships heading toward the planet. A tag on the image reported there being twelve ships. The second image showed some dropships heading toward a factory.

Adams continued, "Whether this is all the ships we're dealing with or not, this confirms where they'll be located. Assuming that's all they have, my flotilla should have no problem taking them out. The problems start on the ground. I have no photos to back this up, but a look through codex entries points out that zauhlons are superior in ground combat. Take into account the lack of cover this world provides, and I think it's warranted to believe Korruk will set up a perimeter around the factory.

"This doesn't bode well for us. Of the fifty ships in my flotilla, ten are carriers, ten are frigates, another ten are corvettes, ten are destroyers, nine are cruisers, and finally one dreadnought. All this is to say we specialize in air and space combat, not ground combat. I have faith we'll cut through their defenses in space, but when the battle moves to the ground, they could wipe the floor with my fighters and gunships."

"Why don't you launch an orbital bombardment? That would take out whatever defenses they have," I said, though as soon as the words left my mouth, I knew what the answer would be.

"I can't risk it. If we set off that bomb somehow, it'll take out all my people. Whatever we do, it has to be the hard way,"

Adams said. "Between all my ships, I have two brigades of marines. I'm willing to send the 10th Brigade down to the factory, but I'm holding back the 15th in case things go haywire. I don't want to lose all my jarheads while they're touching down.

"From there, they'll deal with the perimeter and allow the 15th to land. This should be a good distraction for you. The factory looks like the common make and model from two decades ago, which means there will be a hangar pad on the south side of the building. It's up to you, but the way I see it, there's three ways you can do this. One, the *Sparrow* brings you in hot. Two, we send you off in a Loki dropship. Or three, we send you off in a HALO jump."

Resting my chin against my index finger and thumb, I though over my options. A Loki would be my first choice, but those ships didn't come with any shields, instead prioritizing anti-radar tech. The area would be hot with action though. Even if we couldn't be detected by radar, there's always the chance of being seen by the naked eye. And if that happened …

That left the HALO jump and the *Sparrow* jump. Between the two, I'd rather have the Bird drop us off—I wasn't big on heights. Looking to Arty, I waited for his input. This was his ship we'd be using, after all.

After thinking it over thoroughly, Arty said, "We can fly overhead for a HALO jump. I don't like the idea of having the *Sparrow* that close to the enemy. Sorry, captain."

I nodded. "I understand."

Adams tapped on the factory, which brought up a layout of the building. "The control room should be your prime objective. If Korruk is as smart as they say he is, that'll be his command center. Even if it's not, you'll be able to spot him using the security cameras."

"What about the bomb?" I asked.

"That's what I was about to say. You won't be alone. Another Star Bourn team, Tiger Squad, will deal with the Pale Horse while you handle Korruk. If we get this done simultaneously, that'll raise our odds of success by a lot," she said.

The Pale Horse? It was a fitting codename, but it always amazed me how Command came up with this crap. I nodded, "That works for me."

"Alright then, dismissed," Adams said. Just as we turned to leave, she added, "Oh, and Captain Severre. While you're with the *Poseidon*, you and your team are allowed to train however you see fit."

"Thank you, ma'am."

With that, Arty and I left the bridge and headed back to the *Sparrow*. As our footsteps echoed through the dull and basic passageways, Arty chuckled to himself. "You know, I never thought it would come to this."

He didn't have to elaborate. I knew what he meant. A head-on battle against the zauhlons, trying to acquire a bomb that could destroy a planet ... it sounded unreal. It made me wonder how often such things occurred during the First Contact War, and how often Miller and my father went on ops like this. Regardless, this would be the first full-scale battle for a lot of people here, myself included. Sure, I'd undergone some raids, and I had no doubt the men and women here had roughed it up with pirate flotillas, but nothing like this. If this went sideways, the Zauhlon Legion could declare war on us, and that would start our second war with those brutes. I wouldn't let it come to that.

"Me neither. I just hope we can get it done without losing too many lives," I replied.

15

[Zauhlon Legion Command Center, Klydoon. Four days from the assault.]

[Local system time: 1800.]

Surveillance cameras showed Klydoon's yellow sun setting, creating a red hue around the star. That, paired with the now pink strips of clouds created a view many would love to see. In Korruk's eyes, however, it only brought the planet's flatness to his attention, which served to irritate him further.

Tanks, cannons, gunships and the lone Ragnarok surrounded the factory, acting as its guardians. His zauhlons studied the building thoroughly, familiarizing themselves with each nook and cranny in case a fight broke out. Meanwhile in the control room, Korruk's command center, his more tech-savvy zauhlons were working on getting the factory-wide comm channel operational. Seems as though those bots didn't do as good a job at maintenance as he originally thought.

While factory-wide comms were close to being functional, space-to-planet comms were nowhere near as close. The engineers would get to work on those the next day.

Korruk clenched the edges of a console while he watched the men work. As soon as they were done, he would tell everyone here about the Rahalah, and he would bask in their awe and reverence of him. They would respect him, just like those men before.

One of the engineers came to him and informed him that the comms were online. Korruk brushed him off and walked toward the device. There was no turning back from this. He could get away with those few grunts, but this? This was on a whole other scale. Korruk took one deep breath, then turned on the comms.

"This is Lord Admiral Korruk. I'm sure many of you have questions as to why we're here right now. Or even what the point of all this is. We've been away from Luram for a long time. Too long. I know this, along with the lack of combat, has been frustrating. Believe me, I know. After all this time, I think it's time you know why.

"For the past two decades, Overlord Gorr and I have been building a weapon. One that would start our war with the

Republic not with a mere gunshot, but with a thunderous bang. This bomb has power that the old gods only dreamed of. With this weapon, we will be able to crush entire planets.

"If we're to win this war, we *need* this bomb. Our Rahalah. We've all waited so long for this. Have faith and wait just a little longer. Together, we will watch our enemies burn."

There it was again.

The respect that he thrived for.

After his speech, Korruk felt it all around him. From the zauhlons in the command center with him, and from those outside of it. Some were quiet about their recognition of his will, but he knew it was there. All of them revered him. As they should. He was their lord admiral after all.

Others were more vocal about their respect for him. Shouts of praise reached Korruk's ears, even through the doors of the command center. Cheers such as "Hail!" or "Glory to the Legion!"

Korruk grinned. It had been so long since he felt this respected and appreciated. Oh, how gratifying it was.

———◄◊►———

[Prototype Sim-Room, *Poseidon*. Three days from the assault.]

[Local system time: 0500.]

I found myself in front of the hatch leading to the Sim-Room, waiting for it to unlock. The night wasn't kind to me. Dreams—nightmares, really—of our impending mission kept me from sleeping well. After I woke up the fourth time, I decided to do a little studying. Grabbing my helmet from the armory, I walked on to the Sim-Room, guarded by a single security bot.

Bots in human ships were a rarity, but since these Sim-Rooms were designed by the klex, it was only fitting it was guarded by one of their creations too. I could only hope it didn't become common. Every now and then they were nice, but nothing could replace an organic being. The hatch unlocked, and I walked in. There was a small corridor leading to another hatch. To the left of the bulkhead door was a panel. Removing the memory card from my helmet, I inserted it into the slot under the screen. A minute later, that hatch unlocked.

Upon walking in, I was back in the warehouse where I fought Korruk. The recreation was accurate to the point I had to catch my breath. Knowing this was a battle zone and I was "in" it, I felt naked without my armor. Everything was paused to begin with, allowing me to look around freely without worry of enemy fire. Not that I had to worry about that to begin with; none of this was real, so none of the bullets could hurt me.

I strode over to where Korruk and I fought, and sure enough, the Sim-Room had recreated that as well. Good. This was what I was here for. Frozen in place, Korruk was there with his high guard. I, on the other hand, was in the middle of unsheathing my machete.

Seemingly to no one, I said, "Play." Instantly the action played out before me.

I watched as I made that first and dreadful mistake of charging. Thinking of it made me cringe, but watching it play out was worse. Continuing to watch my downfall, I witnessed Korruk dodge and kick me in the ribs. I told the Sim to pause, and it did. With the way I charged the alien with my machete to my right side, I opened myself up to that kick. I deserved it. As I looked at my recorded double floating in midair, about to hit the floor and undergo the beating of his life, I felt shame. Years of being a Star Bourn, and this was where it got me? Making amateur mistakes like some street thug?

Walking around the scene, my eyes were still on my phantom. I was lucky I made it out of this alive. Considering everyone Korruk has killed, it was a blasted miracle I got by as easy as I did. Just as I was about to continue playing the Sim, something caught my eye. Something I hadn't noticed in my fight with Korruk. How could I? I was on my back gasping for air at the time.

There was a wound on Korruk's hoof.

It was a scar that had long since healed, but it was there.

Curious ...

"Play."

I wasn't paying attention to myself now. No, I was looking to see Korruk's reaction. Sure enough, he stumbled. Now it could have been nothing. Just him regaining his footing. But my gut was telling me it had something to do with the wound. Kicking someone with an injured foot, healed or not, would hurt at least a little bit. My mind was racing with possible strategies for our upcoming fight. A fight that would end differently than the one before me. That much I was sure of.

Watching to the very end, I took notice of my mistakes, Korruk's tactics, and where I could improve. I noted Korruk's flurry of strikes that overwhelmed me and possible ways to overcome them. When Releck entered the scene, I paid close attention to where he stabbed Korruk. And when the fight was over, I replayed the Sim. One could make an argument at how sick this was, watching the life being beat out of me over and over again, and I would agree with them. It was something that needed to be done though. If I wanted to defeat—no, not just defeat, *kill*—Korruk, I needed to learn as much as I could from this footage.

By the time I knew it, it was 0630. The Wolves would be up in thirty minutes. Trying to go back to sleep was pointless, so instead I went to retrieve my data-pad and wrote all this down. When that was settled, I took a shower and got to the *Poseidon*'s gym to get an early start on the others. Studying Korruk was well and dandy, but if I wasn't physically ready, that would mean nothing.

Pushing my body to the limit, my mind went to the old Wolves and Miller. If I failed, all their deaths would go unavenged, and I wasn't going to let that happen. With them in mind, I pushed past my limits. By the time this assault happened, I would be ready.

<hr />

[Cell Twenty, the *Vengeance*.]

[Local system time: 1013.]

Lifting himself off the ground using a ledge in his cell, Orrim began his set of pull-ups. With nothing else to do, Orrim spent most of his days exercising. Thanks to this, his body was recovering nicely. Breathing through his nostrils was still somewhat difficult, but it had gotten easier over the past few days.

While he strengthened his upper arms, Orrim began thinking. Not about what would happen if he lost. That much was obvious; if he failed, he died. No, instead he thought about something he truthfully hasn't given much thought. What if he won? What if he actually killed Korruk?

All this time, his focus had been on getting revenge on Korruk. Yes, becoming lord admiral was the natural progression, but what would he do with all that power? Immediately he thought of the poor state his people were in. There were more zauhlons now then there had been since they waged war with the apes, yet they only had less than two dozen worlds spread across three star systems. With over-population beginning to become a problem, they needed now more than ever to expand and colonize. While waging war was in their blood, turning on themselves now would be foolish. They should conquer the stars first, then they could truly once again be fighting wars.

Orrim smiled. That would be his first act as lord admiral: grow the Zauhlon Legion, and make it as vast in numbers as their enemies.

The guard in front of his cell walked away, and Niruuk replaced him. Their last talk involved planting the seeds of rebellion in the young warrior's mind. While Orrim was going to play the slow game, make sure Niruuk was truly loyal and "believed in the cause," what he said to Orrim next quite honestly surprised him.

"I have good news, Orrim. I've spoken to some other warriors, and all of them agree that there needs to be a change. I told them that your will is as strong as ever and that you want a second chance at taking Korruk's place. All fifty of them agreed to be at your side when you're ready."

Orrim allowed himself to show surprise for a moment. Fifty men was impressive, especially in such a short amount of time. He let go of the ledge and gave Niruuk his full attention. "Impressive, Niruuk. Very impressive. You must be careful, though. Speak to the wrong person, and our plans will be ruined. On top of that, fifty warriors, as good as they might be, isn't enough. Not when so many are undoubtedly on Korruk's side."

The former general began slowly pacing back and forth, thinking of what their next move should be. True to what he told Niruuk previously, he only expected a team of people. If he could amass a true, respectable rebellion, this could go better than Orrim ever imagined. It was then that a glorious idea popped in his mind.

"Niruuk, can you get me transferred to the *Onslaught*?" Orrim asked.

Confused, Niruuk said, "Why?"

"The captain of the ship, Captain Herruk, and I have worked together on more than one occasion. I know he's just as frustrated as I am with Korruk. If I could talk with him, I know he would join our cause. A corvette full of warriors would set our victory in stone."

Orrim wasn't too convinced at the last comment. A ship on their side *would* increase their odds, but unless they co-ordinated a foolproof plan of attack, absolute victory wasn't guaranteed. It was, however, true that he and Herruk were al-lies, and that the good captain was frustrated with their lack of combat. While they weren't friends per say, Orrim believed the two shared enough respect that Herruk would hear him out. He only hoped Korruk's bringing all of them to this spitball of a world was the last straw.

Niruuk hesitantly nodded. "I'll try, general."

The conversation ended, and Orrim resumed his pull-ups. He had to admit, being called "general" once again filled him with pride. Despite the humiliation and defeat he went through, at least some zauhlons still treated him with respect. Before long, it wouldn't only be some zauhlons. Soon, all the zauhlons will not only respect him, but bow down to him as well.

[Prototype Sim-Room, *Poseidon*. Two days from the assault.]

[Local System time: 1130.]

Captain Owens, Rockie, and Crow were pinned down by ten zauhlons. They were receiving too much fire for them to do anything, and they'd already used all their frags. Owens cursed himself for being so nonchalant with his grenade usage. They could have been pretty blasted useful right about now.

The other three members of Tiger—Hatchet, Bat, and Sixteen—were sneaking around the left side of the chamber, using desks as cover. The plan was to bring attention to Owens' team while Hatchet's team went and dealt with the Pale Horse. That changed when Sixteen's T-16 grenade launcher bumped up against their cover. Five of the zauhlons pinning them down turned their attention to the noise and began firing blindly, making gnarly dents in the desk and wall behind it.

"Blast it, Sixteen!" Bat cursed. "See, Black Lung, this is why I didn't want him on the stealth part of the mission."

"It ain't my fault! Besides, we can take these tangos, no problem," Sixteen said while taking out his gold-painted T-16 a little too eagerly.

"Cut the chatter," said Captain Owens, or as Tiger Squad likes to call him, Black Lung. "Charlie team, your objective is still the same. Get to the bomb and shut it down!" Once the order was handed out, Black Lung popped out of cover and with his shotgun put down a zauhlon that was too close.

Hatchet and the others continued to move towards the bomb, only now they had to keep their heads low to avoid the incoming gunfire. While the zauhlons hounding them were reloading, Sixteen laid his T-16 on an empty desk and fired it at their attackers. It hit one of the aliens directly in the chest, blowing the zauhlon to bloody chunks of meat and armor. The explosion also killed another zauhlon and knocked one other to the ground. On Black Lung's team, Crow shot the downed zauhlon in the back of the neck with his Leviathan, killing him.

Just when things were looking up for them, more zauhlons reinforcements showed their ugly faces. This was the third time the zauhlons sent backup to take care of the commandos, and it showed. Bodies with gold armor were littered across the metal floor, blood painted the very same floor, and ammo was low for the Star Bourn.

Sixteen started getting cocky and poked out of cover, firing his grenade launcher at a steady pace now. While the large man was able to kill at least ten more zauhlons, he paid the price for it. The returning fire from the six living zauhlons was too much for him to handle, and he was brought down before he could get back to cover.

Hatchet swore and raced back towards Sixteen. His medical skills would be pointless; Sixteen was already dead. Black Lung didn't need to say anything to Hatchet. He knew that the mission would have to go on, regardless of the loss of their friend.

A risky bullet spray from Rockie's Revenger assault rifle was enough to take the zauhlons' attention off Charlie team long enough for them to reach the Pale Horse. Hearing the smallest of *clanks*, Bat stopped dead in his tracks.

"Hatchet, wait!" Bat called out.

It was too late. Charlie Team's leader was caught off guard by a squad of three zauhlons waiting behind the bomb. The bogies fired their alien guns at Hatchet all at the same time. He didn't stand a chance.

Bat ducked behind cover. This wasn't looking good for Tiger.

"Bat, keep them focused on you. Rockie, take 'em from behind. Crow and I will give you covering fire," Black Lung said in his ever-raspy voice.

Without question, what was left of Tiger played their parts to a tee. The three zauhlons were so enthralled with trying to slaughter Bat that they didn't see Rockie behind them. This would prove to be their downfall. Using his machete, Rockie chopped off the head of the zauhlon to his right, fired his hand cannon at point blank range at the zauhlon in his center, and gave the zauhlon to his left the same treatment.

Bat took this moment to dash behind the bomb with Rockie. He opened the bomb up and tried to disable it. It was no use though. For one, the Pale Horse used a combination of different alien technologies, tech he wasn't familiar with. Lastly, and most importantly, a shrap grenade was tossed overhead and landed next to the two Star Bourn. Before they could throw it back, it exploded, killing both of them instantly.

And then there were two.

Swearing to himself, Black Lung and Crow sprinted to the bomb. Neither of them knew a thing about how bombs worked, so that was out the window. He considered making a last stand, but Tiger's leader couldn't die without at least trying to stop the Pale Horse. Looking into the exposed insides of the bomb, Black Lung unloaded his Punishers into the alien explosive, hoping that would do something. As his drill instructor once said, *When in doubt, shoot.*

While sparks and smoke exited the bomb, it appeared to do nothing. The control panel was still alive and working. Before Black Lung could think of another course of action, he and

Crow were ambushed from both sides. They took out three zauhlons before both men died.

The mission was a failure.

Five seconds later, a feminine robotic voice echoed throughout the deck. "All personnel have been defeated. Simulation will end shortly."

As soon as the sentence was finished, the "zauhlons" shut down. All six commandos of Tiger Squad stood up.

"God, I hate this," Sixteen groaned.

"You're telling me," Crow said, "I'm gonna need to pop some pain soothers after this."

Black Lung nodded. "Let's meet back here in an hour then."

All of them voiced their displeasure, but they nonetheless nodded. They knew they had only two days to get familiar with this factory and these enemies, and that until they successfully completed their op, they would have to do it over and over again. That didn't mean they liked it though. If Black Lung was being honest, he didn't like it either. He knew his boys were the best Star Bourn in town, and that when the time came, they'd get the job done. Still, training never hurt anyone.

Just as they made it to the hatch, in came Captain Adams. They all saluted the beautiful officer in front of them. Civilians would say the scar across her eye was a turn off, but to a Star

Bourn—or any hot-blooded servicemen really—it only added to a woman's charm.

"At ease," she said. "I've received word from the Admiralty. Your mission has been updated, Tiger. Your priority is the same: Disable the Pale Horse and bring it to the designated LZ for pickup. If that's impossible, however, then your new objective is to activate the bomb. A weapon like this can't fall into enemy hands, no matter the cost." She understood exactly what she was telling them, so she reiterated. "If it comes to this, I don't need to tell you that it'll be a suicide mission. Are you all ready for this?"

Black Lung recognized what she was saying. She wanted to know if they were going to back out. He didn't like the idea of dying on some good-for-nothing planet like Klydoon, but if it meant keeping humanity safe, he'd do it. Better to die for something you believed in than to wither away in a nursing home. Besides, they already agreed to the mission, and Tiger never backed out of something they agreed to do.

"Yes, ma'am. We need some more training from the bomb techs, but we're holding up fine," Black Lung said.

Adams nodded. "I'll get them over here in an hour and a half." She snapped a salute to the veteran killers and left the Sim-Room.

That wasn't all they needed, but he wasn't about to throw his men under the bus. Black Lung had no problem admitting that setting the enemies to the highest difficulty probably wasn't needed, as "normal" represented how strong their armor and shields would be in actual combat, but he wanted to make sure his team was ready for anything. Just because this *could* become a suicide mission, doesn't mean he wanted it to end up being that.

The captain of the commandos looked back to his team, his bionic left eye twitching ever so slightly. "Alright, when we start the next sim, all of us are going to carry heavy weapons. Sixteen, you're on 'nade launcher duty. Rockie, you've got the rocket launcher. Crow, you've got the laser ..."

[Zauhlon Legion Command Center, Klydoon. Two days from the assault.]

[Local system time: 1400.]

As Lord Admiral Korruk entered his command center, everyone saluted him with a fist to their chests and a shout of "Hail!"

The salutes were common, of course. Anyone who didn't salute the Lord Admiral faced the consequences. The hails were new though. A nice addition that was added after he revealed the Rahalah to everyone planet-side. This renewed vigor only served to justify Korruk's actions in his mind. For the first time since the end of the war with the humans, his men truly respected him.

It wasn't enough, though.

Even if he had the respect of the hundreds of zauhlons around him, there were thousands up in space that still thought he was weak. Korruk wouldn't be satisfied until every zauhlon in his flotilla knew of the self-control he had to sit out here and deny his deepest desires to wage war. All for the good of his people, and to ensure absolute victory. They needed to know the strength of his will, and they would in due time.

Korruk stood over one of the working engineers. "Is the comm channel to space operational yet?"

"We've connected to five ships, but we still have seven to go, Lord Admiral. These systems aren't like anything we've seen before."

"I don't want excuses. Work faster." Truth be told, Korruk was mildly impressed they were able to achieve this much. Zauhlons weren't known for being technological experts, especially with foreign tech. Regardless, he wanted results, and good ones at that.

The thought crossed his mind to travel back to the *Vengeance* and make his announcement there, but these were tense times. As much as he desired to tell his men of his strength, he couldn't leave until he knew with absolute certainty that this factory was secured. Every part of this building needed to be studied. The defenses, the integrity, all of it. He couldn't trust anyone but himself to oversee this.

Breaking the silence was a comm call from Gorr. He never called unless it was important, so Korruk moved to a quiet corner and opened the channel right away.

"Korruk, has anything changed on Klydoon?" Gorr asked.

He couldn't help but notice Gorr once again neglected to call him Lord Admiral.

He doesn't respect me.

"No. A perimeter has been established, but no one has attacked us."

"Good. I'm putting together a flotilla to join you until the Rahalah is complete. They should be departing by the end of the day," Gorr said.

Gorr couldn't see his face, but Korruk's face contorted for a moment. After all they've been through together—the Valley of Horrors, the Trials of Sorrvuk—Gorr didn't even trust him enough to protect their bomb on his own. Throughout the years of fighting for his life, Korruk learned to harden his heart to feeble things like emotions. Deep inside though, that prospect hurt.

No matter how many grunts respected him, his friend didn't. And no words could fix that.

There was only one thing he could do to earn that.

"That won't be necessary. My men will be able to guard it on their own."

Gorr paused for a moment.

"Korruk, now is not the time to be prideful ..." Gorr started to say.

"Enough! My warriors and my ships are among the best in the Legion. We can handle this by ourselves. Keep your flotilla, Gorr. I'll bring the Rahalah to your hooves, and we will begin our campaign against the Republic as *equals*."

Before Overlord Gorr could respond, he cut the transmission and sighed. Walking back to the center of the control room, Korruk looked at one of the many screens. This particular one showcased the Rahalah being worked on by the old bots.

All this hardship over one weapon. A very powerful one, but a weapon nonetheless. As beautiful as it was, Korruk couldn't help but feel it wasn't worth all the disrespect and pity he faced over the years. An armada of ships and strong warriors would have been just as effective, if not more so. After all, how could you use a planet as a hunting ground if there wasn't a planet at all?

Regardless of his opinions on the matter, he agreed to go through with this plan and he would see it through. No matter what approach they took, the zauhlons would stand tall, and they would all recognize how vital he was to making that dream a reality. By the end of all this, Korruk would be a galactic-wide conqueror, and all would see how worthy he was of the title Lord Admiral.

16

.

Just beyond the door was the control room. For the past twenty minutes I led the Wolf Pack through the factory after successfully landing the HALO jump. I have to hand it to the klex, or whoever added that feature. It really felt like we were jumping from high altitude. While Boomer set up the lock buster, Tenner, Releck and I covered our right and left flanks. Grampa and Bullseye had their sights set on the door, ready for whatever was waiting for us.

"Ready," Boomer called out through the Back Door.

The three of us turned on our heels and piled up on either side of the door. "Go," I said.

Boomer flipped the switch, and sparks flew from the door. A second later, it opened and we tossed frags into the room.

Once the explosions sounded off, we poured into the room, killing targets as soon as we saw them. Korruk, however, was still standing. He said something my audio receptors didn't pick up, and more zauhlons rushed in from the north, west and east hatches.

We moved to find cover, but Boomer went down. If we didn't duck down behind some supercomputers when we did, we would have all been taken out too. The incoming storm of bullets reminded me of the gunship turrets back on Tsello. When the gunfire let up, we popped up to give a little firepower of our own. By the time we got back into cover, we had taken out five zauhlons. It barely made a dent in their numbers.

While I reloaded my gun, a shrap grenade landed at my feet. Thinking fast, I tossed it back, happy that the explosion that followed eliminated a few more red dots from my map.

Taking out his Quaker rocket launcher, Grampa tried to line up a shot into horde of zauhlons. As soon as he popped his head around the computer, he was taken out. I'm ashamed to admit this was getting me flustered. Even if it was just a sim, having my teammates get shot down like this was bringing back bad memories.

Releck quickly picked up the rocket launcher and fired it blindly. The loud *boom* that followed killed six more zauhlons. Thanks to the string of explosions, the zauhlons were dazed enough for us to put down another four. During the firefight, I'd lost sight of Korruk. If it wouldn't have been suicidal, I'd run out there and deal with him myself.

Much to our surprise, a squad of six zauhlons entered through the entrance we came from and caught us in the middle of reloading our guns. They mowed into us, "killing" Bullseye and Releck. Before Tenner went down, he managed to roll a frag right to their feet, killing them all. I was sent slamming into the already smoking supercomputer.

Looking around at my fallen comrades, I thought, *screw it*. I took all the grenades I had, set them to blow, and tossed them in the direction of the control panels in the center. Overall, that meant two frags, two destabilizers, and one smoke grenade. Two seconds later, the entire circle of panels, terminals and screens went up in a blaze of glory, sending strings of tiny explosions rippling around the room. With the enemies blinded and a sheet of smoke as my cover, I grabbed the rocket launcher, and like Releck fired blindly. The walls were painted red and fire began to engulf the room. When the Quaker ran out of ammo, I switched to my Punisher and killed as many zauhlons as I could before I was shot down.

"All personnel have been defeated. Simulation will end shortly."

The factory fizzled away and was replaced with blindingly white walls. The paralysis chips on our armors shut off, and we all got up, sore and beaten. I won't lie, this frustrated me. It seems like no matter what route we take, we always got overrun and killed. "We gotta go back to the drawing board. This isn't working."

"Really? I thought we were doing great," Grampa's voice dripped with sarcasm.

I took off my helmet and wiped away the sweat. "Anybody got any ideas?"

Releck looked confused at my question. I was going to ask what the problem was, but I figured maybe it was a cultural difference. It wouldn't surprise me if anthrum didn't ask for advice. That seemed to fit with their confident and no nonsense way of combat. Unlike them though, I was all for suggestions. Regardless, he spoke up, "I have one, sir."

We all stared at him, awaiting his answer. Just in case, I said, "Uh, go ahead, Releck."

He nodded. "I don't need to tell anyone here that zauhlons have a warrior culture. They live and die by it. They don't know how to function any other way. It's common for lower-rank soldiers or outside parties to challenge a high-ranking officer to a duel for a chance to take that rank as their own. Under the Universal Laws of Sorrvuk, when this happens, all non-participating zauhlons must cease combat and serve as witnesses to the duel."

"So, if we challenge Korruk to a duel, that means we wouldn't get shot to hell?" I asked.

"That should be the case, yes. Anyone who disobeys this law is looked down upon, and seeing as how respect and social status means everything to them, no one would dare to do that," Releck said.

"How'd you learn all this?" Grampa asked.

"School," Releck said, smiling when he heard the old man grumble at the response.

I smiled with him. "Alright, that's a start. Our last practice run had the best route to get there, I felt, so we'll stick with that. Overall, here's the plan so far—HALO jump onto the hangar pad, stick to the south passageway where enemy contact will be minimal, bust into the control room, and I'll challenge Korruk."

The Wolves exchanged looks as if to confirm the plan amongst themselves.

"That won't be a problem, will it?" I asked when no one spoke up.

Grampa shrugged. "You wanna get into a fist fight with a zauhlon, that's on you. Just make sure you watch out for the smaller arms. They pack more of a punch than you'd think."

Releck nodded. "From what I've been told about the origin of this mission, this is near and dear to you. He took people close to you, so it's only right you're the one to challenge him."

Tenner started playing with his mustache. I've known him long enough to be aware he only did that when something was bothering him. "If you have something to say, Tenner, speak freely. You know I'm not the kind of captain to chew you out for having reservations."

He finally relented. "I'm just worried this being so important to you is the problem. You and I have seen what happens when a mission gets personal; people mess up. Hell, it happened at Serpent's Hole," he sighed. "Sorry, sorry. That was a low blow."

I shook my head, "No, you're right. My emotions got the better of me, and I almost paid for it with my life. I got too eager, and I acted without thinking. That won't happen again. I know you've all noticed I've been spending a lot of time in here. I've been tightening up my form and disciplining myself. Next time I face Korruk, things *will* go differently.

"Listen, I know a lot of you don't know me well, and that's partially my fault, I'll admit, but I need you to trust me on this. This is something I need to do."

Tenner shook his head, laughing to himself. "Jim, you know I've got your back no matter what. If this is how you want things to go down, I'm with you."

Bullseye nodded. "I prefer to work alone, but of all the team leaders I've worked with, you've been the best. At least, the most reasonable. Give the word, and I'll watch your back."

"I think I can speak for everyone when I say we're with you," Boomer said, to which they all nodded in agreement.

As cheesy as it sounded, hearing that made me feel more at ease. While the teams I've served with have mostly gotten along, I've seen what it's like when everyone on a squad hates each other. So, to know these guys had my back on this was like a weight taken off my shoulders. There's no better feeling as a team leader than when your squad works like a well-oiled machine. And while we're not quite there yet—that's something you only get when you've worked together for years—the spirit and drive was already there.

I allowed myself a small smile. "Alright then. Let's get some chow, then get back to training."

"Ooh, you think they still serve the green mush? That's my favorite kind," Boomer said.

We all chuckled at the comment. I'd like to think she was joking, but I've seen her go through that junk in less than five minutes. How she did it, I have no idea.

"Do you even know what's in that stuff?" Tenner asked.

"No idea, and I'd like to keep it that way. I'm afraid it'll ruin it for me if I find out," she said.

Grampa snickered. "Challenge accepted."

We all laughed and left the Sim-Room. As the Wolves kept up their banter, I thought back to how things were just two weeks ago. *Has it really only been two weeks? It feels like months.*

Back then, I was ready to give up being a TL altogether. I didn't think anyone could replace my old Wolves. And while I wouldn't say these guys have replaced them—no one ever could—they're still a good team. One I'm proud to be leading.

[Cell Twenty, the *Vengeance*.]

[Local system time: 1900]

Orrim hadn't seen his newfound ally since his last guard post, which made the imprisoned zauhlon nervous. Perhaps he had asked for too much and got Niruuk executed? Without him, he had no way of communicating to his rebellion without drawing suspicion. As much as he hated to admit it, he relied on Niruuk greatly these past few days.

Four zauhlons made their way to Orrim's cell and opened it. As they shoved him out and escorted him somewhere, he repeated in his mind, *This is it. They've found me out and I'm going to be executed.* It didn't take long for him to realize they weren't marching him off to the execution chambers. No, they were taking him to the hangar bay. He smiled inwardly. Niruuk had once again proved himself.

Being paraded around without his armor still brought shame to Orrim, but he didn't let it bother him considering where he was going, and what he would hopefully achieve. He would gladly face some shame if it meant getting revenge and achieving glory.

Throughout the entire ride to the *Onslaught*, no one spoke a word. Orrim because he had no reason to speak to these grunts, and the escort party because they didn't want to talk to the shunned former general. To them, he was another failure in a long string of failures. Yet another man who Korruk defeated. Orrim wondered whether, after seeing his upcoming coup, these men would join him, or if they would meet in the battlefield, only to be killed by the former general himself. It was a thought he didn't have much time to ponder on, as the shuttle landed, and not long after, the door at the back of the vehicle opened.

Waiting for him was a new escort of zauhlons and Captain Herruk himself. Orrim could see a mixture of emotions in Herruk's eyes, first of which was respect. What followed was sadness. The two men greeted each other silently before Orrim was taken to the brig. On his way there, he began to think how he could get that conversation with Herruk. Perhaps, with Niruuk's help, he could break out and visit Herruk in his personal quarters? Or perhaps he could get his rebels on the *Onslaught,* and they could storm the bridge? On a corvette, it wasn't impossible for fifty men to force their way onto the bridge. Ultimately, Orrim didn't think he would have to do either of those things. No, Herruk would come to him.

Captain Herruk, Orrim had discovered through working with him, was a curious man. If he had questions, he would get answers, no matter what. He would no doubt want to hear the full story from Orrim himself, which meant they would be in touch. He just had to be patient and wait.

<hr>

Orrim was woken up by loud bangs. They weren't the bangs of gunfire though. These sounded like someone banging on steel. He rose from his metal bed and saw a guard and Captain Herruk standing before him. Herruk gestured for the guard to leave them, which he did. It appeared Orrim didn't have to wait long at all.

"Orrim," Herruk said, "it's been a long time."

"So it has. How has time treated you?" Orrim asked.

"Not well. Sitting around waiting for orders has never been my cup of gwarg," This was good. Not only did Herruk still treat him like an equal, this was also more confirmation of his displeasure. "I would ask the same, but I see I already have the answer." He shook his head and asked, "How did this happen, Orrim? No more than a week ago you were the Legion's most respected general."

"I got tired of it. Tired of it all. The waiting, the radio silence. I don't need to tell you, but our men have been dying for a real fight. It didn't take me long to figure out that with Korruk as our leader, nothing would change. So, I took matters in my own hands," Orrim said.

"And you failed ..." Herruk said. "Still, you're not wrong. I can see it in the eyes of my crew. They long for the days of old when we could pillage and battle to our hearts desire. This planet we're orbiting ... Klydoon. It hasn't done much to reassure the men."

Orrim grunted. "I heard about that. A flat planet and a factory with pathetic defenses? Is Korruk out of his mind? It doesn't matter how well he fortifies it, should someone decide to raid us, there's not much we could do."

"I agree. If we had to hunker down on a planet, this wouldn't have been my first choice," Herruk said. "If someone does try to raid us, they'll die trying."

Orrim chuckled. "I see your heart is as strong as ever. It's no wonder your crew looks up to you. I'm afraid that won't be enough though. We only have twelve ships in our flotilla. Even the smallest of pirate fleets usually have twenty ships. If a competent pirate gang decided to pick a fight, we would be outnumbered."

Herruk nodded. "I fear you may be right. Even if their ships are rusted and out of date, it would be an uphill battle. There's also the matter of a worse threat emerging."

"Do you suspect something?" Orrim asked.

"It's nothing concrete, but do you remember the ordeal with those apes back on Serpent's Hole? Tell me, Orrim, when have you known the apes to accept defeat and run away? If they're truly adamant about killing Lord Admiral Korruk, as I believe they are, they'll be back," said Herruk.

The train of thought made enough sense to Orrim, but it also made him admittedly nervous. He was right about the humans' tenacity. In fact, he wouldn't put it past them to try again with even more soldiers. While that may prove to be a good distraction, a three-way battle wasn't something Orrim desired. A one-on-one battle was their best bet. If he wanted his rebellion to succeed, he needed to do this as quickly as possible.

Taking a deep breath, Orrim said, "Herruk. You've been on this expedition as long as I have. All we've been doing is sitting around in space waiting for Sorrvuk-knows-what. You know the zauhlons under Korruk's leadership can't thrive. As long as he remains in power, we will never see glory, or battle, or conquest. It needs to change."

When Herruk didn't immediately shut him down, he continued. "I can be that change. Under my leadership, the Zauhlon Legion will expand. We'll conquer the stars and become a true empire. We'll advance technology and replace these hunks of scrap we've been using for centuries. But I can't do all this without you. If we can invade the factory and overwhelm Korruk and his zauhlons, we can kill them and start this new era together. What do you say?"

Herruk was silent for what felt like an eternity. Finally, with fire in his eyes, he spoke up. "If you think you can do this, I'll stand by you. What's your plan?"

Orrim let out a breath he didn't know he was holding. "We'll use the railgun to make an entrance into the factory. From there, we'll send in our zauhlons and kill them all. Once your fighters and bombers are out, fall back. If the old gods bless us, hopefully our coup will inspire other ships who feel as frustrated as we do."

"Very well, I'll get everyone ready. When will we launch this attack?"

"Tomorrow. The longer we wait, the more likely we are to fail."

<hr/>

[Captain's office, *Poseidon*.]

[Local system time: 2350.]

Captain Kaitlyn Adams sat at her desk, going over all the intel and battle plans for tomorrow. Not only was this the first major battle for her and nearly all her crews, this would be the first time humanity had gone head to head against the zauhlons since the First Contact War. Add in the threat of the Pale Horse, and there was a lot riding on her shoulders. She had to make sure everything was perfect. An impossible task, but one she took on nonetheless.

Klydoon was nothing noteworthy. A flat ice world that gangs and pirates used for their hangouts. There hadn't been any activity in years until now. There was no wildlife, so they didn't have to worry about any surprises in that department. Parts of the planet went through blizzards once a month, but so long as all their tech held up, that wouldn't be an issue.

Landing her troops would be the biggest problem, but she was prepared for that. The *Poseidon*'s sister ships would clear a lane for her to send out the 10th. Once that was done, she would join her division in the assault while the *Manta* held back, ready to deploy the 15th. The main concern she had was the 10th being shot to pieces by the enemy fighters while they were trying to land. Even with an escort party, losses were almost a guarantee. It was to be expected, but the more of her people she could stop from dying, the better.

Kait rested her face in her palm. She was tired, and thinking about people from her flotilla dying stressed her out to the point of exhaustion. Between her fingers, she looked at a portrait of her late mother. A smile formed on her face, and she moved to take a closer look.

She always thought her mother was the most beautiful woman in the world. Strong and brave, but also kind and compassionate. Kait looked up to her like no one else. So much so that she followed in her mom's footsteps and became a sailor. That came with its own sets of troubles though. Being the daughter of Admiral Alice Adams meant Kait had a lot to live up to. Despite that, she loved being a sailor, especially a ship's captain, because no matter how stressful situations like these were, it was there where she felt closest to her mom.

Flipping the frame over, she read the words her mother wrote. "Stay calm, be confident, and be smart. I love you always." That was the advice she gave her when Kait graduated from boot camp. They were words she lived by and built the foundation of her leadership on. She would need to continue living by those words tomorrow. That would be when her crew needed her to be all those things the most.

She placed a kiss on the picture and got up to leave for her cabin. Kait had done everything she could do to prepare. Now she needed to get a good night's sleep. While on her way to her quarters, she built up her confidence. On her side were the best sailors, officers, marines and pilots Star Command could ask for, and fifty starships that were the best of the best. She'd like to see Korruk try and beat them. Ground advantage or not, once his starships were taken care of, they could play the long game.

May the best leader win.

PART III

17

[Haunted Reef System, Joro Nebula. Day of the assault.]

[Local system time: 0800.]

That morning was a quiet one. Not just for Captain Adams' flotilla, but for the Haunted Reef itself. There were no other starships in space except for those in the Eighth Fleet. It was as if everyone knew this day would be a monumental day. One that would be etched into history, regardless of the victor. Kait opened a comm link with Tiger Squad and Captain Duncan McCabe. "Is everyone in position?"

"Ready to go. Just give the word," Black Lung said.

"Yes, ma'am," Arty replied. Unlike Black Lung's relaxed tone, Arty was tense, rigid.

Tiger and the Wolf Pack would be vital parts of the fight on the ground. Kait only hoped they got there in one piece. Shifting focus to the helmsmen, she said, "You're clear to go."

As the *Poseidon* led the way to the Slip-Space Highway, the bridge officers began relaying orders to the rest of the flotilla, giving them the green light. Judging by their low numbers, it was a safe bet to assume the Highway would be unguarded. An unwise decision, but given how few ships Korruk was working with, an understandable one. This would give her ships time to get into position.

The *Poseidon* entered the Highway, and the red and blue complexion of slip-space filled their view. It was a beautiful sight as always. One that she would enjoy as much as she could before the battle began. Before the body count started to rise.

The wait was excruciating, and not just for Kait. They all were either eager to fight or counting down the minutes until all hell broke loose. Among the bridge crew, it was definitely the latter.

At the thirty-minute mark, she began checking in on all systems. The 10th was "Ready and dying to stomp some alien skulls in," as Brigadier General Benton put it, which was followed by a chorus of *oorah*s. The space traffic controller informed her that their fighter squadrons were ready as well. One last report confirming all point defense cannons and machine guns were fully operational and she was feeling calmer. The same couldn't be said about the bridge crew, however.

Her poor XO, Lieutenant Commander London, was sweating bullets.

Opening the flotilla's comm channel, Kait tried to cool the nerves of her people. "This is Captain Adams. We're less than thirty minutes away from Diablos Corner and Lord Admiral Korruk's flotilla. I don't need to tell you how important this battle will be. I don't need to tell you the amount of people these zauhlons have killed or how many they will kill if we fail, because I trust you already know.

"If you're afraid, I don't blame you. These zauhlons slaughtered countless humans in the First Contact War. But the way I see it, things have changed. While they've been hiding in the shadows, we've grown stronger. While their fury glows bright, ours is brighter. I don't know about all of you, but I have a chip on my shoulder. I want to prove to these sons of guns that we can bring the fight to them and win. And Admiral Drake gave us that chance. Out of all the flotillas in Star Command, he chose *us*. Why? Because we're the best damn ships in the fleet.

"These zauhlons may have the drive and desire to kill us, but there's one thing they don't have—heart. Heart and compassion. Not for their enemies, but for themselves. It's no secret they're just as likely to turn their guns on their allies as they are on their enemies. Given the chance, they'll sacrifice one of their own or even one of their ships in a heartbeat. All for victory.

We're not like that though. We're better than them. Each and every life on this ship and on every other ship in this flotilla is important to me. And I promise you all that I'll do everything I can to bring you all back home alive. We're in this together. Never forget that."

Her speech seemed to calm the nerves of her bridge crew at least, and judging by the response, all the other bridge crews as well.

The rest of the ride passed much faster. Before they knew it, all fifty ships began dropping out of the Highway one by one. It was show time. A battle group with ten ships including one cruiser, three frigates, three corvettes, two destroyers and a carrier was stationed between Klydoon and the Highway. If the zauhlons attempted to run, they would be met with ferocity.

Upon closing in on Klydoon, two more battle groups were sent out. One was sent to the right flank, the other to the left. If the zauhlon flotilla tried to split up, these battle groups would meet them and push them back towards Kait's battle group. Likewise, their fighter squadrons would protect the main battle group's flank.

All that was left was Kait's group of twenty ships. Her dreadnought, five cruisers, five carriers, three destroyers, three frigates and three corvettes. While on their way, they moved into formation. The *Poseidon* and the four carriers held back while the rest moved into a wedge formation. The tip of the spear, specifically the *Neptune, Atlantis, Mera, Kraken, Julando, Kyoto* and the *Evelyn* would be the ships to clear the way for *Poseidon* to get the 10th Brigade to Klydoon. Protecting their battle group, dubbed the Sea King, would be the fighter squadrons in the process of pouring out of the hangars, and three squadrons from each carrier. If the zauhlons wanted to get to her and the 10th, they would have to get through all of them first.

When they were thirty kilometers away from Klydoon, scouts caught sight of the zauhlon flotilla and pinged their location to Captain Adams. They were directly ahead, as was predicted. Kait gave the order to the tip of the spear to charge up their railguns. As soon as they were within five kilometers of the enemy flotilla, they were to fire at the ships, clearing a lane for the *Poseidon*. By charging now, this would insure the massive weapons were at maximum power by the time they reached the designated firing distance.

As they drew nearer to the zauhlons, it was clear they were trying to make a blockade, though with only thirteen ships that was difficult. At ten kilometers, the zauhlons must have picked them up on their radars, because two of the ships, those in the center of the blockade, turned toward them, no doubt preparing to fire their own railguns. To add to that, they began releasing their Goblin fighter squadrons.

Unlike Captain Adams' flotilla, the zauhlon forces consisted of larger class ships—two dreadnoughts, cruisers, destroyers, and only three corvettes. Next to all the hulking warships, the corvettes looked out of place. While the larger ships would be able to pack a punch and take more than a few hits, they were slow as snails. Maneuvering around the battlefield would be a pain for them. Which also meant it would be better for her smaller and faster ships.

The Goblins looked like a swarm of bees compared to Kait's ships, and when they got into range, began their attempts at stinging her. The Valkyries were there to protect the starships in an instant. As ferocious as the dogfight was, her battle group pressed on, refusing to be stopped by the distraction.

When they were five kilometers away from the blockade, the tip of the spear fired their railguns, creating a beautiful light show of death and destruction. The two zauhlon ships preparing to fire at them, cruisers tagged as the *Inevitable* and *Malice*, were destroyed instantly, the railgun shots firing directly into the barrel of the enemy railguns and tearing them in half.

The rest of the railgun shots destroyed two more ships, both destroyers, and wounded the dreadnoughts. The tip of the spear moved aside and allowed the *Poseidon* to lead the charge through the blockade. This was the most dangerous part of the battle. Valkyries and Thunderbird bombers raced to defend the Sea King and distract the enemies. Still-hot debris bounced off their shields, slowly diminishing it.

To add to this, enemy point defense cannons—PDCs as they were commonly called—were landing shots on them. As they pushed through the blockade and made a wide left flank arc back into the battle, the hangar bay doors opened, and dozens of Odin dropships raced out. Among the heavy dropships was the *Sparrow*, which blended in nicely with the Odins, careful not to race ahead and stand out.

When the space traffic controller reported all the necessary dropships had left the hangar, Kait sighed a breath of relief. That part of the mission went well. Now it was up for them to get out of there and for the dropships to land.

That would be easier said than done.

Their shields were down to sixty percent. The Valkyries were doing their best to keep the *Poseidon* protected, but there was only so much they could do. The Sea King's PDCs were working overtime to combat the enemy starships.

"Captain, problem!" her helmsman called out. "Our trajectory is going to send us right into a destroyer. Orders?"

"How would we hold up if we rammed it?" Kait asked.

"Our shields would take the brunt of it, but after a stunt like that they'll be all gone. If we get hit, we're gonna have to hope the hull holds up."

"And if we fired our railgun at it?" Kait asked.

"We wouldn't be able to destroy it with such a short charge time. Wound, yes, but destroy? No go."

She nodded, "We're ramming it." Kait opened up ship-wide comms. "Everybody brace for impact."

Holding onto the arm rests of her chair, Kait clenched her teeth, waiting for her ship to ram the alien destroyer. It looked like the destroyer realized what was going to happen and attempted to move, but it was too late. The *Poseidon* smashed into the destroyer, ripping the ship in half. Just as the helmsman said, the series of explosions coming from the destroyer depleted their shields entirely. Despite their dire circumstances, things were looking good for the human-commanded ships. Only eight zauhlon ships remained, and there were no casualties for Star Command yet.

As if the universe realized this and attempted to rectify the string of good luck, the dreadnought tagged as the *Titan* fired its railgun at the *Orca*, completely destroying the frigate. It didn't take long for the zauhlons to abandon their blockade and charge them. Not a surprising tactic for a species of strategically inept warriors. Still, even for a bloodthirsty race like the zauhlons, they had their string of good ideas. They formed a wedge as best they could and began firing their railguns, though not at full charge. Regardless of whether they were at full power or not, against a flotilla of frigates, corvettes and carriers, it was bound to do damage.

Along with taking out both enemy and friendly starfighters, the Star Command vessels *Saber* and *Vennergate* were caught in the barrage of railguns. The loss of three ships in the span of five minutes was a tough blow, but they were still winning this battle. By now, the *Poseidon* was in the back with the carriers, its shields fully restored. They were turning around to get a shot at the *Terminator* when she received an interesting report.

"Captain, Blackfire Leader has reported in from Klydoon's atmosphere. You're going to want to hear this."

[Factory 017, Klydoon. Five minutes after the assault began.]

[Local system time: 1145.]

There was utter pandemonium aboard the *Onslaught*. They were being battered on all sides, whether it be by human starfighters or the hulking Ragnarok down on the planet's surface. Despite their shields failing, they still managed to fire their railgun at the west side of the factory, leaving a smoking hole in the building. After they did, the human starfighters, Valkyries, stopped attacking them, instead taking advantage of the new opening.

"Now's our chance! Deploy the Archons and Goblins!" Captain Herruk cried out.

His orders were followed, and the dropships were racing towards the opening they made in the factory. Once there, the battle for control of the landing zone against the humans begun. They weren't doing good, however. That Ragnarok, along with the gunships, tanks and cannon-walkers were depleting their shields. If they stayed any longer, they would be destroyed.

"General Orrim, we've given you the opening. I'm pulling us back until our shields are recharged. May Sorrvuk guide you to victory," Herruk said.

"Thank you. Korruk will die today, Herruk. Just you wait," Orrim shouted over gunfire and explosions.

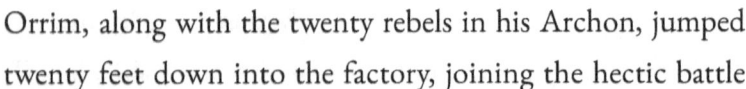

Orrim, along with the twenty rebels in his Archon, jumped twenty feet down into the factory, joining the hectic battle raging on in what looked to be some sort of office. Desks were flipped over, glass was shattered, and bodies were everywhere. Already the humans and Korruk's loyal grunts were fighting among each other. Taking advantage of the chaos, Orrim wailed a battle cry, encouraging his men to fire at both factions.

Korruk's zauhlons seemed somewhat surprised. The humans, however, didn't flinch. They didn't care what side the zauhlons were on; if they were wearing gold, they were going down.

In the chaos, Orrim began moving his zauhlons further south. Not only to get closer to the exit, but to get out of the way of the opening.

This proved to be a wise decision, as more humans came dropping in, pinning down Orrim and his rebels. It was frustrating for the rebel general, who couldn't get a shot in with so much gunfire coming his way. Tossing an inferno grenade towards the new batch of humans, he watched as some, but not all of the apes burned. While the remaining humans made a push to join their allies, Orrim and his warriors gunned them down.

As much as he wanted to just move on and get to Korruk, clearing this room was an important step in winning the battle. Getting too eager and shot wouldn't do him any good. This would prove to be a brutal and long fight, as more humans entered through the north entrance, tossing grenades as they did.

While he refused to take the humans lightly, Orrim knew if they kept up this ferocity that they would see reason and fall back. He couldn't say the same for Korruk's warriors. As such, the focus remained on them. No matter what it took, Orrim would take this room and any other sections that needed taking. He would find Korruk if it was the last thing he did.

[Odin dropship, en route to Factory 017.]

[Local system time: 1146.]

One hundred dropships left the *Poseidon*, carrying marines who were ready to spill some alien blood. A quarter of them were shot down. So far, the Odin holding Brigadier General "Papa Bear" Benton hadn't been shot down yet, but the grizzled general wasn't holding his breath. In his books, it doesn't matter how good you were, when it was your time to go, it was your time to go.

Intel reported that a zauhlon corvette just put a hole in the factory, and that some of his boys were taking advantage of that. That was fine and dandy, but that wasn't what his unit had set out to do. He and two hundred marines were tasked with taking out the enemy perimeter on the north side of the factory. Of course, this was the side that had the only Ragnarok war machine stationed on the line.

Through the smoke of his cigar and the dimmed red lights of the Odin, he saw a private, a young man, who couldn't be older than twenty-two, practically shaking in his boots. He couldn't blame the kid. Chances were he was going to die today. If he didn't grow a pair though, that outcome was all but guaranteed.

"What's your name, private?" Papa Bear asked the kid.

"H-Harry Ortiz, sir."

"You know why they call me Papa Bear, Ortiz?" he asked.

"Oh boy, here we go again," a marine said in the back.

"Stow it, Bronkowski!" He turned to face Ortiz again. "It's because I always take care of my boys. Stick by me and you'll get to see your mama again soon."

"Coming in hot. We're dropping you on the roof," the pilot said.

"Looks like this is our stop! Let's show these alien bastards what happens when they mess with the 10th!"

"Oorah!" his men shouted.

As each marine dashed out of the Odin, they began dropping the zauhlons on the roof. The fighting was hot, and cover was hard to find, but they weren't alone. Two more Odins came in, dropping off Captain Gregor's and Sergeant Turner's men. Together they killed every zauhlon in sight. When the area was clear, they began setting up their weapons. Mortars, Dragonsbreath turrets, T-16s and Quakers. The sight almost brought a tear to Papa Bear's eyes.

More marines from the 10th were on the ground, already dealing enough damage to make Papa Bear proud. Now wasn't the time to get sentimental, however. Once the weapons were set up, he started barking orders. "Keep the Dragonsbreaths and Quakers focused on the gunships! Mortars and T-16s on the tanks and cannons. Turner, you bring that target locator?"

"Yes sir, got it right here," as if to show proof, he held up the small device.

"Good. Paint that Ragnarok red and give the featherheads something to shoot."

"Yes, sir!"

Going down to one knee, Papa Bear opened up the 10th's comm channel. As expected, it was utter chaos. "Oceanus Four, report! Repeat, Oceanus Four, report!"

"I hear ya, Oceanus One!" Major Parker said in between shouting orders. "My men are in the factory. There's a shit load of aliens, but we're killing them faster than they can move. Poor bastards don't know who they're dealing with."

"Oorah. Where are you?"

"Just outside the main offices. Got a distress signal from some of my men pinned down."

"Alright. Get them out of there and link up with Tiger Squad, a couple of Star Bourn lookin' to get to the science chambers down below," Papa Bear said.

"Yes, sir!"

Papa Bear switched to local comms only and grabbed one of the rocket launchers. "Alright boys, let's show these alien brutes how better we've gotten at killing their kind!"

"Oorah!"

"Say it louder for the bastards in the tanks to hear!"

"*Oorah!*" his men screamed, firing their weapons of destruction at their targets. Even skinny ol' Ortiz was firing a grenade launcher.

Firing his own Quaker, Papa Bear grinned under his helmet. He'd go to hell for this, but he loved nothing more than blowing enemies to pieces and watching tanks go up in flames.

Have I mentioned how much I hate heights?

Standing near the open cargo bay door of the *Sparrow*, looking out at how far we'd be falling—fifteen hundred feet, to be exact—I felt sick to my stomach. I had to step back before I got dizzy. Shifting focus to the rest of the Wolves, I looked them over two times each to make sure they had the right equipment and weapons.

Along with our heavy-duty weapons—shotguns, rocket launchers; the good stuff—we were kitted with heavy duty jet packs. These would supposedly help with the jump. They'd never failed before, but that doesn't mean they couldn't now. Shaking away the thoughts of a premature demise, I put mine on. I seriously couldn't imagine having to do this with parachutes. The humans of old were hardcore.

Looking at the countdown at the top of my HUD, I called out over the Back Door, "Thirty seconds."

We were stuck between two battles. Above us, Captain Adams and her battle group were duking it out with the za-uhlon ships. Below us, Valkyries and marines were bringing it to Korruk's warriors. I wished we could join them, but we had more important business to deal with. We had to cut off the head of the snake.

At ten seconds, we lined up on the ramp. I said a silent prayer, and as the timer came to a close, I took a step forward and fell off the ramp. One by one the Wolves followed my lead. I would have liked to say I kept my cool throughout the entire fall, but my mother raised me to tell the truth. My heart was pounding so hard I thought it would explode. It only got worse once we entered the danger zone. Valkyries and Goblins raced past us. One close encounter got a scream of terror out of me. Nobody said anything, but I knew if we made it out of this op alive, I would never live that moment down.

Despite all this, I stayed on course. Focusing on that helped somewhat. When we reached less than a thousand feet, my HUD told me to fire up the jet pack. Somersaulting into an upright position, I activated the jet pack. A quick look told me everyone was doing the same. Not only that, but everyone had made it alive. For now, that is. We aren't on the ground yet.

The clunky jet packs slowed us down enough for us to land relatively comfortably on the hangar pad. When everyone was on the pad, we shrugged off the extra gear and prepared for combat. Below us, the fighting was loud and unforgiving. Gorgon tanks were firing off their large cannons, no doubt at the marines trying to destroy them. Anti-tank rockets fired off, followed by the loud explosion of a tank going up in flames. Score one for the Marine Corps.

Weapons out, we made our way to the door that led inside. When it didn't open immediately, Boomer attached a lock buster on the rusted door. In three seconds exactly, sparks flew and we rushed in. No matter how many zauhlons were in our way, we were reaching Korruk, and I was going to put this to an end. For the old Wolves and for Miller.

18

[Corridor E6, Factory 017, Klydoon.]

[Local system time: 1150.]

A hurricane of death was left in our tracks as we made a bee-line to the control room—a calling card of sorts to let everyone know we'd been there. A shotgun blast to the face took out the last zauhlon in the area. I would have expected more, but I guess they were stretched thin thanks to the marines.

We didn't get far before the corridors started locking down. We were ready for this. Busting all the locks would be too time-consuming, so instead we stepped into the maintenance passageway. It was tight and claustrophobic, but we managed. I was thankful claustrophobia wasn't one of my fears.

Not long after we started using this new path, we ran into a terminal, which we used to open up the corridors. It would have been nice to trap all the zauhlons in small sections of space, but our troops needed to move about freely, not to mention Tiger Squad. Even though the corridors were open, we continued to use the maintenance hallways until we were just outside the control room. The area was protected by a squad of zauhlons. Six to be precise. I motioned for Grampa to come up front. If I could see through helmets, there's no doubt in my mind I'd see a grin plastered on his face.

Rocket launcher in hand, Grampa burst into the main corridor and unleashed a rocket on the unsuspecting zauhlons. Four out of six immediately died. The last two met their end thanks to Bullseye's and Tenner's machetes. Just like in the simulations, the door was locked. We piled on either side of the door while Boomer attached the lock buster.

My heart was racing. This wasn't one of the countless sims we'd trained on. This was the real deal. If we failed here, that was it. Sparks flew and the doors slid open. Twenty zauhlons, including Korruk himself, were inside, guns trained on us.

Before they could open fire, I shouted, "Korruk! By the law of Sorrvuk, I challenge you to a battle to the death!"

This seemed to catch all the zauhlons by surprise. They looked at each other, then to Korruk as if wondering what they should do. Korruk nodded and took his helmet off. It struck me that this was the first time I've seen him without his helmet. Scars from slashes and burns littered his face, and an eye-patch covered his upper right eye. I was going to take pleasure in adding another scar.

Control yourself. Don't let your emotions take control.

He took a few steps back and opened his arms, as if welcoming me into his space. Hesitantly at first, I took a few steps forward. As I did, the zauhlons stepped aside. I walked towards the circular area surrounded by screens and consoles, the heart of the control room. On each screen, fighting was seen. Not only human-on-zauhlon violence, but ... zauhlon-on-zauhlon violence too? That would explain that corvette attacking the factory. It looked like all hell truly had broken loose.

"I'll admit, *Severre*, I'm impressed." Korruk said my name like it stung to say. He unsheathed his sword. "Luring me and my forces here, only to launch an assault ... An impressive tactic. One I'll have to use in the future. As much as this journey has been amusing, let's put it to an end. You and your friends will rot here while I conquer the Republic."

In response, I unsheathed my arm length machete. Like in Serpent's Hole, he took a high guard stance. This time though, I didn't charge like a fool. Instead, I took a mid-guard stance, ready for whatever Korruk threw my way. We circled each other. Everyone in the room was dead silent, the only noise being the background sounds of battle. Both of us came to a stop. It was then that Korruk charged me, unleashing the same battle cry he had shouted on that freighter not that long ago.

———◆◇◆———

[Main offices, Factory 017, Klydoon.]

[Local system time: 1152.]

The battle for the LZ continued. Orrim knew whoever won this battle would control who came in through the still-smoking hole. The humans had slowly repositioned themselves near the north entrance, which made it clear to the rebel leader they were planning on retreating. This was all but confirmed when another squad of human soldiers came into view, but didn't enter the room. They were covering their men while they retreated.

With the threat of the humans temporarily gone, Orrim and his squad, only three in number now, focused on the five remaining zauhlons. Those combatants had the high ground, which made landing killing blows difficult. If Orrim's warriors wanted to gain control of this office, they would need to make a push. Tossing a shrap grenade, Orrim prepared his men for a charge. As soon as the grenade exploded, they rushed the enemy.

One of Korruk's warriors was killed via the shrapnel, the rest were merely wounded. A four-on-three fight would have to do. Orrim grabbed the fallen zauhlon's ax and went for the grunt who looked to be the leader and a more critically wounded zauhlon. Niruuk, who he requested to be on his team, went for the one closest to the ledge, while their third zauhlon went for the enemy on the left.

Fighting two at a time would be a difficult task for most, but Orrim was ready. He hadn't gotten to the rank of general because he remembered names. Going for the injured one first, he swung the superheated ax like it weighed nothing, digging it into the man's chest. For good measure, he swung the weapon once again, this time driving it into the man's neck. Based on how much blood the zauhlon was losing, he was doing him a favor.

The leader was livelier. He fought Orrim tooth and nail, even managing to scar his armor more than once. Upon landing a hit that cut through to Orrim's skin, the general drove the ax into his enemy's arm before following it up with a stab through the chest with his previously sheathed sword. Turning to see how his allies were holding, he witnessed Niruuk beheading his opponent and their teammate defeating his foe.

"Should we go after the humans, general?" Niruuk asked. Like any other zauhlon, he hated letting an enemy escape his grasp.

"No. Our priority is the control room," Orrim said. Opening up his comms, he began commanding his forces. "I need warriors at the offices. Create a defense perimeter and don't let any dropship get in here."

* * *

[Corridor B4, Factory 017, Klydoon.]

.

[Local system time: 1153.]

Bodies piled up as Tiger Squad, accompanied by Major Parker and seven marines, made their way to the science chambers. After passing through a large area with conveyor belts, they arrived at a cargo lift that would take them down to the science chamber and the Pale Horse. Their training in the Sim-Room hadn't prepared them for marine backup, so Black Lung was feeling optimistic with their chances. Even if they weren't as good as commandos, they could still pack a punch.

Upon reaching the conveyor belt area, they were faced with three routes. Two catwalks that gave them the high ground but no cover, and a stairway down to the main level. Apart from it being a maze down there, there was a ton of zauhlon-on-zauhlon action. Killing all of them would be a pain.

"What's the call, captain?" Parker asked. Even though he ranked higher than Black Lung, Star Bourn elicited a certain level of respect from the marines and army. That, and this was Tiger's op.

"Let's save the ammo and take the catwalk. If you take fire, give it back, but otherwise don't engage. We'll finish off whoever is left on our way back," Black Lung said.

With that, they split up into two teams. Black Lung, Rockie, Crow and three marines, and Hatchet, Bat, Sixteen, Major Parker and the other four jarheads. Black Lung's team, Alpha, took the left catwalk, while Hatchet's team, Charlie, took the right. Both teams didn't bother masking their footsteps; the constant gunfire and grenades did that for them well enough. Instead, they kept their heads low and sprinted to the far side of the room. A few bullets bounced off the railings and the grated floor, but no one was hit.

They regrouped at the door leading out of the conveyor belt room and pushed on. Ahead was a long hallway with a cargo lift at the end. Bingo. The downside: a shit ton of zauhlons stood in the way with little to no cover. This was where most of their ammo went dry in the sims.

With no other option, they pushed on, acting as a wall of muscle and valor, killing the zauhlons who had their backs turned to them and using the dead as body shields. One of the marines tossed out a frag, which a zauhlon tried to throw back. Emphasis on "tried". The blast took out another four. Black Lung's HUD read fifteen more zauhlons.

Crow, with his human/anthrum hybrid laser, lined up a shot and watched as the deadly weapon burned a hole clean through three zauhlons. "Hey, Black Lung, can we keep this one?"

"Only if you take care of it," the team leader said as he dropped another alien.

One of the marines went down via an ax thrown into his head. It seemed like the closer to the lift they got, the heavier weapons the zauhlons had. A spiked cannon ball took another marine down; poor bastard probably had all his ribs broken. They were twelve meters away from the lift, and only four zauhlons were left standing. Another laser shot eradicated a zauhlon's head. Black Lung had to admit, the kind of tech the anthrum had was seriously impressive.

The last three zauhlons attempted to charge, but they were gunned down with a collective of four shotguns. *Doesn't matter how tough you are, a shotgun is a shotgun.* Thankfully, the lift was already at their level, so there was no need to wait. While they descended, the group of marines reloaded and checked if anybody was injured. Cuts and bruises, but otherwise everyone was good.

As soon as the doors creaked open, a total of three destabilizers were tossed. It wasn't as packed as it was in the simulations, but it was damned close. Thirty zauhlons, along with a couple of unarmed bots, were in the room with a giant weapon of sorts in the back. With their enemies temporarily blinded, Rockie fired off rocket after rocket while Sixteen fired his grenade launcher. By the time the zauhlons' senses came back, only five of them remained. Those five were shot down by the marines.

The room was filled with blood, armor and destroyed desks. All the while the bots went on like nothing happened. Tiger Squad put bullets in the bots while Hatchet downloaded the schematics for the Pale Horse. This would be a huge edge for them. Unlike in the sims, they almost knew what they were doing. Almost.

"Damn, what is that?" a marine asked.

"Command is calling it the Pale Horse," Black Lung said. He probably wasn't supposed to give that sort of info out, but he didn't care. So what if some people knew the name of something? They only ever slapped him on the wrist.

"Spooky," that same marine muttered.

"Ain't that from the four horsemen or something?" another marine asked.

"Beats me. Let's just get this thing out of here already."

"Alright, I got it," Hatchet said, "Forwarding copies to all of you, just in case."

As soon as he said that, Tiger Squad got notifications from their HUD saying the schematics were received.

"What, we don't get them?" one of the marines asked.

"Sorry, Devil Dog, this is on a need-to-know basis," Hatchet said.

While the marines covered the lift, Tiger Squad lifted the bomb onto two grav-lifts. As they moved the Pale Horse towards the lift, the doors slid open revealing ten zauhlons. The marines unleashed their Punishers on the aliens, but two of the jarheads were killed. Sixteen lugged his grenade launcher to the action, resting it on the shoulder of a marine on one knee, and fired the rocket-guided grenades. The frags that came from the T-16 were enough to kill the scum.

As the remaining marines dragged the zauhlons out of the lift, Parker walked up to Black Lung, who was slapping another magazine into his Revenger.

"Where are we taking this thing? I get you Star Bourn like to do ops your way, but I don't like being left in the dark," Parker said.

"The LZ *was* going to be the hangar pad attached to corridor E6, but I have a better idea," Black Lung said.

"Uh oh," Crow said. "All due respect, Black Lung, but your ideas tend to be downright crazy."

Tiger's captain chuckled. "Can't be crazier than what we were going to do. I say we take it back to those offices we came in from, call in an Odin and get out of here. It's closer, and there's a few good holdout positions in that room."

"Sounds fun. I say we go for it," Sixteen said.

Major Parker nodded. "I can get some marines to rendezvous with us there. The added guns will help a lot."

"I agree. If there is anybody who doesn't like this plan, now's the time to speak up." When nobody spoke a word, Black Lung continued. "Alright then. Let's move out, Tiger. *Poseidon* ordered one large abomination, and they want it in mint condition."

19

.

As good as those Sim-Rooms were, and as accurate as they could be, they could never replicate Korruk's ferocity. And how could they? You can only mimic general experiences or people. Case in point: A lot of people still alive can tell you how a zauhlon fights. Plenty of people can tell you about sky diving. Not many, if any at all, could say how Lord Admiral Korruk fought. No one but me, that is, and I don't know a damn thing about how those simulators work.

Right now, he was on the verge of overwhelming me with some form of sword combat. He was spinning his sword in a figure-eight motion faster than I could keep up with. I was well aware this was merely a distraction—any hits he landed doing this only scratched my armor—but I couldn't judge when the main attack would come. In sudden movements, he would thrust a knife using his upper left hand my way. They had no rhyme or reason; each and every time it would be random. I'd been lucky so far by keeping my distance, but I was running out of fighting room. Sooner or later, one of those jabs would hit me, and it would hurt like hell.

While the name of this sword form was beyond me, I knew from my research it was an ancient type of combat most modern zauhlons didn't use. I managed to learn the utmost basics, but I wouldn't dare call myself experienced. In fact, I found it almost impossible to perform, maybe because my body wasn't used to such an intense form of swordplay. Personally, I think it has something to do with physiology. They've got some crazy muscles. So instead, I added my own twist to it.

I waited for him to strike with that knife of his. When he did, I pushed it away with my machete, pulled out my Sentinel and shot him in the shoulder. Thanks to his personal shields the gunshot didn't do any serious damage, but it did catch him by surprise. Seeing my chance, I went on the offensive. I switched from sword strike to gunshot, picking away at his shields and gaining more ground. Shooting with my left hand took some getting used to, but I was ready for it. He attempted another stab with his knife. I sidestepped, pushed my gun into the spot where his lower left shoulder met his torso and pulled the trigger. His shields couldn't protect him from a bullet that close, and a short grunt of pain let me know I was successful.

Korruk whacked me in the head with the pommel of his sword, which dazed me long enough for him to slap my gun away. Before I could react, he crushed the weapon beneath his hoof. Instead of the methodical approach Korruk used before, he opted for a more brutish, to-the-point style. While each swing had a lot of strength behind it, they were also sloppy, which made it easier for me to block and dodge. When the opportunity presented itself, I would get in cuts and jabs, working away at his armor. One such cut pierced a piece of armor and slashed into Korruk's ribs.

This, topped with his inability to land a hit on me, must have really pissed him off. He grabbed the blade of my machete, its edge still burning hot, and wrestled it away from me. With my weapon out of the way, he chopped my neck. With me gasping for air, Korruk tossed my machete aside. Grabbing me by my chest plate, he raised me high off the ground and slammed me into the unrelenting metal floor.

Moving quicker than I was ready for, he pinned me down and began punching me repeatedly. Thank God I had my helmet on. If not, I don't think I'd remain conscious. That being said, I needed to do something fast. As good as those helmets were, I could hear it start to crack under the constant pressure.

I raised my arms to protect my head, but that didn't do much good against a man with four fists. Feeling myself starting to black out, I acted quick. I grabbed the knife sheathed on my shoulder pad and slashed Korruk's face open.

The blow split him open from his mandible up to under his eye. Another scar for his collection. Blood almost immediately gushed out. I took this time to push him off me and crawl back to my blade. By the time I was on my feet and facing my enemy, Korruk was already rushing me. It seemed like everything I did only fueled him on. He was on me again with his wild, brutish strikes. My mind was struggling to keep up: my defenses weren't nearly as good as they should be, *needed* to be.

Korruk was landing more and more hits. Not just scrapes and cuts to my armor either, punches to the head and body. The tide was turning fast, and if I didn't do something to stop this, I was dead. Using his momentum, Korruk prepared to stab me. This was my chance. I rolled past Korruk, who had foolishly left himself open to such a dodge. With some space between us, I tossed a destabilizer at Korruk, who caught it as he turned around. By the time he realized what it was, it was too late. The grenade exploded, leaving Korruk blind and without hearing. Maybe if I was lucky, he'd be permanently blind. A destabilizer that close would do the trick for any other species.

Using this as my chance to deal serious damage, I circled Korruk and prepared to stab him where Releck did back in Serpent's Hole, only to see it was covered up with extra armor. Smart move, but it needed to go. I ripped off the armor and just barely dodged a swing from Korruk. Moving back around the zauhlon leader, I tore off the last piece of armor, exposing his raw, injured flesh to the world. Once again Korruk swung his huge arm at me like he was swatting a fly, and once again I dodged, taking a leap back.

Seeing an opportunity to bring the pain to Korruk, I stabbed him in the shoulder joint, the same spot where I shot him a minute ago. Before I could pull back, Korruk grabbed my wrist. I tried to force him off me, but his grip was like a snake squeezing the life out of its prey. To my surprise, he pulled me in, further digging the machete into his shoulder, until we were face-to-face. He bared his blood-covered teeth to me, showcasing a rage unlike anything I've seen before.

In an instant, his soup bowl-sized hand was around my throat, leaving me gasping for air. Before any serious damage could be done, he threw me across our makeshift arena into a set of computers. The impact left my back tingling. I was on the verge of blacking out again. In fact, I think I did for a moment, because when I opened my eyes next, Korruk had both his sword and my machete in hand, walking towards me.

"Ah, shit," I muttered, taking out my knife. This was not going to be fun.

⸻◆⸻

[Corridor D7, Factory 017, Klydoon.]

[Local system time: 1155.]

The Battle of Klydoon, as short as it had been so far, was a blood bath, and it didn't look like it was going to end any time soon. Orrim and his zauhlons, which now consisted of seven after regrouping with other rebels, were in a heated fight with the humans. As fragile as they were, they put up a good fight. These past few weeks had given Orrim a newfound respect for the apes.

The rebels were gaining ground, but only in steps. It felt like no matter how many they killed, more humans replaced the fallen. As good as he and his warriors were, they couldn't manage this forever. Orrim motioned for one of his men to toss an inferno grenade, which he did. Focused on staying alive and out of the flames, the human gunfire temporarily stopped. This was their moment. Orrim led his men in a rush to gain as much territory as possible. The charge was more than successful, and they came face to face with their enemies.

The humans stood no chance.

One by one the enemy marines were cut down with swords, axes and gunfire alike. Some of the apes escaped, but Orrim wasn't concerned with them. Looking over his rebels, he saw only one of them had perished. A shame, but only the strong would survive.

Where the three corridors combined sat an old but still functioning terminal. Orrim smiled; just what he needed. While he knew to head to the control room, he wasn't familiar with the layout of this factory. Before any more enemy forces arrived, he downloaded a map of the building.

From where they were, they needed to take five more turns, one elevator ride and a long narrow corridor to get to the control room. With only six allies by his side and with how many enemies were in the factory, he didn't think highly of his chances. If Orrim wanted to leave here victorious, he needed more zauhlons.

Opening a comm link to the rebel team guarding the offices, Orrim said, "Commander Ferrik, how many warriors can you spare? My team is too low on numbers to get to the control room."

"I can send eight grunts. Any more and we won't be able to defend the LZ," Ferrik said.

"Very well. I'm sending you our location. Tell them to ping us when they arrive. I want them here in two minutes." Orrim turned to his rebels. "We need to defend our location until reinforcements arrive. Tear off the metal walls and use them as cover. Kill anything that moves."

His soldiers roared the battle cries of old and got to work. Waiting here killed him inside, but Orrim knew it needed to be done. Looking down the corridor they would eventually need to move through, he wondered what would wait for them. Regardless of who, or what it was, they would die, same as all who opposed them.

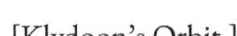

[Klydoon's Orbit.]

[Local system time: 1150.]

Captain Kaitlyn Adams watched the holographic real-time battle intently. They were still winning the fight, but more of her ships were going down. The zauhlon dreadnought *Titan*, while damaged, destroyed the *Julando*. On top of that, the *Kyoto* and her crew met their demise when they moved too close to an exploding zauhlon cruiser. Kait couldn't help but admire the zauhlons' never-wavering dedication to battle. Most flotillas that were at a fifteen-to-six disadvantage would have run by now. These warships, however, clearly had no intention of running. The only way they would be defeated was to destroy them all. So be it.

During the course of the battle, the zauhlons were moving close to her own ships. It was an attempt to keep the humans from firing their railguns, a tactic that worked in the aliens' favor. Most of the human captains didn't dare turn their backs on their enemies in the effort to put some distance between themselves, as that would expose their engines. If those were taken out, they'd be dead in space, making a perfect target. This battle was turning into a boxing match. Whoever had the better shields, armor and weapons would come out on top. Of course, this didn't bode well for her small ships.

The hundreds of starfighters at Kait's disposal were her first line of defense. If they could take out the enemy PDCs, they could help even the playing field. As good as her pilots were, they weren't working fast enough. The *Murso*, her last destroyer in her battle group, had been destroyed. The alien cruiser next to her took a lot of damage, but it was somehow still functioning. One more well-placed hit and it would be toast.

"Lock onto that cruiser and fire our torpedoes," Kait ordered. It was a split-second decision, but one she stood by.

Her officers got to work relaying the orders, and seconds later, ten torpedoes shot out of the *Poseidon* and arched their way to the flaming cruiser. Moments after being fired, seven of the ten speeding missiles hit their target, destroying the ship. She looked back at the display of the battle only to see another one of her ships, the *Hyde*, obliterated by the *Vengeance*'s railgun.

She shut her eyes, pushing away the pain. Kait knew the captain of the *Hyde* well. Captain Halburn was a mentor to her when she first became a captain. He was a good man.

"Captain, we're being hailed by General Benton," her lieutenant commander called out.

"Put him through."

A second later, a holo-image of Benton appeared before her. Behind him were his troopers firing their guns. "Captain Adams! We need some air support here! We painted a target for our fighters minutes ago and they haven't even looked our way. Need I remind you how important destroying this Ragnarok son of a bitch is? I'm lucky I'm still alive!"

Kait sighed. Benton's honesty was a welcome change, but it did nothing to help with her stress. "I'll see what I can do, general. If we have any available fighters, they'll be there in two minutes top."

Before the feed was cut, she could see Benton turn back to his boys yelling, "Alright, ladies, looks like the featherheads missed their alarm! They'll be here in two minutes. Let's show these aliens the Marine Corps don't need starfighters to help kill a bunch of no-good brutes!"

She looked to her space traffic controller and further cemented her command. "Get some bombers and fighter squadrons down to Klydoon."

"Aye, aye, captain."

———◦———

[Hangar Bay Five, *Poseidon*.]

[Local system time: 1150.]

"Come on, gentlemen, you heard the lady! Get in those fighters and get ready for heavy fire," said Captain Tom Taylor of Eden Squadron, watching his twenty pilots hustle on towards their respective Valkyries.

They'd been given a short briefing on their mission: escort Yosemite and Dynamite Squadrons to Klydoon to wreck a

Ragnarok. They wouldn't be alone though, Drifter and Victory Squadrons would escort the bomber squadrons with them, and they would be joined by Blackfire Squadron when they reached Klydoon's atmosphere.

As he secured his helmet with a series of clicks, he began going through the motions he always went through when he was about to take off. First came the giddiness, that feeling when you warmed up your bird's engines and leave the hangar. Then came the butterflies, the realization that no matter how good you or your squadron was, you might not be coming back. Finally, the sense of calmness, knowing whatever happened would happen, and the best thing he could do was continue being the rock his pilots needed, and to put his trust in God.

He climbed into his Valkyrie, which had three red stripes painted horizontally, a nice contrast to the jet black finish Valkyries normally had, if he said so himself. Booting up his systems, he waited for the go-ahead to leave the hangar. Tom took this time to look at the photo of his ex-wife and daughter. Seeing them brought a smile to his face, just as it always did.

"You're clear to go, Eden. Good hunting."

The squadron leader cracked his neck and placed his hands on the controls. "You heard the man, Eden. Let's take to the stars."

Within seconds, all of Eden Squadron were out of the *Poseidon* and into the battle. Thankfully, they had some breathing room. The Sea King was staying back with the carriers, meaning Tom's boys weren't being shot at right off the bat. It didn't take long for Victory and Drifter to show up on the radars. Drifter and Victory Leader's blinked green, signifying their teams were ready to go. Tom made Eden's readiness known as well.

Next came Yosemite and Dynamite Squadrons. Unlike the fighter squadrons, these two squadrons consisted of Thunderbird bombers. Tough as those birds were, they were slow. Escorting them would mean slowing down to their speed. In other words, they would be like snails on a highway in five second's time.

With all squadrons accounted for, they got into formation. Eden maneuvered into wedge formation, Victory took to delta form, Drifter shifted into twin formations on the left and right wings of the bombers, and the two Thunderbird squadrons huddled together into a strike group. Tom wasn't a fan of the strategy. He understood the mindset for it; form a tight shield around the bombers so that no enemies could get to them. If any of the Valkyries were shot down though, the other friendly fighters might become collateral damage.

As much as he disliked the plan, it was better than spreading out and leaving the bombers wide open, he had to admit. There was also the fact that Victory's captain, Eddy Veros, was the head of this op, so it was ultimately his decision, not Tom's.

Once everyone was where they needed to be, they flew off into the fray. Going around the battle would take too long. Their only option was to fly right through the battle to Kly-doon. On the upside, there were more Valkyries than there were Goblins, so if they got overwhelmed, chances were they'd receive backup in no time.

So far so good. Eden got a few shots in on passing Goblins, but none of the enemy fighters paid much attention to them. Evidently, they were more focused on taking down Captain Adams' battle group. *Good luck*, thought Tom. *Even if the brutes get through us, there's still a couple dozen other ships waiting*.

They were halfway to their target when things got hot and heavy. The zauhlons must have picked up on what they were doing, because a squad of twenty Goblins started making runs on them. They caused no serious damage, but the intent was clear.

"They're coming back around. They're trying to flank us," Captain Veros said. "Focus shields on our flank. When they pass by us, dish out as much damage as you can."

All of the Valkyries blinked green in acknowledgment. Tom, along with the rest of Eden, diverted the majority of shield strength to their thrusters. As terrible as the zauhlons were at flying, those Goblins could pack a punch. Worst case scenario, they land all their shots, and they would be out of shields.

The Goblins began laying down fire. Eden Squadron managed to get by relatively unscathed. Some low shields, minor damage, but no deaths. The same couldn't be said about Victory. They were the first to receive fire, so they suffered the most damage. Three of their fighters went down, two from the guns of the Goblins, the last one taken down along with the second Valkyrie.

The featherheads in Eden made sure the aliens paid for it with their lives. With help from the pilots in Drifter, they took down five of the Goblins. Tom smiled. *Looks like the aliens didn't bother to get better at flying.* This was proven further when the zauhlons didn't even try to dodge their gunshots. Instead, they just turned around and prepared for another go at the Valkyries.

A quick look at his HUD told the captain of Eden they were nearing the exosphere of Klydoon, just ten kilometers away. The sight of the Goblins coming for them made those ten kilometers feel like a hundred. Without waiting for Veros' orders, Tom shifted the strength of his shields to the nose of his Valkyrie. The rest of Eden followed suit, along with Drifter, Dynamite, Yosemite and, finally, Victory.

As soon as the Goblins were in range, Tom opened fire on them. He was the first to fire, and all his shots were direct hits. When the enemy shields were down, he switched to the Valkyrie's precision guns. Two hits later and another Goblin went down. Not long after he started shooting at the enemies, the rest of the Valkyries joined him. By the time the Goblins passed them, the zauhlon squadron was down to six.

Before the Goblins could come back around for another attack, Eden and the other squadrons entered Klydoon's exosphere, where they met up with Blackfire Squadron.

"Blackfire, move out with the escort party. These bastards killed some of my men. Victory will deal with them," Captain Veros said.

Blackfire acknowledged the order and took up a delta formation in Victory's place. As the group of fighters neared the factory, they started taking fire from the cannon-walkers, and more importantly, the Ragnarok. As soon as the war machine caught sight of them, Valkyries were shot down left and right. Most of those casualties were Eden pilots. Looking this Ragnarok in the eye brought a strong sense of fear into Tom, but he didn't waver.

"Any time now, Thunderbirds!" Tom called out.

"Just a little closer ..." Dynamite Leader mumbled over the comm, "We've got a lock! Get out of the way, Eden!"

Tom was all too happy to oblige. He and the rest of Eden Squadron arced out of the way. Dynamite was the first to unload their bombs. Leaving a row of fire and devastation, the squadron of Thunderbirds successfully destroyed the Ragnarok and more than a few tanks. To add to the destruction, Yosemite dropped their bombs as well, taking out a dozen cannon-walkers. By the time they were done, no zauhlon vehicle was left functioning.

Captain Taylor opened a channel with Brigadier General Benton. "Did someone call for a bomb strike?"

Not missing a beat, Papa Bear replied, "Took yer damn time. A minute sooner would have worked too."

Under his helmet, Tom smiled. "Everyone's a critic."

20

.

Almost as soon as Tiger Squad entered the conveyor belt area, they drew fire. For a minute, Black Lung wished they cleared out the area when they had the chance, but he realized that wouldn't have done a blasted thing. This place was crawling with enemies. Even if they had killed everyone before getting to the Pale Horse, it still would have been full of zauhlons. The only thing left for them to do was kill everyone standing in their way.

While the Pale Horse couldn't get across the catwalks, those handy walkways didn't go unused. Rockie and Crow climbed up on opposite catwalks and unleashed hell with their rocket launcher and laser. Despite the heavy weapons, things weren't getting easier. Most of the marines were down, save for Major Parker, who was busy calling for backup.

"Shit," Parker muttered.

"What is it?" Black Lung asked, reloading his Revenger.

"That zauhlon corvette that punched a hole into the factory is back, and I'm getting word more dropships are being deployed," Major Parker said.

"That's just great," Black Lung said, "Are we getting backup or not?"

"A squad is on its way. I'm having more squads clear a way to the LZ," said Parker.

Black Lung nodded. "Sixteen, fire up that T-16. We're moving up."

Sixteen laughed and primed his grenade launcher. "You don't need to tell me twice."

Not two seconds later, Sixteen began unloading his weapon into the enemy forces, allowing Tiger Squad to move ahead. The maze-like layout made their trek longer than Black Lung would have liked, but with the rocket launcher and the laser, they were making good progress.

That is, until the rogue zauhlons arrived.

The large windows high above the conveyor belts were blown out, and zauhlons began dropping down. While this wasn't good for Tiger Squad, it was worse for Rockie and

Crow, who were on the catwalks with the new zauhlons. Rockie held his own well. Even if he didn't have the rest of Tiger with him, he was a tough son of a bitch. Along with firing off rockets, he was able to wrestle the zauhlons off the catwalk, sending them falling to their doom. Crow didn't fare as well. Along with Bat, he was one of the leaner Star Bourn in Tiger Squad.

While he was able to keep the bulk of the rogue aliens away from him, one managed to get behind him and stab him in the back clean through the chest. After that, Crow couldn't do much else but watch as the zauhlon who stabbed him prepared to finish the job.

"We have to go help him!" Bat said, already on the move.

Black Lung grabbed his arm. "If we divert from the path now, we risk letting the bomb fall into enemy hands. Crow knew the risks."

Bat knew he was right. As much as he, and every other living member of Tiger Squad wanted to go and bring Crow with them, they had to leave him behind. Fueled with vengeance, Bat turned his attention to the incoming zauhlons. He may not be able to help his friend, but he could sure as hell avenge him.

Tiger Squad, now joined by Rockie, had gotten through the twists and turns of the machines in the room. All that was left was to walk the rest of the way to the bulkhead door. Nothing was ever that easy though. The rogue zauhlons were behind them and were laying down heavy fire. Thankfully, no one had gone down by gunfire, but they didn't dare try to back up towards the door.

"CB out!" Black Lung shouted. The bomb exploded with the might of a thunderbolt, taking out four aliens in the process. Rockie followed this up with a shot from his rocket launcher.

"I'm out," Rockie called out, switching to his Punisher.

Despite the sudden casualties, the zauhlons pushed forward, closing in on their prey by the second. Tiger did their best to hold them off, but there was only so much they could do. Black Lung tossed his last destablizer into the group of enemies. As soon as the grenade ignited, Tiger fell back to the door.

Black Lung frantically looked over the control panel, tapping buttons at record speed. When a red message popped up saying "Door locked, please insert keycode." He audibly swore.

"Parker! Where's that squad?" Black Lung asked.

To his credit, Major Parker, who was simultaneously on the comm and firing at the zauhlons, replied to Black Lung. Knowing how hectic the comm channels no doubt were, it was an impressive feat, "Two corridors away. We just need to buy them some time."

The Star Bourn captain nodded. "Alright, you heard the man! Form a defensive perimeter."

Each marine started knocking over nearby large equipment, using the machinery as cover. It wasn't ideal, but it was good enough. Their next course of action was to kill as many za-uhlons as possible. If Black Lung calculated right, some of them would be regaining their senses any second now, so they needed to take advantage of this while they could.

As he expected, the rogue brutes finally began returning fire and find cover of their own. Even with their depleted numbers, the zauhlons still outnumbered them by twenty. On a good day, Black Lung liked those odds, but ammo was getting low. If those jarheads didn't open that door soon, this wouldn't end well for Tiger.

Evidently, things were already going from bad to worse. Parker tried to get a shot in on a zauhlon, but got a volter round to the chest. The electricity-laced bullet immediately took Parker out of the fight. Black Lung didn't know if he was dead or not, and he didn't have time to find out. The doors behind them opened, and a squad of ten marines entered the room.

Rockie and Sixteen took control of the Pale Horse, while Bat and Hatchet joined the marines by providing covering fire. Black Lung meanwhile dragged Parker. By the luck of the universe, Tiger made it out. Now all they had to do was get to the LZ ...

[Zauhlon Command Center, Factory 017, Klydoon.]

[Local system time: 1157.]

One massive knee to the face knocked me onto my back, looking straight up at the ceiling lights. My head was pounding, and felt like it was going to explode. On top of that, my visor was shot. One more hit and it would shatter. I took off the useless piece of equipment and tossed it aside. This allowed me to see Korruk leaping at me, threatening to lunge both blades into my chest.

I rolled back, barely avoiding both weapons. Korruk attempted to kick me in the face, but I saw my chance. In that moment, everything moved in slow motion. My knife in hand, I plunged it into the cracked bottom of his hoof. Korruk shouted in pain and dropped the machete and sword. The attack sent him tumbling down, groaning in agony.

Grabbing my machete, I brought it down onto his upper right hand, chopping off his fingers. He pushed me away with what strength he had, earning him enough time to get to his hooves with the help of a nearby console. Korruk stomped a few times with his injured hoof, no doubt trying to get feeling back into it.

Despite the beatdown, and despite my bones being more sore than I thought possible, I was optimistic. My blocks were good, and I didn't let him get any serious blows in, minus that knee to the face. Korruk on the other hand, now had a few less fingers and a bad hoof. With that disadvantage, I could get away from his attacks easier.

Blood trickled down my face, resting at the corner of my mouth. Taking a deep breath, I waited to see what his next move would be.

Through sharp breaths, Korruk chuckled. "This ... This *battle* of yours is pointless."

"You think so? We've got you outnumbered. Your ships are getting their asses handed to them, and so are your men. Even your own people are fighting against you."

"They're weak. Only the strong survive in this galaxy. Reinforcements are on their way. We only needed to survive until they arrive," Korruk said. "After that, you'll be wiped out like the monkeys you are. A shame you won't live to see it, and what will follow."

It was a hundred percent possible he was delusional from the sudden influx of pain. That he was talking out of his ass here. Still, if what he was saying was true, I needed more information. "And what's that?"

Korruk chuckled again. "The fall of your capital."

I raised an eyebrow. "Milara? You really are insane. How do you expect to get close to it? We have dozens of fleets. You only have, what, three?"

Lord Admiral Korruk slowly let go of the console, standing on his own. He carefully made his way toward his sword. I should have struck him down. Instead, I awaited his response, intrigued at what bullshit he'd come up with.

"This is much bigger than your feeble mind can comprehend." With his sword in hand, Korruk took a few steps back. "I have allies in higher places than you think."

Trying to not let the implications of what he said get to me, I took the initiative and attacked. Korruk's guard was sloppy to say the least, which allowed me to get a few good hits on his arms. His armor took the brunt of it, but the sight of blood told me at least some of the slashes pierced his skin. It was then I noticed something interesting: Korruk was using his upper left hand. The thought almost made me laugh. *The bastard was right-handed.* If he wanted to keep his distance, he had to use his upper left arm.

Perhaps it was this fact that made me get a little cocky. My attempt at a thrust was parried by Korruk, who pushed it outward. This opened me up to an elbow to the nose.

An audible *crack!* echoed throughout the room. As I fell to the ground, blood began pouring from my nose. There was no doubt in my mind that it was broken. Before I could get back to my feet, Korruk was on me. He drove his sword into my left arm, pinning it to the floor. What followed was a beatdown that threatened to knock me out or worse.

With each punch, my mind blacked out for a moment. My sight was going fuzzy. If I didn't do something quick, this would be it. Rolling onto my left side as best I could, I feigned an attempt at blocking. This fooled Korruk, who forced me onto my back. When he did, I had my knife in hand, ready to slash his face even more. I managed two more cuts and a stab into his wounded lower shoulder before he got off me.

As much as I wanted to just lay there and rest, I pushed myself on. One misstep and that was it. With all the strength I could muster, I heaved the alien sword out of my arm. The pain and burning sensation that followed brought me back to Serpent's Hole. Unlike last time, though, this wasn't life threatening. This wasn't a defeat. I could still win.

Not missing a beat, I rolled over to grab my machete. When the edge of the blade reached its maximum temp of five hundred degrees, I brought it down onto Korruk's sword, cutting the weapon in half. Upon turning to face Korruk, the anger and frustration on his face was apparent.

Korruk balled his hands into fists multiple times and stomped his injured hoof again. "I don't need a blade to kill you, ape. I'll use my bare hands!"

Resting my wounded arm behind my back, I pointed my machete at Korruk, ready for the attack that was sure to come. Even with one good arm, I still had speed on my side.

One thing that was certain in my mind was that the end of the fight was drawing near. We were both injured, but most importantly, we were both vulnerable. One well-placed hit would end it. I was determined to be the one to deliver the final blow.

For the Wolves. For Miller.

21

Major Parker was dead. The Volter shot stopped his heart, and time was of the essence. Just like the late major told them, marine squads were busy clearing the way for Tiger Squad and their cargo. As good a job as they were doing though, the influx of rogue zauhlons, along with the already present zauhlons, made it impossible to make the corridors completely clear.

Tiger's string of bad luck continued further. Right as they entered the main offices where the Odin would pick them up, Bat took a cannon ball to the skull. He was killed on impact.

Black Lung fumed in anger at the aliens who took his teammate to Valhalla. He was only twenty-two. Bat knew the risks when he signed up, sure, but no one deserved to die that young. Tiger Squad, along with the two squads of marines accompanying them, cleared the LZ and covered the entrances.

"Tiger One to Golden Eagle, the LZ is clear and ready for pickup," Black Lung said.

"We'll be there in T-minus one minute. Things are hot up here, so be ready for a hasty retreat," Golden Eagle reported.

"Got it."

Things were calm for that minute, which to Black Lung felt like an eternity. The drums of war raged on, but things were getting much quieter. Tanks were no longer firing rounds, everyone who wanted to join the battle were already here, and starfighters were dropping out of the sky one by one.

Finally, the Odin was in sight. Black Lung watched it get closer, turn around with its ramp already down. A risky move, but it would save them time in the long run. Rockie and Sixteen stood by with the Pale Horse as Golden Eagle lowered itself into the opening. Black Lung's relief turned into dread when he saw a zauhlon bomber—a G17 Genocide—race into view.

Golden Eagle must have noticed the bomber too, because the pilot reversed the thrusters, trying to get out of the death trap they found themselves in. By the time they were ready to exit, it was too late. Two V1070 bombs left the Genocide bomber and crashed into Golden Eagle. The force of the impact sent the Odin crashing down into the hole and right towards Tiger.

Black Lung didn't need to give the order. They all scrambled, desperate to get away from the falling dropship. The bombs cracked the Odin in half, leaving their ride on fire and totally wrecked. Not only that, but the opening to the outside world was effectively blocked off.

A quick look at where the cockpit should be told Tiger's leader the pilots didn't survive. The back half of the Odin folded in onto the cockpit, crushing it and anyone inside.

"Well frack," Black Lung cursed.

"What do we do now?" Hatchet asked.

That was the question everyone was asking. Black Lung knew the answer, but he dreaded voicing it. "Rockie, Sixteen, bring the bomb around to the back of the wreckage. Hatchet, get the marines over here and set up some cover and traps."

His Star Bourn froze for a moment. They knew what this meant.

"Go!" he ordered. With the rest of Tiger getting to work, Black Lung opened the comm channel he and Captain Adams set up in case this very situation occurred. "Captain Adams, do you copy?"

"Loud and clear, Captain Owens." She paused. "Is the Pale Horse ...?"

"Safe, but our ride has been destroyed. The way I see, we got no other choice."

"You're sure?" Adams asked.

"Positive," Black Lung breathed.

"Very well, I'll send out the order. It's been an honor, Owens," Kait said.

Black Lung grunted and cut the channel. He never was one for honorable goodbyes or anything of the sort. At the end of the day, the commando knew none of it mattered. They wouldn't be given any awards for this. Chances were, they wouldn't even be mentioned. Tiger Squad would disappear and this factory with them.

He looked back at the office. Most of the desks were moved closer to the crashed Odin. Those that weren't were used to barricade the doors. They may not actually keep them shut, but it'd be an obstacle for the zauhlons to get through. The rest of the room was barren. No cover was provided for their enemies. If they wanted a taste of human blood, they would have to come and get it.

Electro-nets were laid out beside the doors and just beyond the desks, along with mines. The area had been truly transformed into a death trap. Black Lung smiled.

A large message flashed on his screen: CODE RED EVAC. ALL PERSONNEL HEAD TO DESIGNATED LZ POINTS.

The marines looked to one another, no doubt questioning what they should do. Black Lung took the initiative. "Go on. You did good setting up the traps, but we can handle the rest."

"You sure, commando?" one of the marines asked.

"Positive. Besides, our armor is better than that weak crap you guys have on." That comment got a few laughs from the rest of Tiger.

The marine who spoke up scoffed. "Almost makes me wanna stay and prove you wrong. But, if you think you can do it on your own ..."

Black Lung nodded. "We can. Don't worry about us."

The jarhead shouldered his weapon and saluted, and the rest of the marines made their way to the nearest LZ point.

Hatchet stood next to Black Lung. "It was a headache to work with, but the timer is set to five minutes. That should be enough time for everyone to get out of here. That being said, some of us will need to stay behind in case any brutes show their faces."

Owens swallowed, looking back at his team. "I'll stay behind. The rest of you go on and get your pretty selves outta here."

"Like hell we are," Sixteen retorted. "I don't know about the rest of these guys, but no way am I going to let you do this on your own."

"I should stay back too. To tell you the truth, I don't trust any of you to repair that bomb if it gets damaged," Hatchet said.

"Yeah, and I'm not going alone. Leaving you behind would've been bad enough, but leaving you all behind? Not an option," Rockie said.

Black Lung looked at each of his fellow Star Bourn. They'd been with him for years, and as much as they got on his nerves, if he had to die with anyone, it would be these men.

"All right then," he said, getting into cover behind a desk. "Let's do this."

[Zauhlon Command Center, Factory 017, Klydoon.]

[Local system time: 1200.]

As I expected, dodging Korruk's attacks became much easier thanks to his injured hoof. That being said, we were at a sort of stalemate. With my machete, I had range. Match that with my speed and I was able to stay away from Korruk. On the other hand, the lord admiral of the zauhlons still had strength, despite his injuries. Even with his wounded hoof, he could still swing his fists pretty quick, which made getting close to him a risk.

Getting a little too eager, I stepped inward, attempting to further damage the armor protecting Korruk's abdomen. I was punished with a series of punches to the face and chest. Before he could land any more blows and knock me down, I rolled forward, dodging a particularly painful-looking left hook.

With his back to me, I heaved my blade into the wounded spot on his back. Korruk cringed from the pain, which made him lose his balance. Now on his knees, I twisted my machete. I should have just thrust it deeper into him and killed him, but I wasn't thinking straight. In that moment, vengeance crept into my soul. He needed to feel the pain Miller felt.

The creak of the bulkhead doors opening behind me snapped me out of my trance. A squad of five zauhlons with red war paint on their helmets stood there. While it was hard to say thanks to their helmets masking their faces, it felt like the leader—a zauhlon wearing silver armor—was deciding what they should do. Thank God for their ancient customs, or else I'd say a firefight was about go down.

Before I could turn back around to face Korruk, I felt four armored arms as thick as logs wrap around me. It didn't feel like Korruk was trying to crush me though. No, he was trying to steal my machete. A part of me wanted to laugh. *So much for not needing a weapon.* The more common sense filled part of my brain told me to get out of this scenario. I couldn't wrestle my blade back with only one good arm.

Using the size difference to my advantage, I wriggle myself around so I was looking at Korruk's bloody face. The heat emanating from my machete caused enough discomfort to Korruk's leg that he loosened his grip on me, now trying to get the blade away. With this newfound space, I whipped my head back and with what little strength I could muster in such a small space, I smashed my forehead into Korruk's mouth. The sound of teeth falling to the blood-stained floor filled my ears as I tried my best to stay conscious.

Korruk staggered back, thankfully nearly as affected by the blow as I was. I felt my legs wobble in their attempt to keep me standing. Before they could finally buckle, I leaned forward and channeled my energy into one last attack before I went down. Holding onto my machete for dear life, I lunged the heated blade deep into Korruk's chest.

Instead of staying upright, my body began tumbling forward past Korruk until I rested on a console, blinking away the sleepiness I was feeling. Looking back at where my enemy was, I watched Korruk fall down to his knees. While his face was hidden from me, there was no doubt in my mind shock painted his face. Perhaps the most shocking event of all followed.

The silver-clad zauhlon leveled his rifle at Korruk and shot him in the head. His lifeless body collapsed onto the floor, pools of blood forming from his chest and head.

Korruk was dead.

Everyone in the room froze. That is, everyone but the Wolves. Before the zauhlons could react, Tenner picked me up via a fireman's carry and hauled ass out of there, along with the rest of the Wolves. I'll be honest, I wasn't used to being picked up, nor was I a fan of it.

"What the hell's going on?" I asked. In my mind I was yelling it, but in all likeliness I only mumbled it.

Thankfully, Tenner's audio receptors picked it up. "No time. This place is gonna blow."

I had a million questions running through my mind, but I managed to put the pieces together. *He must be talking about the Pale Horse.* That was a question in and of itself. What was Tiger Squad thinking? Did they even have clearance to pull a stunt this big?

Even though we weren't out of the fire by a long shot, relief washed over me. It was over. The old Wolves and Miller could finally rest easy.

It was over.

<hr />

[Zauhlon Command Center, Factory 017, Klydoon.]

[Local system time: 1202.]

As Orrim expected, the humans bolted out of the control room. As strong-willed as they'd proven to be, the sight of so many enemies was clearly too much for them. Even the strongest have their breaking points.

Not Orrim though.

He persisted. He refused to break, and it finally paid off. As he walked to the center of the control room, Orrim stared at the fallen lord admiral. Of all the warriors who stood up to Korruk, he was the one who put him down.

Orrim raised his sword high. "I, Orrim of Drenobar, have slain Korruk and declare myself Lord Admiral of the Zauhlon Legion! Bow down before me or face my wrath."

"Be silent, coward! You haven't earned the right to be lord admiral," a zauhlon said.

The zauhlons appeared torn, confused at what they should be doing. It was true that Orrim delivered the killing blow to Korruk, thus "earning" the title of lord admiral, but to do so in such a cowardly way was enough to cause doubt.

Slowly though, each of the zauhlons began to bow before Orrim until everyone did so. The new lord admiral smiled. "For the past three decades, we've stagnated. Our colonies are overpopulated, and we've allowed the Republic to disrespect us. No more! Today will mark a new era for the Zauhlon Legion. Under my rule, we will colonize the stars and control countless planets! The superpowers of the galaxy will be crushed beneath our hooves, and the restraints Korruk forced on us will be a thing of the past. I only ask that you all stand by my side when this happens."

Niruuk was the first to bend the knee. "Hail Lord Admiral Orrim!"

One by one every zauhlon in the room fell to their knees, "Hail! Hail! Hail!"

A grin washed over Orrim's face. This moment was even greater than he imagined. Even though he hadn't got to fight Korruk nor defeated him himself, he delivered the killing blow, which was good enough for him. Orrim had risen from the bottom and held ultimate power. It would be a story told for generations to come.

The moment was cut short by an incoming transmission from Captain Herruk. As infuriating as it was, Orrim accepted the call. "What is it?"

"Orrim, thank the gods! The humans are evacuating en masse."

"What of it? They've obviously realized the error of their ways and want to get out while they can," Orrim said. Herruk sounded panicked. Scared, even, which wasn't like him at all. Despite this, Orrim wanted to get this over with and go back to soaking in his newfound glory.

"That's not it. We're picking up abnormally high nuclear readings not far from you. This has to be why the humans are leaving," Herruk said.

Orrim stood there, trying to piece together what Herruk was telling him. Ships and the like often used nuclear energy, but high enough for the apes to run? Multiple possibilities raced through his mind, but one terrifying proposition stood above the rest. The humans must have known they couldn't take them on in a straight fight. *They must have brought a ...*

His eyes widened. The fear Herruk felt now coursed through Orrim's veins. "Herruk, aim your rail gun and fire it at these coordinates!" Orrim quickly sent the captain the series of numbers he would need. "Send a dropship to pick me up as soon as it's done!"

"Are you sure? The risk of you being—"

"I don't care about the blasted risks! Do it now!" Orrim shouted. This couldn't happen. Not when he finally achieved his goal. He wouldn't let these apes take it all away from him.

22

[Corridor E5, Factory 017, Klydoon.]

[Local system time: 1203.]

Back on my own feet, I trailed behind the rest of the Wolves. I told myself it was because as a leader I wanted to make sure everyone got out safely, but truth be told, my aching body and lingering dizziness no doubt played a role.

Zauhlons, both dead and alive, greeted us at every turn. With the marines mostly gone and the two opposing alien factions apparently cooperating, that meant we were in deep shit. For the first part of our run, more time was spent shooting rather than sprinting. That changed when Tenner told me through gasps of air how much time we had left. After that, I put every ounce of energy I had into running.

We made one last turn into the passageway that would lead to the hangar pad. Two minutes until the Pale Horse went off.

I prayed that was long enough for the *Sparrow* to get us out of the blast zone.

My lungs were burning, but that didn't deter me. I pushed on, even surpassing some of the Wolves in the process. The doors slid open and there hovered the *Sparrow*, cargo bay doors open and waiting for us. A few marines which were stationed on the Bird were at the bottom of the ramp, ready to help us should we need it.

Training kicked in and I came to a halt, watching each of my teammates jump onto the lowered ramp. Something was wrong though. Someone was missing ...

I looked back and my heart stopped. Releck sat by the door in a pool of his own blood, shooting at the zauhlons attempting to follow after us. In the heat of the moment, I must not have heard him go down. Racing after him, I tried to pick him up, only to be pushed back.

"Forget it, Cap," Releck wheezed out. "They ... they got me good. I can't feel my legs."

"I'm not leaving you behind," I said, but again he shoved me away.

"Yes, you are. I'll hold them off. Don't deny me this, Severre. Let me die a warrior's death."

Behind me I could hear the Wolves calling for me. In a split-second decision, I turned and ran. Everything in my body told me to stop, but I ignored those instincts. My desire to live outweighed the code to never leave a man behind, and I hated it.

As best I could, I leaped toward the *Sparrow*. Tenner and Grampa were there to catch me and pull me in. With just enough time to get away from the ledge, the Bird shot off, desperate to outrun the grim reaper. The large ramp sealed shut, denying any of us a view of what was to come.

I found myself resting on a nearby crate, desperately trying to catch my breath. The entire time my mind went back to Releck, then his father, a man my dad and Miller knew well, and finally the possibility of us being caught up in the explosion. On one hand, I'd hate for it to end like that. We made it all this way only to be engulfed in that devil of a bomb. On the other hand, though, maybe it would be better that way. At least then I wouldn't have to face Orthin and tell him his son wasn't coming home.

The next twenty-four hours were stressful, to say the least. Even though we managed to get out of the kill zone, the Pale Horse ended up scrambling our systems, meaning we were on our own. On our way out of the system, we ran into one of

Captain Adams' battle groups. When asked, they said they couldn't hail her, but that they would wait to see if she showed up. Regardless, we were on our way to the Haunted Reef. If Adams survived, we would meet there.

During the wait at the Haunted Reef, there was plenty of scuttlebutt making its way throughout the ship. Talk of who lived, who died, and what was next. I couldn't say I blamed them. I wanted to know who perished myself. Call it morbid curiosity. That being said, I spent most of that time in the med-bay.

My left arm would be fine with a few cybernetics, and the tecronim helped with my bones and muscles. While everything healed, I watched a video of the battle via the Republic drone in the system. It wasn't everyday you got to watch a battle like this. Most footage like this involved rival gangs duking it out, or Republic flotillas taking care of terrorists, and that wasn't the type of stuff that you could find on the net.

I was only half interested in the naval combat. While a sailor could no doubt appreciate it more than I could, there was something else that I wanted to see. Around ten to twenty minutes in—the old drone didn't have a time keeping feature—I saw what I was looking for; the Pale Horse's apocalyptic explosion.

It was more of a bright flash than an actual explosion. One second, Klydoon was completely normal. The next, giant chunks of the planet were floating away and off the screen. Three large cracks formed on the surface, which made way for a dozen smaller cracks.

In all honesty, I was mesmerized. The fact that it had so much power while still being incomplete amazed me. Imagining the same outcome on Milara, which had a hundred times more people, shook me. Pushing the data-pad aside, I put those thoughts behind me. That wouldn't happen now that the Pale Horse was gone.

The door to the med-bay slid open and in came Arty. Upon seeing the captain of the ship, I got to my feet. "Any word?"

He nodded. "The *Poseidon* and her flotilla have entered the system. Be ready to board her in ten."

Considering the occasion, I wore a black suit that resembled an officer's uniform. All Star Bourn were given them in case the occasion ever came. Nine times out of ten, they were only ever worn at funerals.

Yet there I was, alive and kicking next to Captain Arty and Captain Adams, wearing their typical white uniforms. Next to them I stood out like a sore thumb. While we waited for Admiral Drake to hail us, none of us spoke a word. I reckoned no one knew what to say. Adams no doubt knew just how many of her people died, and if she was anything like me, that would be a subject she didn't want to talk about. I was still processing Releck's death and the subsequent end to my two-month long mission. And Arty ... well, he and his crew *did* just barely avoid a prototype planet killer. Situations like that had a way of making you not want to talk.

Just when I'm about to take the bullet and try to break the ice, Admiral Drake's blue-tinted image appeared before us. He returned our salutes as soon as he got them. "At ease. I've received the footage of the battle and the aftermath, but I expect your debriefings nonetheless."

Captain Adams went first. She went into detail about her battle strategy, how the fight played out, and how she and her battle groups escaped. "We were left with two options. Either risk staying near the planet and wait for the dropships, or move farther out in the system and let them find us. I had no idea how far the effects of the Pale Horse would extend, so I chose the second option."

It didn't get past me that by doing what she did, she left the marines to fend for themselves. I understood why Adams did it, lives of the many and all that. Still, it didn't sit right with me.

Arty didn't have much to report, since the *Sparrow* didn't play a big role in the battle. That meant I was next. As Captain Adams did, I detailed every part of my mission, down to when that rogue zauhlon shot Korruk in the face and when I left Releck behind.

Admiral Drake nodded. "How we got to this point is by no means 'by the books.' We took some risks, and there will be repercussions, but you have my word none of you will be affected negatively. These were my orders after all.

"That being said, what you all achieved was nothing short of incredible, and while there won't be any grand ceremonies, you have my word each of you will receive Galactic Crosses of Honor. Now if you'll excuse me, I need to speak with Senator Bennett about all of this. Good job."

We saluted until the hologram disappeared.

After a brief pause, Captain Adams turned to address us. "Gentlemen, it's been an honor."

Compared to Drake's speech, her simple words were a welcome change. As nice as the admiral's words of praise were, they felt scripted. Adams offered both of us handshakes, which we accepted.

Walking back to where our shuttle was docked, Arty spoke for the first time since the debriefing. "You'll be getting deployed elsewhere, right?"

I smirked. "What, you looking to get rid of us already?"

Arty chuckled. "Actually, I was wondering if you'd like to stay. I'm not sure what the regulations on it would be, but the crew likes having you all around. On top of that, the *Sparrow* is quick, so we could get you in and out of ops without trouble."

Like I haven't been on the ship long enough to know that. The thought made me smile. "I'll bring it up to Admiral Drake and HQ. Having a place to call home is pretty enticing."

As we neared the shuttle, Arty said, "Well, until the higher-ups say otherwise, you're still a part of my crew, and we're long overdue for some shore leave. Know any good bars for a celebration party?"

"Yeah, I know a real good one."

EPILOGUE

[Comm Room, *Sparrow*. One day later.]

[Local system time: 1530.]

We were on our way to one of the older cities on Earth—London. It would take us another day to get there, so I took that time to connect with Senator Din. Earlier in the day, I prepared video messages to the families of the old Wolves. I considered doing the same for Releck, but I felt compelled to tell Orthin in real time. Maybe it was the fact that the senator had ties to my father and Miller, but simply leaving a message didn't feel right. Hell, I already felt bad enough doing that for the Wolves' families.

After a few seconds of waiting, a holographic image of Orthin appeared. Before I could get a word in, Orthin was speaking a hundred miles per hour.

"Where's Releck? Is he okay? He's not hurt, is he?"

I looked down and swallowed. *All that talk about wanting to tell him in person and I can't even look at him. Get ahold of yourself.*

"What, what is it?" Orthin asked.

Pushing away my nerves, I spoke up. "Senator Din, I ... Releck didn't—" I felt myself stuttering. Taking a deep breath, I slowed down. "Releck didn't make it. He died protecting us."

Orthin was quiet for so long I thought for a moment the call was interrupted.

"W-what?" he finally muttered.

"Your son was a hero," I said. It sounded generic and stupid, and Orthin deserved to hear something more assuring, but it was all I could muster to say.

"I don't care! Why didn't you save him? Your father would have!" Orthin's voice was wavering. He sighed, "I'm sorry, captain. I think I need to be alone right now."

Orthin cut off the transmission from his end. Putting my weight on the cane Dr. Holiday gave me, I pinched the crook of my nose. While I knew this wouldn't be easy, it was so much more difficult than I could have imagined. My respect for the police officers who have to do this has grown significantly.

Limping on out of the comm room, I made way to my bed. According to Dr. Holiday, the tecronim should do its job and bring me to a good enough state by the time we reach London, but rest would help speed up the recovery. At least that's what he said.

When I carefully laid my battered self onto my not-so-comfy bed, I was tempted to just push aside that feeling of remorse and sense of mourning, just like I did throughout this whole mission. But I remembered the words I knew Miller would have said from back when this mission wasn't even official. *There's still a job to do.*

That was the thing. The job was done. What's the point in holding back anymore?

I hid my face in my hands and sighed. A rush of emotions swept over me. Sure, they've been avenged, but my friends of nearly a decade were really gone. They weren't coming back.

Crying was never my forte. Miller taught me not to early on. For the first time in a long time, however, I wanted to. If anything, just as a way to get these pent-up emotions out. Seems I trained myself too well, though. No matter how much I wanted to, it wouldn't come out. So instead, I took up Holiday's advice to get some rest. Maybe after a few beers those tears would come out.

<hr>

[Bridge of the *Judgment*, Diablos Corner.]

[Local system time: 1100.]

In front of Overlord Gorr was a sight that made him sick to his stomach. The scarred world of Klydoon lay in front of his flagship and his escort party. The molten core of the planet was exposed to space, and the icy, flat world Korruk told him about was riddled with cracks, bodies of water and even lava.

Gorr didn't care much about the planet itself. It was the implication that made him nervous. The only thing that could cause destruction on this scale was the Rahalah, which meant all that hard work was wasted. That alone made him grit his teeth. What was more concerning to him though was the silence from Korruk.

His lifetime friend had been acting strangely recently, so the radio silence wasn't completely out of the picture. Whatever he was dealing with, it was clear to Gorr that he needed space and needed to deal with it on his own. The least the Overlord could do was grant him that wish.

Something felt wrong, though. He couldn't quite figure out what it was, but something told him Korruk was in trouble. A gut feeling, perhaps. When this sense of dread fully encompassed his thoughts, Gorr decided to give his friend three days. If Korruk hadn't reached out by then, he would go to Klydoon himself. Deep down he knew he was being overbearing, but if their war was to be won, he *needed* Korruk. He couldn't do this alone.

Now, seeing the state of Klydoon, everything started to make sense.

Phantom had set them up. He led them out in the open to be attacked. To get rid of the Rahalah, and to get rid of Korruk. There was no way anyone survived that cataclysmic explosion. Korruk was—

No, Gorr thought, *There's still a chance. Maybe he escaped in time.*

Turning his attention to the captain, Gorr commanded, "Send out a request for communication across the system." If anyone was still in Diablos Corner, they would receive this call.

The captain relayed that order to the proper officers, and the waiting began. Unbeknownst to him, Gorr held his breath. The prospect of his closest friend dying without him ate away at his soul. They had promised to die together in battle. This couldn't possibly be how it ended.

"We're being hailed by the *Onslaught*," an officer said. "They're requesting permission to board."

After a nod of approval from Gorr, the captain gave the green light. It wasn't Korruk's own flagship, but maybe that ship was destroyed and he fled on any starship available. That's what Gorr told himself to ease his mind.

———◆◇◆———

Gorr, along with his loyal Centurions, waited at the hangar bay for the *Onslaught*'s dropship to land. If Korruk was alive, he would be in this Archon.

He made sure to hide this from his warriors, but Gorr was getting anxious. If he was being honest with himself, he never imagined Korruk dying in a scenario like this. Throughout all their years of knowing each other, Gorr always knew him as a survivor. Whether it be against the packs of Ash Ravors they faced in the Valley of Horrors, or the waves of apes he slaughtered during the Great Hunt, Korruk always stood tall.

Within no time, the Archon passed through the shield and landed. Its doors creaked open, and the zauhlons within the dropship exited one by one. They lined up in single file on each side of the doors and held their swords in front of them. Gorr let out a quiet sigh of relief. This was customary when a lord admiral boarded a ship.

When the lord admiral emerged from the Archon, however, that sense of relief was replaced with confusion. The man in front of him wasn't Korruk, but instead ... Orrim? He never personally interacted with the man, but he was one of Korruk's generals. One who, if memory served him right, was sent to the brig for a failed assassination attempt.

"What is the meaning of this?" Gorr demanded.

Orrim continued walking until he stood directly in front of Gorr. His demeanor wasn't one of an underling, but of a leader.

"Overlord Gorr, I don't blame you for your confusion. Allow me to sum it up for you," Orrim grinned, "Korruk is dead by my hands. Per the laws established by the warrior god Sorrvuk, I am the new lord admiral. I look forward to working with you."

Orrim moved past Gorr, accompanied by the zauhlons who were with him on the Archon. Gorr's Centurions gave questioning glances at one another while the overlord himself stood there, shocked.

Korruk really was gone.

His shock turned to sadness, which transformed into anger. He turned around to see Orrim leaving the hangar bay. That low-life general had not only killed his friend, but had the nerve to show his overlord no respect? Gorr snarled. If that was how Orrim wanted to start off his reign as lord admiral, that was fine with him.

He would pay for what he did to Korruk, even if it was the last thing Overlord Gorr did.

⸻◆○◆⸻

[London, Earth. Two days later.]

[Local system time: 2100.]

Most of the *Sparrow* crew were either spread out across London or visiting family. The majority of the partying happened around an hour before at a nearby club. As it turns out, the bar I had in mind was smaller than I remembered. When the crew split up, Arty and I decided to hit up the bar I mentioned, a nice joint called Reina. The Wolves tagged along, egged on by Tenner's constant praise of the place, as did the senior officers of the Bird.

Back in the day, Reina became a regular stop for the old Wolves and I. Something about the contrast between the royal decor and the drunken sailors made it hard not to love the place.

We Wolves were holed up in the back of the bar, enjoying mugs full of Plinton Whiskey—the best damn whiskey among the Core Worlds, I might add. Boomer, who already fit in here

358

with how drunk she was, raised her glass, "To Releck, and all th' good bastards who died."

The rest of us followed suit. "Cheers."

Chugging down my drink, I could feel my senses begin to dull. Even though I knew I'd feel like hell tomorrow, I was content with dealing with it. I was honoring Loudmouth, after all. No better way to honor a friend like him than to get piss-ass drunk at our favorite bar.

Out of the corner of my eye though, I saw Engineer Walker sitting at the bar. She was a few seats separated from the others, and she looked like a fish out of water. Looking between my commandos and her, I decided to go keep her company. The Wolves could go on without me for a little while.

When I reached the bar, she was just staring at her drink. If I hadn't said anything, I'm sure she wouldn't have noticed me. "Everything alright?"

She nearly jumped out of her seat at the sound of my voice. "Oh, c-captain. Sorry, I didn't know you were there."

I waved it off. "Don't worry about it, I just got here." There was a brief moment of silence between us. "So? How are you doing?"

Twiddling her thumbs, she finally sighed. "Remember Ensign Gregor?"

The name sounded familiar, but my buzzed state made my memory foggy. After thinking hard on it for another second or so, it hit me. "The man who died back in the Vorka System?"

She nodded. "That's him. I've been trying to forget about him, but he's been in my dreams. Nightmares, more like it. I just—I just see him. His body, I mean. He broke his neck when he fell. Every time I close my eyes, I can see him and his lifeless eyes."

"Was that the first dead body you've seen?" I asked.

Walker sheepishly nodded.

"The first one is always hard. It's human nature to be afraid of death. You just have to find your own ways of coping with it. For what it's worth, I think you're doing it wrong."

She raised an eyebrow. "How so?"

"You shouldn't forget the dead. You should remember them. Not the way they went out, but how they were when they were alive," I said. "Take me for example. Whenever someone close to me dies, I make sure I honor them by doing something both of us loved. It's a way for me to say goodbye."

"That's actually a good idea, for a Star Bourn," Walker said, grinning when she saw me feign heartbreak.

"Here I was trying to help you feel better," I said with a shake of my head, which elicited a chuckle from her.

"So how are you honoring your old teammates?" Walker asked. Not a second after the words left her lips, she apparently realized what she just said, and covered her mouth. "Sorry, I shouldn't have said anything."

"It's alright. I'm actually honoring one of them right now," I said. Seeing her questioning look, I continued. "Loudmouth was a party animal. The rest of us would hit up this bar after a big op, so he tried to make every op out as a big deal. Out of all of us, he was the heavyweight drinker." I laughed, "You'd swear it was impossible for that man to get drunk. In short, I'm saying goodbye to him by getting drunk."

Walker smiled. "That doesn't sound like that bad of an idea. Mind if I steal it?"

I matched her smile with one of my own. "Go right ahead. Besides, now that I think about it, I promised we'd drink to Gregor."

"Shall we then?" Walker asked, raising her glass.

I waived the bartender over and ordered a drink of my own. While it was being prepared, I scanned the room and watched my Star Bourn laughing about something.

My *Star Bourn, huh?* I was brought back to the beginning of this mission, when I promised myself I would go lone wolf after this. After serving with the same Star Bourn for so long, I didn't think I could connect with others as well as I did them.

Even though I wouldn't say my bond with the new Wolves is as strong as with the Wolves of old, I'm still proud to call them my team. *Maybe I could stick around for a while longer.*

The bartender slid my drink over to me and my attention was back on Walker. She raised her glass. "To the fallen."

I couldn't think of a better toast. All the people who died along the way—my old Wolves, Miller, Releck, and everyone else—they didn't die in vain. They can rest easy knowing that bastard Korruk is dead.

"To the fallen."

Continue the story of James Severre and the Wolf Pack in ...

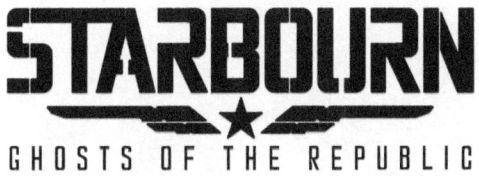

Preorder by clicking the link below if you're reading via ebook,
or scan the QR code if you're reading via paperback.
https://a.co/d/5SP0gVG

THANK YOU FOR READING!

To everyone who made it to the very end, from the bottom of my heart, thank you. You took a leap of faith in reading my debut novel, and I want you to know it means the world to me, even if you didn't end up liking it. My goal in writing *The Pale Horse* and every book that comes after it is to give whoever reads it a little bit of escapism and entertainment, which is sorely lacking both when I wrote this and when it's been published. If this book gave you some enjoyment, then all the effort was worth it.

About the Author

Fueled by at least two cups of coffee, his vivid imagination, and a love for science fiction, David Hart is devoted to delivering the following: fun stories, quality writing and escapism. If that sounds like it's up your alley, strap in and watch out for stray blaster bolts. You're in for a hell of a ride.

Sign up for David Hart's newsletter and get a FREE short story; *Star Bourn: The Final Day*!

https://davidhartauthor.com/free-book-here

Acknowledgements

Special thank you to my editor Martin Roy Hill, without whom this book would be yet another amateur outing to add to the ether. Thank you to the people who read much earlier versions of *The Pale Horse*, especially to an old friend, Xander. Without his blunt critique, this story wouldn't be where it is today.

I'd like to thank my proofreader, Kevin Eddy, for helping out with *The Pale Horse*'s final stretch and cleaning up the book even further.

Lastly, I want to thank my mom. Without her support and encouragement, I likely would've never gotten this far.